RANSOM

PEACEKEEPER'S HARMONY - BOOK 1

MAGGIE M LILY

Oh, family. What a year we're having.
With love and gratitude to all those waiting patiently for this story.

OH, SHIT

"Oh, shit," I mumbled as I felt the sword slice through my neck.

Time slowed as I slid to the ground.

Sam was right. I was wrong, I acknowledged to myself.

It wasn't a happy realization.

I heard Jen screech.

The power of my circle flared. But I was pretty sure it was all for naught. I couldn't feel my body.

I thought I heard William yell something, but William wasn't here with me, so maybe it was the synapses firing in my brain?

Why would I hear William? Seems like Matthew would be the brother to shout through my dying mind...

The world went dark. My time was up.

IN-BETWEEN

I didn't wake up. I became aware. It was a mental thing, not a physical thing.

I didn't have a body to go with the awareness. I had no sense of space, no feeling. There was no smell or sound. I couldn't see.

Nonetheless, I was there—wherever "there" was.

And I wasn't alone.

"Hello?" I didn't speak the word. It was more of a mental projection. But I wasn't sure I had a head to do mental things within.

Startled laughter rolled back to me, genuine amusement that my energy recognized.

Oh. My energy works here. That's interesting.

"Hello?" I tried again.

"Well, you've made a mess of things, Luke."

I knew the voice. "Where am I?"

"In-between."

"In-between what?" I asked. "Am I doing some kind of heaven and hell life-flash montage? I'm not into that."

"Nah," he said. "Between life and death. We're in a holding pattern. Why don't you tell me what happened while we wait to see if they can pull it off?"

"You know what happened."

"No, I don't," he disagreed. "I don't know what you perceived happening. It doesn't work like that."

"Huh." I wished I had a body so I could fidget. "How does it work?"

"There's no fidgeting here."

"Caught on to that," I muttered sullenly.

"So, are you going to tell me?" he asked.

"No."

"Why?"

"Because I'm talking to myself—at least figuratively. You're me. I know it."

"Well, yeah. But no. I'm only part of you. Or, more accurately, you are part of me. It doesn't matter."

I did the equivalent of a sigh.

"You sigh too much," he complained.

"Sorry," I muttered, considering the possibilities.

He cut into my thoughts before I could speak them aloud. "Nope. Right track, wrong idea. I'm not a possible future. Your mind doesn't work like that. Don't make this harder than it needs to be. And don't sigh again."

"Fine. What are you?" I asked, decidedly not sighing. I was pretty sure I knew who I was talking to.

"Tell me what happened. We don't have anything better to do while we wait."

"Why don't you tell me what you know, and then I'll tell you what I know?" I offered.

Silence.

"Hello?" I asked again.

"What I know doesn't matter, Luke. This is your show-and-tell. So, what happened? What really happened?"

"I got betrayed," I summarized.

"The sword chopping through your neck gave that away?" There was more laughter. "Start at the beginning."

"No. I feel like you're going to nitpick if I explain. I know I'd nitpick myself. Just let it go."

He sighed at me.

"Now you're sighing," I said, vindicated.

"It's rubbed off on me," he admitted. "Sighs convey a lot of things."

"So, you're me, but not me?" I asked, fishing. Maybe he'd admit it.

Silence again.

"We have this opportunity to talk, just you and me," he said, sounding tired. "There's real potential to do something amazing with this time. There's an opportunity to affect things for the better. But only if you tell me what happened."

I could feel my awareness rolling backward in time, preparing to tell a story. If I'd had eyes, I'd have rolled them at myself. I wasn't planning on playing along, but it seemed I might not have a choice.

I wasn't sure I wanted to talk about what led us here. I'd done things wrong, despite my best efforts.

"I'm waiting."

"And you'll keep waiting," I snapped. "You want to talk about this? I need a minute."

I WAS JUST GOING to say it. Peace was the worst superpower.

My brothers gave me a lot of crap because my lot in life seemed comparatively easy.

But at the end of the day, all I was left with was the feeling of "meh."

I come from a family of empaths. I mean that literally, not just that we are emotionally aware. We are true empaths with control over emotions.

William could sense and influence fear. I had a brother who worked with rage and another brother who was all joy. With all eight of my siblings present, there were a lot of emotions and a few other interesting twists of power hanging out around the family dinner table on Sunday evenings.

But my schtick was peace. I could feel peace in myself and others, in the world around me, even in the placement of objects. Everywhere I went, there had to be peace, or my internal triggers went bananas.

I couldn't sit still at the dinner table if the saltshaker was out of place. I couldn't sleep at night if my dirty clothes were on the floor. Those things were not at peace. They were not where they should be. I had to fix them.

Because that was me: The physical embodiment of peace itself.

My siblings and I gathered with other empowered people to stand energy circles, sharing our power with the world around us. The end goal of our circles was a matter of perspective. But, in my opinion, our circles brought harmony in the shitstorm that was modern life. They were a place to pause, take a deep breath, and recenter the distribution of energy.

In my circle, I was called Peace. Or, if I was being addressed by an ass-kisser, Lord Peace. Depending on who you asked, I might also be the Peacekeeper. I wasn't sure how that whole Peacekeeper thing shook out in the end, given they tried to lop off my head.

My mind stalled out at the thought.

Now wasn't the time to think about that. For now, I'd ignore it. I had a gift for ignoring the obvious. My headless state would just be another thing to deny.

I moved on to happier thoughts.

There weren't a whole lot of people who were a pure emotion like me. It was the *Highlander* rule— "There can be only one." There could only be one true physical embodiment of a particular emotion at a time.

There was only one Peace, and I was it.

Given my current neck-chopping predicament, maybe I shouldn't have been making *Highlander* references.

Anyway...

I was a sedative in human form. Just my presence would clear minds and ease worries.

Not bad, right?

So what if I was a bit obsessive-compulsive about things and was often mistaken for a neat freak? Big deal.

There were worse things than offering peace to the world around me.

And I agreed with that for the most part. My gripe was about the utter lack of all other emotions.

The only emotion I seemed to inspire was peace. I couldn't hold on to anger for more than a minute or two. Fear rarely touched me—what would I fear? I instinctively knew how everything should be. Joy and hope weren't part of my natural makeup, either. Sure, I felt other things, but only in small bursts. Only for a minute. After that, if the emotion wasn't peaceful, it wasn't for me.

It was fine. I accepted that reality for the most part, with one major exception—love. I couldn't fall in love or inspire love.

Well, that wasn't totally right. I could manage familial love and the love shared between friends. The default sort of love taken for granted every day was part of being at peace. That sense of acceptance and appreciation was at the very core of what kept humans balanced and peaceful. I could do familial love and friendship better than just about anyone.

But romantic love? Fire, passion, and the stuff of legend.... the love that bound people together for their entire lives? That love wasn't part of being Peace.

And I knew it. I could see the bindings of love between people. Technically, I could see a few different types of bindings. But love shone brightest when I looked for the things that bound people together. It was like my powers were trolling me by showing me what I couldn't have.

"I don't know where to start," I admitted to the me that was me but was not me—the other me. "You know, peace is really the worst. All I feel, all I inspire in others, is a great big pile of 'oh well.'"

"The power's not the problem, Luke. It's the way you let it run your life that's the problem." My disembodied friend sounded smug.

I went back to silence.

"What happened with Candy, Luke?"

"I tried to save her. I tried to pay the ransom on her life by giving up my own future. I failed," I muttered.

"Let's start there. What really happened with Candy?"

1

"Oh, come on!" Candy yelled as we walked back to my house. My brother, Jake, had just gotten married in a small ceremony at my parents' house. "You can't be mad about that. So what if I announced you're a sex god during your brother's wedding? Your family thought it was hilarious! No one minded!"

"I minded," I muttered, throwing the front door open.

"Why?" she demanded. "I didn't say anything bad! Sex is part of life. There's nothing to be ashamed of. Why let it bother you?"

"I just don't want our personal shit spread around, Candy."

She groaned. "Spoiler alert: Your family knows we fuck, Luke. The only neighbors you have for miles and miles around are your family. They know I stay the night all the time. And they know you're at my place when you're not here."

"I know they know."

"So?"

"Candy, I just don't want it shared."

"You don't want to talk about sex. At all? Or like, just not in front of your parents? Let's keep in mind that your parents have nine children. They know what sex is."

I sighed, my anger already fading into peaceful acceptance. We'd reached the point of no return. "It's not the sex banter, Candy. I don't care about that. My family jokes about sex all the time. I didn't want to discuss sex in front of them because every last adult in that room knows it's *only* sex for us."

Her mouth dropped open in shock. "What are you talking about?"

"Candy," I started.

Her eyes narrowed. "That better not be the tone of voice I think it is, Luke! I'm crazy about you."

Crazy about me, not in love with me.

"Well, at least you're not lying to yourself about things. Candy, I can see the bindings between people. Adaline can see them, probably Sam too. Adaline's sister, Jessica, can see everything about a person at a glance. She has all-sight. Are there legends of all-sight among the shifters?"

Eyes focused on the middle distance, decidedly not looking at me, she shook her head. She knew where I was going with this.

"Anyway, more than a few of us can see the bindings between people. You don't love me. You're attracted to and turned on by me, but there's no love. We've been together a few months now. The colors haven't changed. The bindings haven't shifted at all. We're friends that have sex. That's all you feel with me."

"Luke, I'm not like you and your family. I'm not empowered

like you guys are. I'm a shifter. Maybe the bindings always look different."

I was shaking my head before she could finish her thought. "No. I can see the love binding your brother to his wife. I can see the love binding pets to humans and animals to their mates. Love is love. The binding doesn't change. You feel friendship toward me. And I feel like you're family. Amber binding from you to me; silver binding from me to you. Not a smidge of romantic, gold, love bindings between us. And everyone in that room knew it."

"Why didn't you tell me?" she whispered.

"Because you already know it."

She moved her head in a so-so gesture. "I did, but I didn't know that you knew it."

I stayed silent, waiting for the next objection. I didn't wait long.

"It might change," she offered. "We haven't been together that long, Luke."

"I kept thinking that when I dated Talise too," I replied. "It doesn't change."

I had thought Talise, who'd been part of my circle for almost a decade, was going to be the love of my life. I had been determined to make it so. She had been my perfect woman in every way. When a relationship had finally become possible, it turned out I couldn't see her as more than a sister and part of my family. Much to my annoyance, she'd ended up in love with my least favorite brother shortly after that.

Candy snorted, actually laughing at me. "Oh, please. The nature of love changes all the time. Are you really trying to tell me that the love my parents felt for each other at twenty-five is the same as the love they feel for each other at fifty-five? No. Love evolves."

I didn't bother responding. I just waited.

"So, this is it? We're ending things? No more great sex?" she asked. "I'm not opposed to friends with benefits."

"I am," I murmured. "We've been through this. I know you think my peace shit means that I'm going to end up with a harem of shifter lovers, but that's just not who I am, Candy."

"Luke, if you get mixed up with the beast affinities like me, you'll be prime breeding stock—all the women you could ever want. I don't mind the idea of being part of that."

"I do," I said, voice firmer. We'd been over this repeatedly. "It's not who I am, Candy. I don't want to be part of the shifter stuff. But, even if I did get roped into your little corner of the world, I wouldn't participate in that bullshit. Even if it didn't bother my sensibilities, my mother's head would explode."

Candy snorted again. "Darla would be delighted. There'd be grandbabies everywhere. They'd shift into little animals at the drop of a hat, but she doesn't spook easily. It'd be fun."

I sighed.

"It's over?"

I nodded.

"We need a better breakup story than this."

"What?" I asked, startled.

"'I dumped Candy because she didn't love me' is lame Sunday dinner fodder. No. If we're breaking up, you're going to make it good. I'm going down in epic fashion. Let me get some paper. We gotta sketch this shit out." She flounced out of the room, not even pretending to be heartbroken.

"I'm serious, Luke," she said, coming back to the living

room. "You need to make this good. Pull out the acting lessons you took in high school."

"I didn't take acting lessons in high school."

"What? What's wrong with you? Everyone takes acting in high school."

I shrugged, laughing at our tangent.

"Can you dig up some angst for me? Like, Shakespearean tragedy?" she asked, eyebrows raised.

"Think about who you're talking to," I suggested, slipping a bit of peace into the words.

She shivered. "Don't do that unless we're allowed to have sex. That's the new rule. No peace if there's no nookie. Deal?"

I winced. My peace energy affected shifters like Candy and her brother, Charlie, differently. It calmed their human emotions, giving their more beastly natures space to breathe.

The extra mental space left Candy with a sense of euphoria that led to energetic sex.

"Okay, so you don't do angst. You do doldrums. That's not much to work with." She was silent for a moment, thinking. "I'm going to have to blow up your car."

I sighed again.

2

"—And then the car blew up. She was so mad about the way things ended, she firebombed it. I tried to get her to stop, but she was a woman on a mission." My voice was monotone.

There was no way anyone would buy this shit. My natural energy would've calmed Candy out of a true rage, and we all knew it.

My entire family—eight siblings, their assorted significant others, my parents, and our extended loved ones—sat in stunned silence at the Sunday dinner table for a moment.

Sunday dinner was a thing with my family. Every week, my immediate family and a smattering of those dear to us gathered round to share a meal and gossip. Our weekly headcount was now upwards of thirty people. It didn't matter. My parents' house had been built for this. Their dining room was bigger than some gymnasiums. My mother lived for Sunday afternoons with the family.

Matilda's peals of laughter broke through the silence first. She laughed so hard she was tearing up as she bent at the waist while trying to catch her breath.

"That is a festering pile of bullshit," William said, throwing his head back in laughter while ignoring a glare from my mother.

"The best part of this is that she really blew up the car!" My dad had to yell to be heard over the laughter. "He had to call me to pick him up."

More laughter.

Sigh.

"No, really, what happened?" Matthew asked. Matthew was my closest brother by age and disposition. He was my exact opposite as an empath, though. I was Peace; he was Chaos. Or, more precisely, he was Pandemonium. He was also a giant nerd.

"No!" Matilda yelled. "Don't ruin it for me! I know she worked hard on this story. I want to savor it."

"Why would you even ask? We all know what happened," My brother, Jake, said. He and Matilda were still in newlywed bliss, holding hands at the table. "Luke got grumpy that Candy talked about great sex at our wedding. They broke it off. I'm guessing it was over within an hour of them leaving the wedding."

Noah gave a mocking sigh, smirking as he put his arm around Talise. "Luke, you don't end relationships because the sex is great. You end relationships when there is no sex and no connection. No wonder you—"

"Stop," Talise cut in. "You know I won't allow you to bait him. Why do you do this?"

Noah frowned. "I keep hoping to slip one in. It was going to be funny. I feel like you used to enjoy my humor more."

"I love your humor," she agreed. "But not at Luke's expense, and you know it."

"Tali, who's your best friend?" Noah prodded.

Talise, Adaline, and I narrowed our eyes in unison before Tali smacked her boyfriend upside the head. "Stop it."

Once upon a time, I had been Tali's *only* friend, a best friend by default. But she had become closer to Adaline.

"You know she would have said you if you were still the BFF, right?" Noah stage-whispered to me, enjoying the nonstop laughter at my expense.

I sighed again. I couldn't even bring myself to be upset. Candy had concocted the breakup story to bring laughter to the table, and she'd succeeded. I was glad. I'd rather they laugh at me than feel sorry for me.

At that moment, I realized Candy had made the whole thing up and blown up my car, so I wouldn't have to be pitied. She'd done it for me, and I loved her—in that friendship way—a little more for the thoughtfulness. I had not thought this far ahead.

"Anyway," I shouted, "we broke up."

"Yeah, we got that part," Matthew said, still laughing. "Thank her for the tall tale, please."

"Will do," I agreed, nodding.

"I'm glad she made you park at the back of that lot, so no one got hurt when the car blew," my dad acknowledged.

"We wanted the long walk to and from the restaurant," I deadpanned.

"It was an empty lot, Luke," my dad disagreed.

"There was a Chili's about a half-mile down the road."

"I love that you're sticking to this." My mother grinned. "This is so good for you. I love her even more for making you tell this ridiculous story."

"I'll send you the bill from the fire department, Mom."

"I'll pay that bill!" Sam called from the other end of the table, laughing harder.

I rolled my eyes. The bill didn't matter any more than the car did. Sam had long since made us all disgustingly rich. As a time-walking oracle of sorts, he'd had a bit of an unfair advantage when it'd come to picking investments. The money had accumulated over the last decade. Still, we hadn't understood what he was or what we were until the past summer.

"We shouldn't laugh at this," I scolded as everyone continued to laugh at me. "Someone could have gotten hurt. Could you imagine if a firefighter had been injured?"

My dad actually snorted. "How much gas was in the tank of that car?"

"That's not the point."

"I bet you even drained the oil," Matilda said, grinning at me.

"You know Luke wouldn't even know where to start. *Candy* drained the oil." Will laughed.

This was getting annoying.

"Wednesday is Christmas. What's the plan?" I asked, trying to change the subject.

"Dinner here at three o'clock," my mom yelled over the din. "Everyone's welcome for Christmas Eve too, but good boys and girls need to be in bed and asleep by eight for Santa to come." She looked meaningfully to the children at the table.

Excited giggles about Santa saved me from further humiliation.

"Practice on Tuesday," Will said, eyeballing me.

I'd called the end of humiliation too soon.

My eldest brother had recently decided I needed to get

stronger and learn how to fight. Since then, he'd been beating the shit out of me twice a week.

I was terrible when it came to actual combat. I could make people fall asleep by flexing my energy. Why fight when sleep came easily and didn't hurt anyone? The problem with my dependence on the energy was that it didn't always work. When I couldn't knock someone out, I was in deep shit. So, Will was teaching me to fight. In the process, I took a lot of beatings.

"I don't want to get beaten up on Christmas Eve." I wasn't whining. I'm Peace. I can't muster a good whine to save my life.

"Stop whining," William retorted. "You need to learn how to use the energy to heal yourself. Once you figure that out, it'll be easier. You're just too stupid to use the circle's power."

"Gah!" I yelled. While I was distracted by Will, Matthew had stabbed me through the hand with his steak knife. "What the fuck?"

I waived my bloody hand at my favorite brother—WHO HAD STABBED ME.

He didn't seem impressed.

"Lucas!" Darla bellowed. My mother did not tolerate swearing at the table when little ears were present.

"He just stabbed me!" I yelled at my mom.

Yelling at my mother was not advised. She had nine children and didn't take crap from anyone. While she wasn't empowered like the rest of us, we lived in fear of her wrath.

"Heal it," Matthew said calmly. "You can pull power from us to fix it. Heal it."

"Really? Doing this with Will twice a week isn't bad enough? You're going to randomly stab me at dinner too?"

Noah made yapping motions with his hand like I was needlessly whining. Talise glared at him.

"I will stab you if it helps you learn," Matthew agreed. "Will is right. You should know how to do this by now. Pull the energy."

"Adaline!" I called, getting out of my chair and heading her way, knowing she could heal this in no time.

"Nope," she refused. "You can heal that in a second without my help."

"You apologize to the children!" My mother was losing her shit because I swore after I got stabbed.

"I'll apologize right after Matthew apologizes for stabbing me!" I shouted back at Darla.

"Whine, whine, whine," Will muttered. "Your entire power base is right here, Luke. Pull the energy from us and heal it."

"Healing is not a 'Peace' thing! Overcoming pain is not a 'Peace' thing. No one's stabbing fucking Noah over dinner!" I yelled, diving to smack Noah's yapping hand.

But I'd been careless. I'd sworn. Again. The table went still and silent, waiting for my mother's reaction.

"Get out," Darla said, voice cold. "Leave my house right now. If you can't respect my rules, you will leave."

"Hey!" Jake yelled. "When I swear at the table, I have to do the fucking dishes for like thirty people!"

Darla sniffed. "He can't do dishes. He'll get blood all over them. But it was wonderful of you to volunteer, Jacob."

"Oh, for fucking shit's sake! I walked right fucking into that fucking trap!" he yelled.

"Feel better?" Mom asked him.

"I figure if I'm doing dishes anyway..." Jake shrugged. "Sorry, kids."

"Uncle Jake has a potty mouth," the kids chanted in unison.

"It's creepy how they all say the same thing every time. Do

you coach them on that?" I asked my mom, my anger already gone, lost to peace.

Oh well. I was wounded. It would heal.

I poked my bleeding hand with my napkin. It was spilling blood at an alarming rate.

"I told you to go," my mom said, unamused.

"What did you do?" Adrian asked Matthew. "Am I going to have to stitch his hand?"

My second eldest brother, Adrian, was a pediatrician by trade. We roped him into all sorts of *"does this rash look alarming"* crap, sometimes making it up as we went, just for fun.

"I twisted the knife once it was in there good. Tore up some tendons, but I don't think I broke anything," Matthew said, still watching me. "You're not even going to try healing it?"

"For the nine thousandth time, it does not work for me! I know you all can do it. I know Beth can do it without help. I know Noah's done it a few times. It does not work for me. The circle energy does not heal me. It just makes me feel weird."

"I'm playing the world's smallest violin for you, bro," Will mocked. "Mom's right. Get out."

"KNOCK, KNOCK," my brother, Ethan, yelled as he walked in my front door.

The door wasn't locked. We lived in a gated, guarded community made up of just our family. There were no neighbors around for miles. There was no point to locking the doors.

For the record, I was not a huge fan of family compound living. But Sam had demanded we build a family compound.

No one in their right mind bet against Sam, who could move

through time. So, we had a family compound with armed guards.

In fairness, William was responsible for the armed guards. Sam rolled his eyes at the guards.

"I'm in the kitchen," I yelled back. My senses told me both Micah and Ethan left their coats on the stairway rather than hanging them in the closet. They weren't staying for long. They slipped their shoes off, though, saving me from having to clean up snowmelt.

A moment later, Micah and Ethan walked into the kitchen.

"We wanted to check on you on our way home. Is it still bleeding?" Ethan asked, brows furrowed with concern.

"Yep," I said, back to resignation. "I'm icing it and applying pressure. It's slowing down."

"Sit," Micah ordered.

Like William, Adrian, and Matthew, Micah could heal his wounds. Millenia ago, he had stood in energy circles as Lord Hate and managed to outlive his circle. He'd spent almost two thousand years alone before joining our circle and our family, finding love with Ethan.

As part of accepting his love for Ethan, Micah had also accepted a change in his base nature and power. He was no longer Hate. He now stood as Redemption.

"It's not going to work," I muttered, sitting. "I can feel the energy. I just can't make it *do* anything."

Micah exhaled, sitting next to me as he unwrapped the dishtowel from around my hand. "Try anyway."

I rolled my eyes.

Ethan lifted his eyebrows. "You're going to give him attitude? I will let him beat you. You know that, right? He's trying to help you."

I blanched. The only person in our circle scarier than William was Micah. Well, maybe Sam too. It depended on the day.

"Pull the energy," Micah prompted.

Using my sight, I found the circle of energy that always enclosed my family when we were within range. With Ethan and Micah in the room with me, I had no trouble finding the power that healed.

I tried to pull it into myself.

The energy didn't move.

"You're pulling it through the circle," Micah muttered, thinking.

"That's what I'm supposed to do, right?"

"Yes," he replied, drawing out the word. "That's the easiest way to do it when you have a circle. You help yourself to what's available. Try again—"

"Micah," I started.

"No. Try again, but pull it from me, from our familial bond," he suggested. "Don't use the circle. Use our bond."

"What?" Ethan asked, crinkling his nose. "It doesn't work like that, does it?"

Micah shrugged. "You and I share energy through our bond all the time. I have shared power with others through bonds and without a circle before."

The binding that went from Micah to me was a thin silver bond of familial love. We weren't close.

"I know," Micah murmured, "it's not a deep bond yet. But try it."

Gently, I tugged on the bond, pulling energy from Micah.

"Ech!" Micah yelled.

I stopped immediately.

"No, it's fine. Just strange. It startled me." There was an apology in Micah's voice. "I have not directly shared energy with someone that was not a lover in a long time. It's different, not bad."

I nodded, pulling at the energy again.

Ethan gasped, watching as the swollen, bruised puncture wound on my hand healed.

"You're right. You can't use the family circle," Micah acknowledged. "I used that circle before I was a part of it. Why can't you use it?"

At a loss, I stared at my hand. My energy was roaring through me, trying to calm my anxiety.

"Luke?" Ethan asked. "Are you okay? You look...not peaceful."

My eyes shot to his face. "I'm your brother." My voice shook. My statement warbled like a question.

Ethan nodded. "You are my brother. You are absolutely part of our family. Don't go there. There's just something off about your binding in the family circle. We'll straighten it out."

"Until then, you know how to heal yourself without Mistress Life's assistance," Micah murmured, using Adaline's formal title, *Mistress Life*.

I nodded.

"You need to know how to do this, Peace," Micah continued. "Your energy does not heal physical wounds, only mental ones. You must know how to work with the rest of us to keep yourself well. You can't use the circle for it. Fine. Use the other bindings. Your bindings to your brothers are much stronger than your binding to me."

"Thank you," I mumbled, still at a loss. While I had insisted

I couldn't use the circle for healing, I felt sick once it was confirmed.

"Okay. We're going." Ethan tugged at Micah's hand.

Before he turned to go, Ethan hugged me.

Through the contact, I felt the spark of his joyful energy flow through me, reinforcing my own peace. This would work out. I was part of a family that loved me. I smiled, accepting that truth and finding joy despite the situation.

"G'night, Luke," Ethan murmured. "Love you."

"Love you too." I meant it. Ethan was easily the best person I'd ever known. I'd love him even if we weren't related.

While joy was his thing, Ethan took it beyond simple happiness. It was his goal in life to help people understand their worth and value their uniqueness. Joy went beyond smiles, turning on the light within each soul and celebrating it.

"You owe your mother an apology," Micah scolded as he followed Ethan out of the kitchen.

3

$\mathcal{I}$ had not realized I felt bad before connecting with Micah's energy. My hand hurt a bunch, but looking back, there was also a feeling of general I-don't-feel-good that I had not bothered to articulate. After my hand was healed, I noticed the absence of malaise and wondered if I'd been fighting off a cold.

I slept like a log on Sunday, not even sure I rolled over during the night. Monday morning, I woke up to a quiet house, looking forward to the day.

I started with the exercise routine William insisted accompany his other "training." He demanded I be fit and strong, so I was packing on the muscle.

Running on a track or road was too easy for Will's liking. Couldn't have that. I was expected to full-out run over uneven terrain on the open land around the family compound. He called it "trail running." I objected to that phrasing. There was no trail. It was just me, hauling ass over open ground like my

24

life depended on it. Because, one day, my life might depend on it.

That Monday, the run went faster than usual, so I covered nearly twice the normal distance.

Back home, the weights were easier too. I blew through my normal sets and wondered if Micah's power had made me stronger. Either that or William was about to up my routine again.

Done with the workout, I had nothing but happy things ahead for the day. I'd spend my morning with music and my afternoon with Matthew and his girlfriend, Miranda. Then, we'd do a Monday night circle with a large group of people.

Music was a part of my soul. I needed it every day in some form. Without it, I couldn't rest. A day without music was worse than knowing something or someone was not at peace. I could control the peace to an extent. A lack of music in the day disrupted my sense of self in a way even my energy couldn't override.

Having said that, music came into my day whether I created it or not. When the world was quiet around me and my energy was calm, I could hear the music of the world, of life, as my own personal symphony.

But I planned time for making music every day. I had no obligations other than teaching some after-school music classes. I had all the money I could ever want, thanks to Sam. Planning time for what I loved wasn't a challenge.

That morning, I tinkered with a saxophone. Learning new instruments and feeling their subtle personalities was a favorite hobby. Soon, the sax would be added to my ever-growing list of mastered instruments—piano, guitar, violin, clarinet, bassoon, and cello.

I loved them all, but the piano was my first choice, the keys an extension of who I was. When my world went to shit, you could find me at my piano.

After lunch, I went next door to glare at Matthew.

"I'm not sorry," he said as soon as I walked into the house.

I applied the glare.

"Glare all you want. I don't care."

"Micah and Ethan stopped by last night," I said conversationally, still glaring. "We confirmed I cannot use the family circle for healing. I healed my hand in about a second when I pulled energy directly from Micah."

Matthew blinked. "Say that again."

I explained what happened again, then explained it again to Miranda.

"But you're in the family circle. I can see you in it," Miranda disagreed.

"Get up," I barked.

"Huh?" Miranda asked.

"Please stand up, just for a sec?"

She stood up.

I scooted around her, picking up the end of the couch she was sitting on. I threw a dirty sock at Matthew. "Why do you do this to me? Why do you take strange delight in putting shit in weird places for me to find?"

"I've been looking for that sock!" Matthew grinned. "Thanks."

I glared some more.

"I didn't do that one on purpose," he admitted.

"Is whatever's going on in the fridge an accident or a test?" I asked, suspicious.

Matthew and Miranda shared a look of confusion.

"Something's wrong in the fridge. It's not one of you trolling me?" I asked.

Head shakes.

I groaned in frustration, headed for the kitchen.

"I thought we were talking about the circle issues?" Matthew called after me.

"We are," I yelled back. "You're smarter than me. So is Miranda. Figure it out while I sort the fridge."

A minute later, I walked back into the room with a dust rag and wood polish. "There was a piece of moldy cheese. You're going to ask me how I differentiate healthy cheese mold from funky cheese mold. I have no idea. I just know you don't want the black, moldy cheddar. Moving on. The circle?"

I felt Miranda's eyes on me. "I just dusted the end tables, Luke."

"I know," I muttered, slightly ashamed I couldn't suppress the instinct that told me to fix the furniture polish.

Matthew was grinning at her. "There was a streak. He was trying not to stare at it before."

"Sorry," I murmured. "It's just... Anyway, the circle?"

"You're in the family circle. I can see the tie," Miranda said again.

"And yet, I cannot heal myself from it. No need to continue stabbing me. We confirmed it last night."

"Can you heal yourself from the full Harbor circle?" Matthew asked, voice distant as he thought through things.

"I've never tried, and I don't care to try tonight. Please don't stab me again."

He shook his head. "We need to know. You're going to take some sort of injury tonight. Sorry."

"You're not sorry. I can tell," I muttered.

"That's crap, and you know it. I don't want you to be hurt. But you need to be able to take care of yourself. Everyone else has done this at least a few times now. Randa pulls healing energy when she breaks a nail."

"That was one time!" Miranda objected. "It split down to the cuticle."

"I'm not suggesting you shouldn't have done it," Matthew said, an apology hiding in the words. "I'm saying that you can do it without issue. We need to figure this out."

"Why? I truly just don't think healing is part of peace. I don't think I'm supposed to be able to do this."

"You think you can be Peace when you're in pain?" Matthew asked, eyebrows raised.

"Yes. I do it every time Will beats the crap out of me. Calm acceptance just takes over."

Miranda was shaking her head. "My earth energy also has nothing to do with healing, Luke, but I can heal myself. This is something specific to you."

I shrugged again. "I can feel the power there. I can pull it toward me. I can use the emotions in it. It will not heal me. I think that means the circle won't help me."

"We'll look at it tonight in the bigger circle," Matthew said. I tried not to take his words as a sign of an upcoming injury, but I also knew I was kidding myself.

I'D STOOD circles with some understanding of my energy since I was a teenager. Matthew and I had worked through our different energies together while comparing and contrasting our weirdness with comic book superheroes.

28

But other than working through things with Matthew, I hadn't felt the need to enlighten my family about how my energy worked. We'd kept what little we understood about our abilities to ourselves.

In an effort to control my power, the circle elders had tied my energy without my knowledge when I was a teenager. Afterward, my energy hadn't seemed particularly noteworthy. Plus, I'd expected my parents to freak out about the idea of circles and life energy.

In retrospect, I was wrong to keep my knowledge to myself. For all my family's superpowers, we were mostly ignorant of what we were until last summer.

We had all known Sam was creepy. Sam had always been slightly out of step with reality and never pretended otherwise. It'd turned out Sam was the Walker, a being of legend that could control time and space as well as the elements.

Left to his own devices, he'd introduce Adaline as his wife because somewhere in time, they were married. Sam didn't care about the formality of it. They would get married at some point, so in his mind, they were married.

Adaline was Sam's fated match and balance, Mistress Life. She held power over all living things and emotional states.

Truth be told, I didn't understand how either of them was sane, but I guessed "sane" was a relative term in their cases. They were both weird. It was impossible to be around them and not know that they were different.

Other than Sam, each of my siblings had lived their own version of not-quite-normal before last summer. We just hadn't compared notes.

Will had figured out he had some control over fear when he was a little kid. But he'd had no idea where it came from and had never thought to discuss it with the family. He'd joined the military in an attempt to put his mojo to good use.

Adrian had realized he had some serious rage issues in middle school. Forever the scientist among us, he'd tested his powers on his own and discovered his rapid healing and ability to create mental compulsions. Adrian had gone to medical school looking for answers. He hadn't found any and hadn't talked about his issues with anyone.

So, William, Adrian, Sam, Matthew, and I had each kept our own little secrets and hadn't compared notes. It had shocked the fuck out of all of us when it'd turned out all our siblings had some sort of special energy and that all our assorted significant others did as well.

Standing circles together now kept us all balanced and healthy.

Think of a circle like a circus tent. Sam and Addy were the center pole. Each pillar—each member of my family, as well as their significant others—stood as a support pole on the circumference of the circle, holding things steady. The other members of the circle filled the gaps. They were the covering to our tent, giving purpose to the structure my family provided.

My family could produce a tremendous amount of energy. The other members of the circle made it easier for us to share that energy with the world.

Harbor was the most extensive circle of empowered people in the Chicago area. And, with my family involved, it was the strongest circle in the world.

Gathered as a group, each person in the circle took a turn swapping negative for positive energy. Stressed out and exhausted? Offer the stress to the circle, letting it go from your mind. Then, take someone else's manic energy and put it to better use.

When everyone had spilled their excess and addressed their deficiencies, the remaining energy was offered to the world around us. We usually released some form of life energy to help with growth and understanding throughout the world.

No matter how wet and cold it got, we never missed a circle. I couldn't imagine skipping out on the soul cleansing—even if I knew I was about to get hurt.

"HE'S COMING," Talise called from the backyard as I walked into the farmhouse, passing through on my way to the field we used for circles.

I sighed, knowing it was pointless to try to prepare myself. I could feel the members of the circle shifting uncomfortably. Something was waiting for me.

As I opened the back door, William slammed his fist into my face, knocking me unconscious.

Adaline had already closed the circle when I came to, and was now hovering above me, scowling at William.

"You told me to knock him out!" Will complained.

"I told you to give him a minor injury before I knocked him out," she replied. "I'm sorry, Luke. We wanted to study how the circle affected you without your mental blocks getting in the way."

"J—," I started before my face exploded in pain.

"Don't talk." She glared at William. "He broke your jaw. You'd still be out if I hadn't woken you. We've studied the bindings between you and the family circle, you and Harbor, and you and Micah. There's nothing unusual about any of them. They're identical to Noah's bindings in every way we can see.

"Can you pull Harbor's energy to heal your face?"

"He's pulling the energy," Jess said, saving me the words. "I can see it flowing into him. But no dice. It won't mix with his natural energy."

"Okay," Adaline breathed, gently touching my face. "It's done now. I'm sorry."

I could feel the bones in my jaw knitting back together under her touch. She stayed there, waiting until it was fully healed before moving her hand away.

"I'm sorry," she said again. "I caused that pain."

"No!" Sam roared, already turning on William.

I winced. "No, Addy."

Part of being Mistress Life meant Adaline didn't intentionally harm life. Causing pain caused her real pain, magnified several times over.

"Oh, shit," Will muttered, realizing his error too late. "It wasn't your fault Addy. Don't! Don't do that. I purposely misunderstood. You didn't do anything wrong."

It was too late. She'd already accepted responsibility for what had happened. Mistress Life was weeping in misery as she held her face.

"Fuck," Will muttered, head hanging as he tugged at his hair in frustrated guilt. "I'm so sorry."

Through the circle, we felt his guilt and remorse for hurting Adaline by hurting me. It washed through the group twice over before Jake changed it to be raw life energy.

"Lord Fear," Samuel's voice rocked the clearing with power as he addressed William formally, "how will you make amends to my Mistress? And it had better be good."

"I'm so sorry, Addy," Will muttered, collapsing next to Addy and me in the circle and pulling her into a hug. "Can you push the pain to me? Will that work?"

Adaline shook her head, still weeping as she tried to roll herself into the fetal position.

"Addy, what can I do?" Will begged. "I'm so sorry."

"Godparents," Adaline croaked out between sobs, face contorted in agony.

I bit back a smile. William's wife, Emma, was due to have twins in February. We had been arguing over godparent rights from the moment we'd found out Emma was pregnant. This was a new level of manipulation.

"Okay," Will said, nodding immediately. "Okay, of course. We'd be honored, Addy. Honored. You and Sam, okay?"

Addy nodded, smiling even as she cried.

Standing over us, Sam bent to touch Adaline. The tattoo markings they shared on their arms flared bright white.

Adaline exhaled, her pain gone. She grinned. "That worked out well."

The color rose in William's cheeks as he realized he'd been played. "That was slightly evil."

"And effective." Sam nodded in agreement. "It was always going to be us, and you know it. Beth and Hennessy for the girl, Addy and me for the boy."

"That's bullshit," Adrian yelled. "It was *not* going to be you. You just made sure to work things in your favor. I call dibs on the next kid!"

"The circle can't heal Luke," Adaline summarized, getting back to the point. "You need to learn how to heal yourself from us directly, Luke."

I nodded, moving to my place in the circle so we could get

back on track. I spent about thirty seconds feeling incredibly embarrassed that the entire circle saw me knocked out and broken. Then it dawned on me that they also knew I couldn't use the circle properly.

But I was almost to my place on the perimeter. My peace energy flowed freely.

Oh well. At least I didn't piss my pants.

4

"*I*f you pass out, I'm going to piss on you before you wake up," Will threatened. "Pull the fucking energy, Luke. You can't use the circle. Fine. I'm right here. Pull the energy."

Tuesday morning began much the same way Monday night had gone. I was sprawled on the mat in William's basement, on the verge of passing out again.

"Ah con feel da bending," I slurred, unable to focus my eyes.

"You don't need to feel the binding. Pull the energy."

I searched for the energy, but my brain wouldn't focus. I definitely had a concussion.

Will bent, touching the back of my neck gently. That helped. I pulled at his power.

"Don't pull the fear, Luke. You'll scare the shit out of yourself. Literally. Just the energy, not the emotion."

I didn't know how to separate them.

William sighed with frustration. "This needs to become

second nature, Lucas. You can't pause in the middle of a fight to go searching for a good power source. Addy, would you fix his head? I didn't mean to hit him that hard. I think he actually landed badly."

"You cracked his skull," she admonished, scowling at him. "Didn't we *just* do this last night, He-man? You're trying to help him, not kill him, right?"

Will nodded, head hanging again. Being scolded by Adaline wasn't fun. When she was mad at you, the very essence of your life energy wiggled uncomfortably.

She sighed, but her words came out strong. "He can't focus his thoughts to learn if you break his head, William. If you can't be deliberate, stop hitting him. Let Matthew, Hennessy, or Adrian do it. You don't know your own strength."

My vision cleared after a minute. I blinked. Addy was sitting next to me, holding my hand. "Hi," I slurred, trying to smile at her.

She smiled, then kissed my hand. "Be brave."

"Can you sit up?" William asked, voice subdued.

I nodded, pushing myself into a sitting position. I hadn't bled on the mats, which was a pleasant surprise. Will made me clean it up when I bled everywhere.

He folded his arms, staring down at me. "You're going to need to learn to do this with all of us...or at least Adrian, Micah, Matthew, and me. You need to be able to pull the healing energy without the other energies. You have a new thing to practice until we figure out the circle issue."

I stared at him, knowing this meant I was going to get beat up more often.

"This means you're going to take a lot of beatings." He smiled a bit, knowing his words aligned with my thoughts.

"Not right this minute, okay?" I asked, still slurring. I'd bitten my tongue somewhere along the way, and my head ached miserably.

"I didn't heal it all the way," Adaline muttered, going back to her spot next to Talise. "You can practice with the wounds you already have."

"Thanks?" I asked, not sure if I should be happy or not.

Will held out his hand. "Don't search for the binding. Just pull the energy. Just the healing energy, not the fear."

I did as I was told.

"Luke, you keep pulling on the fear. If you do it again, I'll let that energy go, and you'll be sorry. *Just* the healing energy."

"I don't know how to separate them."

"You better learn quick," he replied.

Shortly after that, I lost some time rolling around in terror on the mats in William's basement. For the record, it takes pure peace longer than you'd expect to shut down full-blown terror.

While I'm not sure how long Will let it go on, it was too long. I actually pissed myself that time. Eventually, Emma came halfway down the stairs to yell at us for all the noise.

Will pulled the fear back, shaking his head as he climbed to his feet. "You're healed, but you're cleaning up piss. You better work that shit out, Lu—"

Shoving peace directly through our bond, I dropped Will to the mat, dead asleep in my urine.

He meant well, but damn. He was an asshole.

I was due for more beatings anyway. Might as well earn them.

MY FAMILY HAD three small children to dote upon at Christmas. Ree was Adrian's girlfriend's nephew. Mia and Meg were Adaline's nieces. Since the eldest of the kids was only six, we were in prime Santa years.

My mother was in heaven. And, when Darla was happy, we were all happy. There would be at least two more children next year. William and Emma were expecting twins in February. While the twins would be the first biological grandchildren, my parents didn't make such distinctions. Family was family, blood-related or not. And little kids got a Christmas to remember each and every year.

With nine kids and one income, my parents had not been wealthy while I was growing up. We'd had all we needed and never worried about our next meal. But Christmas had not meant excessive gifts in the Trellis household.

Even now that we were wealthy beyond imagining, our gifts were nothing more than tokens of love.

Because, in our family, Christmas meant love. It was an occasion to celebrate all the beautiful things in our lives and express gratitude to each other.

There were gifts, especially for the kids. But there was also hot chocolate, family stories, a new annual tree ornament, and a big meal. We sat at the dining room table for more than four hours, first eating and then teaching the kids to play cards as we laughed and talked.

Stuffed with more food than I would typically eat in a week, I felt like I was rolling myself toward the door when it was time to go home.

"It's Christmas," William said from behind me. "I won't back over you with my car. We'll train tomorrow."

"Your house is six houses away. You drove?" I asked, amazed

at that level of laziness coming from William, my hardcore, former military brother.

Emma snorted, following us. She had an adorable pregnancy wobble with the sort of belly that made it look like she'd swallowed a giant beach ball. "He's worried I'll slip on the ice. He drove, then literally carried me into the house. Because, you know, *he* can't slip on the ice."

"Seriously?" Matilda rolled her eyes at William. "You could have just asked."

"What do you mean?" Will replied, confused.

"Here. I'll demonstrate." Matty walked out onto my parents' front stoop and made all the ice and snow dissolve within five feet of her.

Matilda was Lady Light. Her energy manifested in variations of light and fire, among other things.

"I'm more efficient than a snowblower." She laughed, walking down the sidewalk as she melted the snow with enough heat to make steam. "I'm pissed I couldn't do this when I was working in the Chicago Loop. I can't tell you how many times I fell on the damn ice."

"Carrots," Will breathed, using his personal nickname for Matty, "that's amazing. Can you do our walkways? Just so Pip has a clear path?"

"Sure," Matty said, smiling. "But only if I get to start referring to Emma as Pip too. It's adorable."

"Boo!" William yelled. "No Pip for you. Only people who knew her when she was Pip get to call her Pip."

There was a grunt of agreement from somewhere in the entryway. Hennessy, Will's best friend and my sister's fiancé, obviously agreed with Will.

"Fine," Matty muttered. "But I'll still melt the snow. It's

fun."

"You go that direction? I'll go this direction?" Jake asked, walking the opposite way, melting the snow as he went.

"Holy cow!" I called. "You're getting good at that, Jake!"

His shoes started on fire. "Fuck you for distracting me!" he yelled back.

I grinned. It didn't take much to distract someone new to their powers.

5

The week between Christmas and New Year's involved a lot of beatings. The family business was closed for the week. Everyone was home, creating a bigger audience for my ass-kickings.

"Get up." Matthew sighed, resigned.

"Mmrgurmh."

"Get up," he repeated, unmoved. "Put the tooth back where it goes and do the healing thing."

"Should I do this one?" Adaline asked, sitting on the sideline with Tali, Matty, and Emma.

"No." Matthew, William, and Micah spoke in unison. They were taking turns. So far, the only one I could pull energy from with any sort of confidence was Micah.

Micah's primary energy had to do with redemption and self-awareness. Truthfully, I wasn't sure if I was pulling the emotion with the healing. The last time I'd pulled from him, I'd gotten a good dose of his secondary energy, hate.

My peace had swallowed it quickly enough, but we'd moved on to the next available source. Undiluted hate was not something to mess with.

Matthew was the yin to my yang. At times, we seemed to share thoughts. I could calm his energy without effort. It would make logical sense for the healing to flow easily from him to me.

Six burst water pipes, a small fire, and a busted television later, it was clear I couldn't separate the healing from Matthew's chaos. And I couldn't manage the chaos either.

"He did this correctly when I let him look for the binding," Micah offered. "Maybe we should let him do that until he gets a feel for it."

"Peeze," I groaned, fishing the displaced tooth out of my mouth.

"Fine," Will groused, resigned. "Try it with me."

I rolled onto my back on the mat, then closed my eyes. My skull wasn't cracked, so I could find the links to my brothers without looking. I opened the binding from William. The healing energy poured into me. I didn't even have to pull it. He was so eager to see me succeed, he was pushing the power at me.

Adaline gave a surprised yelp.

"Yeah, I noticed that too," Will acknowledged. "He didn't pull a damn thing. He just opened the path. Why are you strangling your side of all the bindings, Luke? That's gotta be the problem. You push your peace shit out nonstop, but you don't let anything else in?"

I lay there, thinking about it. "I don't know."

"Get up," Matthew repeated, still not impressed. "You're going to learn this."

"I'm not sure beating knowledge into me is working," I admitted.

"You still need to get up. You still need to learn how to protect yourself in a fight," Matthew argued.

I pushed peace toward him to knock his ass out.

"Nope," he said, instead of dropping like a stone. "Unlike you, I know how to open *and* close my bindings."

"Teach me?" I asked. "If you can do it, I can too. Show me how?"

"I am," he replied. "Get up."

By New Year's Eve, I wanted a break from family. Everyone else was married or on their way to being married. I had no desire to be one of two singletons at a celebration of couples and kiddos ringing in the new year. I made pulled pork in my slow cooker and had a day of bingeing the *Lord of the Rings* Extended Edition. I still don't regret it.

By ten-thirty, the movies were done, and I was contemplating bedtime. It wasn't midnight yet, but I didn't care. It was a pointless milestone anyway.

I had just finished straightening up for the night when I heard a car squeal to a stop outside. I wasn't quite to the front door when someone pounded on it with enough force to shake the doorframe.

No one knocked on my door. It wasn't even locked.

"Who is it?" I called.

"Open this fucking door and let me in!" I knew the voice, but the power and magnitude of it rose the hair on my arms. The words sizzled and snapped like a live electrical wire.

"Uh, Ellie?"

"NOW!" she roared.

Eleanor Hapner was Matilda's best friend and Candy's sister-in-law, married to Charlie. She was also some sort of energy vampire I didn't fully understand.

She didn't appreciate being called a vampire. She preferred siphon. But, as she stood outside my house demanding entry, I had trouble thinking of her as anything but a vampire.

For the first time in my life, I was afraid of her. The sound of her voice and the snap of her non-threatening words made me shake a bit.

"I-It's not locked," I stuttered, experiencing a flashback to rolling around on William's basement floor in terror. My energy went batshit crazy, trying to soothe me.

I heard her growl with impatience before she took a deep breath. "Open the door and let me in, Luke. It's important. No harm to you or yours."

"Ellie, I don't mean to be a dick about this, but your words are literally rattling around my house. Like Sam does with his voice sometimes, but different. Darker. I'm not sure I believe you."

"They've taken Charlie, Candy, and their parents. They're all going to die if you don't help me. Open the fucking door, Luke. It's time to repay a favor."

I dove for the door.

6

"Invite me in," Ellie demanded.

I stared at her.

"It gives me access to more of your energy. If we end up fighting here, I'll need access to it, Luke. I'm already welcome at Hank and Darla's, as well as Matty and Jake's. If I intended you harm, I'd just rip you out of your house and take care of things in the street. This is a formality."

"Who are we going to be fighting?" I asked.

She smacked my head.

"Sorry," I grunted. "Please come in and tell me what's going on, Ellie."

Taking a deep breath, she stepped over the threshold. "Ugh. Your power tastes like tepid tea. Anyway, get dressed. We have to go. I'll explain on the way."

"How about you explain while I get dressed?"

"Here's the short version, moron: Someone took a video of Charlie and Candy transforming into animal forms in

November. Most of your family was visible in the video. Shifting in front of 'normal' humans is a big no-no. Their lives are considered forfeit unless we can demonstrate there was not a normal human present when they shifted."

"So, you need my whole family?"

"No. I need you, Peacekeeper of legend, to quit being a fucking coward and make yourself known. They've been looking for an excuse to get at Charlie since he got involved with me. Even if we trucked out everyone visible in the video, they'd argue there could have been someone off-camera when Charlie shifted. We can't *prove* there were no normal humans there. So, we're making it clear exactly why he shifted.

"Charlie is an extremely powerful shifter. He was the heir apparent until I came along. Now he won't play their power politics. And he won't defend himself because he knows you don't want to be involved with the shifters. Someone set him up to remove him from the power struggles. Put on your fucking clothes. We're going to get my husband and your ex-girlfriend out of shifter jail before they get executed."

"You're not exaggerating, are you?" I asked, eyes wide.

"Luke. I'm trying to be calm. Please. Go get clothes. We don't have a lot of time. They die at three a.m. unless someone makes a case for their survival."

AT TWELVE-THIRTY IN the morning on New Year's Day, Ellie pulled over on the street beside what appeared to be an estate. We were in the far northwest suburbs of Chicago. Like my family's compound, there was not a neighboring house in sight.

"I can't be in there. After I get out, take the car up the drive-way, hit the button on the speaker box, and tell whoever answers that you've come to speak to the Beast Overlord. It's a proper name. Say it with respect, even if the dude is a fucking lunatic. He is, technically, the head of all people with beast affinities."

"The head of all shifters lives here?"

"No. This is his residence in the midwest. He was called here because of the video. He and his entourage arrived yester-day. They took Charlie and his family this afternoon.

"Don't call them shifters. They hate that as much as I hate being called a vampire. Beast affinities, Luke. You are a fucking god to them. Be polite but contemptuous. Do not bow. Do not show obeisance of any sort."

"When you say they took—"

"I mean exactly what I said," Ellie snapped. "Stop wasting time. Someone will meet you at the building entrance. Push your peace shit for all you're worth. They need to know who and what you are. Don't be shy about it.

"Walk around like you fucking own the place because this estate actually belonged to the last Peacekeeper. The Overlord inherited it by tradition, but it is yours by rights. Make it known that Charlie and Candy were fighting in your defense. That should do the trick."

"And if it doesn't?"

Opening her door, Ellie glowed in the same way a blacklight does. "If it doesn't, stay out of the way."

I got out of the car, walking around to the driver's side. "Ellie—"

"Be careful. Be polite. But again, you're a god to them, Luke. Act like it. I won't be far away if it goes to shit."

She wasn't in the mood to answer questions, so I did as I was told.

I had to buzz the speaker three times.

"What?" a voice finally barked out at me.

"I'm here to speak to the Overlord."

"The *what?*" The tone was disbelieving, like the guy was sure he'd misunderstood me.

Were we at the wrong place?

"I'm here about Charles and Candace Hapner." I tried again.

"That matter has already been settled."

My stomach dropped. Ellie said three o'clock, but what if she'd gotten that wrong. What if it was midnight? Anxiety and rage poured through me in a flash, making my next words sharper than usual.

"I'm the Peacekeeper. Open the fucking gate and let me in."

There was a derisive snort from the speaker. "Whatever, man. Your funeral if you want to join the traitors."

The gate buzzed, opening slowly.

I drove through the gates and down the driveway, pulling in the circular, covered parkway. Before I opened the car door again, I took a few deep breaths, pulling my peace forward. If they'd been visible, my already muted emotions would have been dull shades of grey.

Calm settled around me. Candy and Charlie weren't dead. If they did die, the world would keep turning, and life would go on. None of us were here forever.

I knew the power was flowing when even the thought of dear friends dying didn't ruffle me. I got out of the car.

I wasn't even to the door when it opened. A security guard scowled at me. "I don't know who you been talking to, man, but you don't want no..." His words trailed off into silence as his mouth went slack.

Huh. I had the power forward, but I wasn't pushing it out yet. I was about five feet from the guard. When I wasn't pushing, it appeared my range was about five feet. I probably should have tested that before now.

"I want to see the Overlord," I said, my voice quiet and calm, almost monotone.

The guard's head dropped, chin to his chest. "As the Peacekeeper wishes." He didn't try to meet my eyes again as he led me through the house, out a back door, and into some kind of stadium gym.

"Please wait, Peacekeeper. I will tell the Overlord you've summoned him."

I gasped. "No, I..." My words trailed off as I remembered Ellie's coaching. I gave a sharp nod. I could do contempt if I had to.

My escort disappeared, leaving me alone. I wandered farther into the space. The center of the room was shaped like an oval with stadium bench seating along the sides. It made me think of the Roman colosseum on a smaller scale. There was a roof on the building, but I couldn't begin to guess the height.

And, for all the space, it was empty, except for me. I wondered if I was about to put on a show. Walking out to the center of the floor, I tried to gauge the size of it. I came up blank. It was smaller than a football field, but not by much. There was seating for hundreds of people.

"What the hell do they do with this space? Shifter battle royale?" I muttered to myself, barely a whisper.

My energy pinged. Someone I couldn't see was disturbed by

my words—decidedly not at peace. I smirked, looking for the source. I couldn't find whoever was hiding.

I wasn't in the mood for games, especially with lives at stake. I let my power answer the disruption and soothe my new friend.

Far overhead, a hawk shrieked before dropping into a dive, aimed right for me. I froze, unsure what to do. Had I just blasted a bird? I felt guilty right up until the would-be bird dropped into a giant panther form, pacing around me.

"Holy shit," I breathed. "That was amazing."

I had seen Candy shift into a few cat forms. Cats of any type were her specialty. And I'd seen Charlie shift to a giant wolf form.

Theoretically, I understood that Charlie had the power to shift into other animals.

It had not occurred to me that he could shift into a bird (AND FLY!) and then shift directly into a cat in the blink of an eye.

After the third lap around me, the cat sat directly in front of me, staring.

I lifted my eyebrows, unsure what to do. "Hello."

The cat smirked at me. The fine details of its expression were lost to the lighting. Hanging far overhead, the lights cast deep shadows everywhere. But it was definitely a smirk.

I smirked back, dosing the cat with another wave of peace. It seemed like the thing to do at the time.

The cat roared in my face. If I hadn't been steeped in my own power, it would have been terrifying. I let a larger pulse of peace free, watching the cat rock back on its hindquarters.

"Enough," a voice called from the entryway.

THE CAT SHIFTED BACK to hawk form, flying off toward the entrance faster than my eye could follow.

I could hear quiet murmurs but couldn't make out words. The acoustics in the building would give me a headache before long. I gave a loud, put-upon sigh.

A moment later, a giant furry man entered the arena. I don't mean that figuratively. He had fur covering all visible areas of his skin, including his face. He had to be close to seven feet tall, and he lumbered instead of walked, bent at the waist, arms longer than they should be.

In his wake, a more ordinary appearing couple followed. The man appeared to be in his late fifties with frown lines around his mouth and sagging, pale jowls. The woman was young and fit, though barefoot and wearing nothing but a silk slip that left nothing to the imagination.

"I am Nathaniel," the man introduced himself. "This is my daughter. I understand you claim to be the Peacekeeper."

He held up a hand before I could respond.

"This is Edgar, my brother and advisor." He gestured to the furry dude. "It takes much effort for him to transform. He's been trapped between forms for too many years to count. If you are the Peacekeeper, you can help him. Do it."

My eyes darted between the woman and two men. "How would I help him? I've never been asked to do anything like this. What would you have me do?"

Nathaniel tilted his head, smiling, his doubt obvious. "The Peacekeeper of old, my father, would know what to do. It was a natural byproduct of his power. Surely, a new Peacekeeper would have that same capability?"

I took a deep breath, thinking through all the conversations Candy and I'd had about shifting and what my energy did to her transformations. I came up blank.

"We're waiting," Nathaniel said.

"And you'll keep waiting," I replied, remembering Ellie's advice.

I didn't open my eyes to see the reactions.

Instead, when I opened my eyes, I opened my sight, looking for bindings and ties on Edgar.

I wished I could take a picture for Jess, Adaline's sister, who could see all ties and bindings.

Our Edgar was a mess. There was one tie in particular that strangled his life force like a python. I could see it slowly pulsing, draining life energy from him.

It was worth mentioning that I had never broken a binding or tie before. Sam had done it to me once; it was the worst experience of my life. A few weeks later, he'd done essentially the same thing to Talise. Other than experiencing it and witnessing it, I would be winging this exercise.

But I was guessing I'd be in trouble if I couldn't help Edgar.

"Edgar, may I touch your hand?" I asked.

After shifting his eyes from me to Nathaniel and then back to me, he nodded.

I walked toward him, arm outstretched. He met me halfway, grabbing my offered hand.

"Please help me." His voice was guttural and difficult to understand. "Or kill me. Either is fine."

I blinked, wondering how long he'd been stuck like this. "I have never broken a tie before. If I can't do it, I know someone who can."

Without another word, I sent peace coursing through him,

dropping him to his knees but not entirely knocking him out. My peace made everything looser, like untying a knotted shoelace.

His healthy bindings shifted away from the tie, making space for me. I gave a mental shrug, then willed the constricting tie to break with another pulse of pure energy, sans the peaceful after-kick. It snapped like a rubber band.

Edgar yelped as Nathaniel screamed, the sounds echoing in the vast space.

Edgar lay at my feet, shifting back to a more human form as I watched.

"Well, that was fun. There was a tie strangling his energy," I said, voice flat as I watched Nathaniel wipe the blood from his nose.

"I cannot feel the others," Edgar groaned. "I can't feel the elders."

"I can't feel you either," Nathaniel murmured, helping Edgar to his feet. "Rest and heal. We'll reestablish a tie when you are stronger."

"Peacekeeper," Edgar bowed to me, still stumbling a bit. "I am forever in your debt."

Turning to Nathaniel, he continued. "His peace is unlike anything I've felt. He is what he says, Nate. The Peacekeeper has returned to us."

"Rest," Nathaniel said again as the guard that brought me in came to help Edgar.

Once they were gone, I stood before Nathaniel and tried not to look at his daughter. It was beyond awkward.

"I feel the peace from you, but it's not what I would expect," Nathaniel commented. There was a challenge somewhere in the words.

I sighed at him and then dosed him with a giant wave of peace. His eyes dropped to half-mast as he staggered drunkenly.

"Anything else?" I asked.

Righting himself again, Nathaniel watched me through narrowed eyes. "You certainly have the energy. But you've not been offered or taken the name. We've not completed that process."

"Great, let's do it. I am the Peacekeeper," I said, monotone. "Time is ticking."

"Ticking toward what?" the woman asked, confused.

"He's here regarding the traitors," Nathaniel muttered.

She rocked back on her heels, watching me. "You were there. She bit you that night. They both tracked you that night. The video was unclear, but it could have been you."

I nodded. "They shift—" I paused, reconsidering my words at her frown. "They transformed at my request. My family was in grave danger. They went into the danger, intending to keep me safe."

"Then they are not traitors," she said as if it was obvious. Nathaniel raised his hand to silence her. "No. You need five to sentence a beast lord. I will not vote for his execution if he transformed in defense of the Peacekeeper."

"He's not the Peace—" Nathaniel started.

"The Peacekeeper does not need permission to exist. I have felt his energy myself and will attest to it." Her words were quick, like she was seizing on an opportunity.

Nathaniel looked startled. "I am not suggesting he needs to ask for permission. I'm suggesting we cannot honor him appropriately as we are. We shall gather; all of the elders will join us."

I cleared my throat. "My interest at this moment is in the Hapner family. I will not allow them to be harmed. They may have violated your rules, but it was done at my request. Where are Charlie and Candy?"

Nathaniel smiled innocently. I wasn't fooled. He was no friend of mine. I could feel his deep distrust and rapid heart-beat as parts of him not at peace. "You are not Peacekeeper. Yet. You may claim their innocence after our ceremonies are done."

"Except they're scheduled to be executed in about two hours," I replied.

His eyes narrowed as he searched the room. "The vampire either has a spy or a way around our wards."

I crinkled my nose. "She dislikes being called that."

"She is a parasite, infesting our line of succession," he snapped.

Wow, he was strongly opposed to the Charlie and Ellie love match. I'd seen their bindings to each other. There was no divorce in their future.

"I will not vote to destroy Charles. You are a vote short." The daughter crossed her arms over her chest. I still wasn't looking.

"What does that mean for Candy and their parents?" I asked.

In my peripheral vision, I saw the woman shake her head. "The parents will pay a fine for opposing our team this after-noon. They are not held on pain of death, just restrained until... things are finalized."

"And Candy?" I asked.

The response was slow in coming, but the woman answered me. "By our laws, her actions open her to claiming. As Charles's sister, someone will claim her as a mate. Her genes make her excellent for breeding."

Candy was going to be "claimed" against her will? *Over my dead body*.

"She belongs to me. We've been together for a few months."

Nathaniel gasped. "Go! Now!"

I didn't see the woman move, but she was gone.

7

"She'll be back in a moment," Nathaniel said. "May I know your name?"

I lifted my eyebrows, smirking. He was the one that refused introductions earlier.

His lips lifted into something akin to a smile as he guessed at my thoughts. "Over the years, many have brought 'Peace-keepers' to us that were no more than people empowered to give peace. There is a difference. You demonstrated that difference with Edgar."

"My name is Lucas. Luke."

"Please call me Nate. 'Nathaniel' is a mouthful."

I nodded, still not fooled. My presence disturbed this man. He appeared calm, but I would swear he was having a panic attack.

"How do you know Charles?" Nate asked.

I blinked. "I told you. I am involved with his sister. Where did your daughter go?"

"She went to get the Hapners."

"They'll leave with me?" I meant it to be a statement, but it came out a question.

"No, Luke. I cannot allow that. There are very few rules we insist upon. Secrecy is one of them. They put us all at risk, and on video, no less. No. They will remain as my guests until we can verify your abilities and honor you properly."

"Why keep them here?" I asked. "They're not going to run away. They know what I am."

"Ah. That's a question with a complicated answer. Would you care to sit?"

I looked at the bench he'd gestured to. "No."

I didn't know why, but I knew sitting with this man would make me more vulnerable. We would stand.

I thought of the tie wrapped around Edgar, drawing out his life energy.

We would stand, and Nate wouldn't touch me.

He nodded, seemingly unfazed by my rudeness. "There are a few varieties of beast affinities within our culture. Most are weak, barely able to form a mental bond with an animal. Beast affinities like your Candace, who can transform into many animal forms within the same family, are rare. Once mated and a mother, Candace would be among our nobility—a Beast Master in title. She is gifted with strong genes to produce progeny with powerful beast affinities."

"Progeny? We're not going to call them children?" I asked, almost laughing before my peace ate the humor.

Nate lifted his hand, pointing like he was correcting an answer in a classroom. "Ah. They are not children. They are more than just children. They carry beast affinities."

Okay. The Beast Overlord was a snob. Noted.

"If we are lucky, once a generation or so, one is born like Charles, who may transform to any animal, any form, without notice."

"I believe I saw your daughter do that."

He nodded. "My Sianna is a miracle in many ways. She waited a long time for one such as Charles. He is a Beast Lord in truth: fully human, brilliant, strategic, and capable. He was meant to be Sianna's mate and my successor. Then, when he finally came into his full power, he snubbed his destiny. He fights his true nature, aided by the vampire."

"She prefers to be called a siphon," I cut in, just to see how he'd react.

His sense of self went batshit crazy, triggering my peace without conscious thought. This man was not entirely sane.

Nate took a deep breath when it hit him but didn't otherwise acknowledge my energy.

"No. It is not within my power to release them without a vote to acquit them of wrongdoing. Charles will stay among us. He will remind himself who and what he is. Without the vampire, he will reconsider his choices."

Somewhere to the right of where we stood, I felt Ellie's emotions flair and heard a tiny snort of amusement. If Nate heard it, he didn't react to it.

"They will stay as my guests. Candace will not be further injured. We were unaware of you. We certainly didn't know of her involvement with a potential Peacekeeper. In a week's time, we'll gather a larger group to discuss your status among us as well as Charles and Candace."

"Go back to 'further injured.'" I grated out, anger flashing through me.

Watching me, Nate actually took a step back. "Our customs

are not yours. She stood at her trial, was found guilty, and sentenced to death. She is a female with strong bloodlines. We will waive the death sentence if she is claimed as a mate. She will be released from custody once she produces at least one offspring, rebalancing the scales."

I stared off into space, processing. My inner caveman reared his head. I hoped my mother never heard about it. "She is mine." The words were flat. My rage managed to edge out my natural peace for longer than usual.

"I understand that now." Nate nodded. "There is something I do not understand, though."

Still breathing through my anger, I nodded, inviting his question.

"Charles and Candace know our laws. They know our customs. She knew her fate. They both knew that the protection of a true Peacekeeper is a justifiable defense for their crimes. Why didn't they mention you? Why didn't they summon you? If the girl is yours, why did she not claim you?"

They didn't claim me because I'd told them I didn't want this.

I remained silent.

"Perhaps you are not truly the Peacekeeper?" Nate asked, eyebrows raised. "Perhaps you are an empowered person loaded with stolen energy and the gift of sight. We shall see. It will be impossible to hide what you are when we are gathered."

I didn't bother responding. I heard the door open and feet shuffling toward the center of the arena.

"Luke," Charlie breathed, shaking his head. "You shouldn't be here."

I was not looking at Charlie, the nerd, Ellie's husband and Matilda's friend. I was looking at Charlie in truth. Adonis

60

Charlie—well over six feet tall and built like William, with white-blonde hair and turquoise eyes. His face was severely beaten with blood dripping from an ear. He was naked, whip marks, bites, and bruises galore marring his body.

Candy followed in his wake, holding his hand and looking at the ground. She appeared unharmed but was also naked.

I ran for her, pulling her into a hug and lifting her eyes to mine. "It's going to be fine," I said with more confidence than I felt as I threw my coat around her.

"You can keep sending them," Charlie yelled, taunting Nate. "I'll just keep killing them. The insane ones don't stand a chance, and you know it. There will be a pile of dead bodies before the witching hour. I won't allow her to be claimed against her will, and you don't have a cell that can hold me."

"You are not meant to be a prisoner, Charles," Nate barked. "I gave you an option. You refused. And now, after all of this, a potential Peacekeeper appears, claiming her and defending you! You are not a traitor, but you have kept secrets that should have been shared."

Candy's eyes went huge, staring at me. "You didn't claim me?" she breathed.

I shot her a look, saying, *"You really want me to take it back?"* without words.

She thought for a moment, chewing on her lip, then shot me an apologetic glance. "It's been less than two weeks since we were last together. I could be carrying his child, even now."

It was good Nate couldn't see my face; I was mighty confused. There was no baby on the way. We were careful to ensure there were no babies.

"Of course," Nate replied, now all kindness and smiles. "I will convene the other elders. We'll meet again in a week's time to test and honor the Peacekeeper and acquit you both of wrongdoing. Charles, your actions in defense of the Peacekeeper and in defense of his potential progeny are fully justified, as you know. Until we can convene, you will all stay as my guests."

"No," I said, thinking of my mother's potential freak-out and Sam's subsequent search through time and space to find me. "You will not recognize me as Peacekeeper at this time. You have no right to my company."

I could hear Nate's teeth grinding from ten feet away.

"Luke, you misunderstand. I wish to ensure your safety. If knowledge of you spreads, those with beast affinities will want to test the truth of your claim. As you so aptly demonstrated your peace to our security guard, word already spreads."

"He's not wrong," Charlie muttered. "Announcing yourself and walking out of here without protection would be foolish."

My eyes cut to Charlie. I glared as I muttered, "I'll stay home for the week." The family compound was heavily warded and guarded. And Charlie knew it.

His head gave a minute shake. "Not good enough. Wrong types of protection."

I turned to the woman, still standing behind Charlie in her stupid almost-naked slip. "Go away. Go stand by your dad."

"What do you want me to do?" I murmured without moving my lips once the woman was out of earshot.

"She can hear you no matter what you do unless you can do the telepathy trick," Charlie said in a normal voice. "You need to stay here, or there is going to be—"

"We have a solution!" Nate yelled, seeming pleased. "Sianna has offered to be his guard and protector. Luke, you may go so long as she is with you. There is no better protector."

I paused to look at the woman again. The idea of her as a

fighter seemed absurd. Then I remembered she was still just about naked and turned away, blushing, before peace swallowed my embarrassment.

I looked at Charlie again, then at Candy.

Candy shrugged. "Probably great sex."

"Candace!" Charlie and I growled together.

There was a snort of muffled laughter from the direction of Nate and Sianna. I couldn't tell who made the sound.

"She's not your friend," Charlie said. "But she's not an enemy, either. We have history—"

"I heard."

Charlie exhaled, scrubbing his hand through his hair. "We have history but have always kept in touch. She's fair. And she will kill anyone that gets within ten feet of hurting you if she's volunteering to protect you."

"What does her absence, and mine, mean for you?" I asked.

He shook his head, thinking. "Edgar?"

"Resting. Better. I helped him."

Charlie nodded. "No one will touch Candy while we're on baby watch." He shot his sister a look. "They don't want me dead. I'm the bait in the trap." He stared, waiting for me to get it.

They didn't want Charlie dead. They wanted Charlie free of Ellie. He was the bait in a trap for Ellie.

I snorted. *Yeah, right.* They were severely underestimating Eleanor.

Charlie's lips quirked. "Edgar is an ally if he's back to himself. We'll be okay for a week. Go home. Don't trust her, but don't fear her, either. She's not out to *hurt* you."

I stared at Charlie, waiting. There was more to what he was

saying, but I wasn't getting it. He looked at Candy again, tugging his scraped and bruised hand through his hair.

"Offspring of the Peacekeeper are always Beast Lords, Luke. They're always like me. And they're always sane, at least at the start. The return of the Peacekeeper means the rise of beast affinities again. She's not out to *hurt* you."

My mouth dropped open in shock. I was going to have shifter babies one day?

"I'll be right back," Sianna said, walking by us on her way out of the stadium. "Rest, Charlie. They won't bother her again."

Before my eyes, Charlie dropped to his wolf form, all signs of injury gone.

I guessed we were done talking.

Candy hugged me, holding on for all she was worth. "I do love you, Luke. If this isn't what you want, I don't want it for you, regardless of the cost."

I ran my hand down the back of her dark blonde hair, smoothing it. "It'll work out," I muttered. "Love you too."

She smiled into my chest. "It's like when I tell Charlie I love him. I admit you're right about that."

"Did they hurt you?" I couldn't help asking. The thought made me ill.

She shook her head. "Charlie hates fighting, but he's a great brother. There was no one here tonight that could match him. By next week, though... I guess we'll see. But, Luke, if you come back next week, there will be no way to escape what we talked about. Don't come back."

"It'll work out." I said the words, knowing she was telling the truth. There would be no way to escape the Peacekeeper thing if I made myself known. But that ship had already sailed.

The alternative of letting Candy be "claimed" and Charlie be cornered was not an option.

She banged her forehead into my chest, guessing my thought. "We're two people, Luke. Don't let them ransom two people in exchange for your eternity."

"I am ready," Sianna said. I hadn't heard her approach, but there she stood in a baggy dress with a backpack and what appeared to be a sword over her shoulder.

"Is that a sword?" I asked.

She smirked. "I'll show you my sword if you show me yours."

I could feel Candy shaking with laughter in my arms. I glared at them both.

"I know this isn't funny, but it's kind of funny. I can't wait for Darla to meet her," Candy said, letting go of me. "Go home, Luke. Remember what you are to us and let her see where you come from."

I tilted my head, not understanding. Candy was looking at Sianna. Her voice was taunting, even threatening, but I didn't understand the subtext.

"Let's go." Sianna was talking to me but looking at Candy. "This place will be hip-deep in beast affinities within an hour. Promises of strong progeny only bring out the crazies. Rumors of a true Peacekeeper will draw in everything. I would like to limit the body count."

8

We were silent walking to the car. I realized I didn't know whose Toyota I was driving. Ellie and Charlie didn't have a car. I paused, considering what to do about Ellie.

"Keep moving," Sianna muttered, eyes never stopping as she kept watch. "I was baiting the kitty, but not kidding. They will come in droves to test and feel your power, Peacekeeper. We need to lie low."

I didn't respond, finally walking around to the driver's side door of the car. There was a note on the windshield.

Park outside the guardhouse. Make her walk through the wards.
Leave the car keys in the ignition. Don't fuck her.

Holy shit, Ellie, I thought, rolling my eyes in the darkness.

"From the siphon?" Sianna asked.

I didn't respond, shoving the note in my pocket as I fished out the keys and unlocked the doors.

"I know she is around somewhere. I could feel her energy outside the arena. I could not find her, even from a birds-eye view. She is a powerful one."

I started the car.

"Are you just going to ignore me for the next week?"

"Would you mind opening the glovebox and looking for a registration? I don't know who this car belongs to."

The glovebox was empty, as was the cubbyhole between the two front seats. It was either a rental or stolen. I was guessing Ellie didn't stop to rent a car.

"Just go. You're sober. It's almost three o'clock on New Year's Day. You are not who the cops are watching for," Sianna said. "Or I will drive if you prefer."

I shook my head, pulling through the carpark and out to the main driveway, then out of the estate.

"Where do you live?" she asked, trying to make small talk.

"Cornfields," I muttered, not interested in chattering.

"It's winter. You live in a barren field with dead cornstalks?"

"No. I live with my family in an estate compound similar to this," I answered, seemingly incapable of being an unresponsive ass.

"You have a family? You are married?"

"No."

"You live with your parents?" She was silently judging me.

I sighed. "You'll see."

I hesitated.

"What?" she asked.

"Am I bringing danger to my family? If we're set upon by people wanting to test me, will they threaten my family?"

"No," she answered immediately. "We will be besieged by people wanting to feel your natural energy and confirm what you are. Those who dance on the edge of madness, those who know they're losing control, will come first. My purpose is to ensure they leave you in peace - no pun intended. They may feel your energy. They may not try to claim you as their own."

"So, it's just me they're interested in?"

"I will not allow harm to you or yours, Peacekeeper. We do not need to hide from your loved ones. We just need to lay low until next week."

"Things will improve next week? After they acknowledge me?"

"You are sacred to us. Your wishes will be respected. Drive, Peacekeeper."

FORTY-FIVE MINUTES LATER, I pulled into the parking lot outside the family compound. The guard was already walking toward the car, flashlight shining.

"Luke?" a woman's voice called.

"Hi Joann," I answered. "It's just me. And someone else."

Joann huffed a laugh. "Why park out here? Did you finally get a new car?"

"It's not my car. Someone will pick it up by morning." I hoped. A stolen car outside the compound would be hard to explain.

"We can register your friend quickly—"

"She's not a friend. Just staying for a few days," I said. "I don't want her registered. She's not welcome unless she is accompanied."

That gave Joann pause. Then, I felt her internal triggers fire, probably at the sight of the sword. There was a click in the darkness that likely involved a gun.

"That is an illegal deadly weapon. You will surrender it now and may claim it when you leave." Joann's voice had lost all humor, all traces of emotion, as her hackles rose.

"It's fine," I murmured, pushing peace into the words. "She's a cosplay actress. It's a prop—nothing to worry about. We're just going back to my place. Would you leave notes for the team that I have a guest for this week? She won't be coming or going without me."

"I will," Joann replied groggily, not reacting to the strange request. "Have a good night, Luke."

Sianna and I walked up the sidewalk, around the guard-house, and toward the subdivision compound. About five feet from the ward line, she froze. I kept walking, crossing the line.

I wasn't sure in the darkness, but I thought her eyebrows rose.

I waited.

"These wards will not stop me," she said softly, ensuring Joann couldn't hear her. "They would not stop me any more than that guard would. But there is more to this place."

I nodded, still waiting.

"Would you explain it?"

"No. Cross that ward line, demonstrating you have no intention of harming me or mine. After that, we'll walk to my house, and then I'll answer your questions."

She considered her options for a moment, then crossed the wards to continue walking with me in silence.

My house was dark. Ellie had ushered me out so quickly, I hadn't left a light on. The lights were out in all the houses; everyone had long since gone to bed. I thought about waking William but decided it could wait until morning.

I hopped up the two steps and opened my front door, turning on the lights with the sound of my voice.

"Your door was not locked," Sianna said, offended.

"The only people who live here are my family. There's a fourteen-foot wall around the 'subdivision' and armed guards. There's no point in locking the doors. No one has been in my house since I left."

"You will lock your door, Peacekeeper. Those coming for you will not be stopped by a wall or a guard, though those wards will give them pause. Tell me about your family." She closed the door behind herself, walking down the main hallway and looking around.

Reaching into the front hall closet, I grabbed the dry mop to wipe up the shoe prints we'd made. "I have a family. My parents, Hank and Darla, live at the bottom of the cul-de-sac. I have seven older brothers and a sister." I wasn't going to volunteer anything beyond the basics.

"The Time Walker and Mistress Life are here," she said. It wasn't a question, so I didn't respond.

She lifted her eyebrows, waiting for words that weren't coming.

"I can also feel fear, love, your opposite, fire, earth, and water. I know there are more. I have not sorted them out yet."

I nodded. She wasn't wrong. She wasn't entirely right, either, but not wrong. And there still wasn't a question.

"If trouble comes for you, will your family help you?"

"Of course," I said without hesitation.

She shook her head. "You cannot assume protection from anyone, even family. Family can be your worst enemy. You are confident they are on your side?"

"Yes," I said again.

She nodded. "It will keep until morning. Rest well. Lock the door behind me." She made for the front door again.

"What? Where are you going?"

"I am going outside," she said. The "duh" was implied.

"Why?"

"Peacekeeper—"

"Luke. My name is Luke," I snapped, annoyed for a moment before it washed away again.

"Peacekeeper," she said again, emphasizing the word. "When danger comes, I do not want it within reach of you. I will meet it outside the walls."

"There are people here—the guards in particular—who don't understand what we are. You cannot keep calling me that."

"What would you have me call you?" she asked, pulling a confused face.

"Luke!" I almost yelled my name.

She shook her head. "You do not wish to be friends. I will not use your given name, though you are welcome to use mine. I will hear you if you call for me. Charlie was right about that. Good resting, Peacekeeper."

As I watched her disappear into the darkness, I realized I had been a touch rude to someone who had offered to protect me. Though, I wasn't sure if she was my guard or my jailer. Maybe both?

MY CELLPHONE VIBRATING on the nightstand woke me on Thursday morning.

"Mhufrmp?" I answered.

"Since when do you sleep past seven in the morning?" William demanded. "Get up. What's with you and this cosplay woman showing up in the middle of the night?"

"Time is it?" I groaned. My head felt like it was going to split open from the pressure. That was new. I was not prone to headaches.

"Oh-seven-hundred." I could hear the smile in Will's voice. I hung up and turned my phone off.

"Ugh," I groaned into my pillow, rolling over on my stomach.

"Peacekeeper?" Sianna asked softly. "It is your head?"

"Why are you in my bedroom?" I asked into the pillow.

"I heard your phone vibrate. I intended to silence it before it woke you, but you are sensitive to sound."

That was true. I had a musician's ear.

I turned my head but didn't otherwise move. "I apologize for being rude. Please call me, Luke?"

"You are sick?" she asked, ignoring my words.

"My head."

She made a tsking sound. "I thought it better that you left my father's presence last night. I did not expect to affect you as well. You have spent time with Charlie. He and I are near equals."

"I make Charlie woozy. He doesn't make me sick," I muttered. "But there's a real chance I'm going to puke. Please don't tell my family."

"Your family will worry if you are ill," she said knowingly.

I actually laughed at that. "No. My family will take great joy in adding new words to my name. When last it came up, I was 'Poor Persnickety Puking Peace.'" I wondered if they'd come up with a new one since Candy blew up my car.

"Your family is not an ally, then?"

I sighed. "Don't you have a family? Brothers and sisters?"

She nodded. "Many."

"Don't you give each other shit?"

Her brow furrowed. "No. They do not speak to me often."

Before I could respond, there was slamming on the door downstairs. Sianna was suddenly gone. I didn't see her move.

"It is a large blonde-haired man that emanates fear. Not a danger to either of us."

"It's my eldest brother," I responded. "Not a danger to either of us, but a pain in the ass."

The pounding continued.

"I'm coming!" I shouted, hoping he'd stop pounding on the door.

I rolled out of bed and fell flat on my face. "Oh, shit," I muttered. "I don't think I can stand up."

I heard something give way in the front door, and then Will's feet pounded up the stairs.

Sianna had her sword at his throat before he made it into my room.

"My brother!" I yelled, right before my stomach gave way and I puked all over my bedroom floor.

Dry heaving too hard to speak, I heard Will and Sianna fighting. I saw her sword go skittering down the stairs, followed almost immediately by William's gun. There was a lion's roar followed by complete silence.

"Oh," Will muttered. "New girlfriend? It stinks in here. Holy shit. You puked everywhere."

I managed to turn my head. He was bleeding from what looked like a stab wound to the abdomen but didn't seem to care. Whatever.

I puked again for good measure—too much head movement.

"I'm just about healed. Pull the energy, Luke. I'll hold the fear back."

I tried. I really did. I felt the energy move into me, but it didn't help. I puked again, surprised. I didn't think it was possible to puke once you started dry heaving. You'd think I would have had this puking thing down pat by now.

"He is not injured," Sianna said, back to human and pulling her dress on. "Let me help." She offered a hand.

There was no discord coming from her, nothing out of balance, no lack of inner peace. She wasn't plotting anything. I took her hand.

The weight of my sick stomach lifted first, making it easier to breathe. The pressure in my head gave way, giving me chills as my body temperature dropped back to normal. I hadn't realized I was running a fever.

I sat back, leaning against my bed. Meeting her eyes, I squeezed her fingers a bit. "Thank you. Better."

She nodded. "He is not a threat?"

I shook my head.

She disappeared again. I could hear her futzing with the front door.

"What the fuck is going on?" Will asked.

9

I gave Will the short version of the previous night's events, skipping over the ugly details—like Candy being forced to have children against her will and Charlie being beaten and whipped.

If my brother realized the stakes, he'd hunt down Nate and storm the compound, regardless of the repercussions. If I could end this without anyone getting hurt—or more hurt—I would.

"I get the feeling you're leaving out details."

"I am," I acknowledged.

He nodded, understanding. For all our differences, Will and I had reached a strange understanding and respect for each other.

I still cleaned up the puke on my own. Asshole.

"So, you're going to do the Peacekeeper harem thing? Mom's going to need to adjust her Sunday dinner seating arrangements."

I glared as he grinned.

"Who's the woman?"

"She's supposedly here to guard me. I think there are a couple reasons for her presence. Apparently, I make good shifter babies. And I think they realize there's a chance I won't play ball with the Peacekeeper thing. But I want Charlie and Candy out of trouble. So, we'll see where it goes."

"Shifter babies?" Will threw his head back, laughing. "I don't recommend sleeping with her, Luke. She's faster and more dangerous than me—way out of your comfort zone."

"Noted."

"Where's Ellie now?"

I shrugged.

"The car you brought home last night was gone at sunrise. Joann couldn't remember what happened to it."

"Makes sense."

Will waited for more information. I shrugged, not offering anything.

"You stink," he said, nostrils flaring.

I groaned, knowing what was coming.

"Poor Pathetic Persnickety Putrid Puking Peace." He grinned, proud of himself.

"I hate you."

"Shower before you come over. You're foul. You'll make Pip sick. Training at ten."

"Tell Micah and Hennessy?" I asked. Will, Hennessy, and Micah formed the trifecta of protectors and warriors for our little family circle. I didn't want anyone to get hurt.

"Headed that way now."

"Tell Mom?" I figured it was worth a shot.

Will laughed again, headed for the door. "That's funny. No. Don't lock your fucking door again. We'll switch the locks out with something biometric before nightfall. But I will rip that fucking thing off the hinges if you lock me out again."

"Noted. I wasn't expecting a visitor at seven-thirty in the morning."

Will turned, shooting me a look. "You showed up in the middle of the night with a sword-wearing woman you wouldn't name."

"I asked Joann to leave a note," I said, realizing how stupid it sounded in retrospect.

"Get cleaned up. Eat something. Then I get to beat the shit out of you again!"

I WAS SCRUBBING my face when I heard Sianna's voice. In my bathroom. Where I was naked in the shower.

"You said you hate your brother."

I yelped, covering myself in a hurry. "Privacy?" I scolded as the face wash stung my eyes.

She actually laughed.

"Please go away," I begged, feeling my entire body flush with embarrassment. My man bits were trying to hide on their own.

"This bothers you?" she asked, obviously surprised.

"YES!"

Through the glass wall of the shower, I saw her frown. "Apologies, Peacekeeper."

She was gone again.

It occurred to me that I didn't hear her coming or going until she chose to make her presence known. My modesty was lost on her.

After I was clean and dressed, I stood in my room, debating

what to do. "Sianna, I'm decent," I said in a quiet voice, not calling for her.

A heartbeat later, she was in front of me. "I apologize," she said again. "Nudity has never been uncomfortable for me."

"Where were you just now?" I asked, curious.

"In the fields behind your house, outside the wall." She said it like the answer should be obvious. "There is a small gap in the stone wall encircling this place. I will show the guards so it is repaired. But the wards are thorough, thick and strong, encircling all the houses as well as the entire compound."

I nodded. "How do you move so quickly?"

Confusion flashed in her eyes. "Charlie does the same, yes?"

"No."

She rocked back on her heels, surprised. "I apologize again. It must be jarring."

"Surprising," I said, smiling. "But nothing to apologize about."

"I am the fastest beast affinity on the planet, when it comes to speed as well as transformations."

My eyebrows shot up. "You're shifting forms that quickly?" She nodded.

"Where do your clothes go?"

Her brow wrinkled again. "They stay here."

"Is that some sort of magic?"

She was trying not to laugh at me. I could tell. "No, Peacekeeper. I take them off before I transform."

I looked down, noticing her clothes. She was still wearing the dress. Easy on and off, I guessed. She was barefoot.

"Don't you get cold?" I asked.

She shook her head again. "I can regulate my body temperature and circulation. The cold does not affect me."

"Huh. Neat."

"You do not seem to know much about beast affinities," she noted.

"I know almost nothing about beast affinities," I agreed. "Beast master, lord, overlord something. Whatever. You can shift to animals."

She flinched, displeased.

I frowned at the reaction. "I'm sorry. I didn't mean to be offensive, just flippant about my ignorance."

She hesitated. "It is not important when it is just us. I will not take offense. But it will be important next week. Many would be glad to take offense and test you. You understand?"

I nodded.

"The Overlord is Nathaniel, my father. He has invited you to use his given name, but I do not recommend using his title as a joke. I would likely die defending you. It is a title infused with power to us, much like your kind treat the Walker with deference."

I busted out laughing. "Sorry. I know. I know what you mean. But Sam... is different. I'm sorry. Go on."

She nodded. "At his core, my father is like Charlie and me—a Beast Lord. But his human intelligence remains when he is in animal form. That is exceptionally difficult for us to do. So, he leads. Charlie and I also keep our intelligence as beasts. Most of the elders that still transform can do it when they focus.

"Otherwise, when we move from human form to beast form, the transformation is complete. Our human minds give way to animal instincts. When Candace transforms into a cat, she is a cat in truth. The word 'shift' indicates that human instincts come along for the ride. For the most part, that is not true. That is why we transform, not shift."

"Candace understood me when I talked to her that night in November. When we fought for my family, she had enough humanity left, even in her cat form, to understand and express humor," I disagreed.

"You were there, Peacekeeper. You 'kept' her mind, her peace, for her. I would wager she could not transform back without your permission."

That threw me. I'd had to close the bond to Charlie and Candy to get them back to human form that night.

I shook my head again. "She and I talked about this. She said the cat psyche never had complete control because she'd lose her human self. That the peace thing I do gives the cat psyche more space in her mind. I don't think she truly loses her human self."

"I do not know. You can have this conversation with her next week. But I suspect she avoided full transformations when you were not around. Maybe she only partially transformed?"

I thought of the night I met Candy and her hand shifting to a paw.

"I don't know," I said, acknowledging I was missing pieces of this puzzle. "Hungry?"

Sianna's eyebrows shot up.

"I'm going to make some breakfast. Would you like some eggs?"

Her mouth opened and closed twice before words came out. "I apologize for not attending to your needs. I can make food— eggs if that is what you would like."

I narrowed my eyes in suspicion. "Is this some kind of weird ego trip?"

Her head tipped to the side in confusion. "No eggs?"

"I'll make eggs," I said. "I'm the one that offered to do it."

"You are Peacekeeper. You do not do such mundane things."

I burst out laughing again, walking toward the stairs. "I'm Luke, Sianna. Luke. And if you tell my mother I made you cook eggs for me, she'll gut me like a fish. I'm a modern man. I'll make breakfast."

She was still at the top of the stairs, looking confused when I turned into the kitchen.

10

MICAH: Outside training today.

LUKE: It's freezing.

MICAH: Outside training.

MATTHEW: Why am I included in this text thread?

MICAH: You are required to attend if you are on this thread. Happy New Year.

SAM: Me too?

MICAH: You especially.

"Why are we outside?" I heard my sister, Beth, ask as I approached the field we used for outside training.

"We need more space," Micah said, tone flat and severe. Ethan was not in sight, which probably meant Micah was freaking out.

He exhaled hard when he saw Sianna and me walk toward the group. He pressed his lips together before giving me a look that threatened severe pain.

"Huntress," he greeted Sianna without offering any sign of welcome. "I suspected William was speaking of you when he mentioned your little tussle."

"Micah," Sianna replied, ducking her head a bit but not moving her eyes from him. "I knew you were here. I felt your power last night."

He exhaled again, more slowly, as he nodded. "We'll wait for the others. Lucas, you do not understand what you've brought here."

Sianna actually rolled her eyes, the most casual expression I'd seen from her yet. "I serve as guardian. He waltzed out in front of my father, declaring himself Peacekeeper."

Micah's eyebrows shot up. "Your father means him harm?"

Sianna's expression went blank. "I do not believe so."

"I can do introductions," I started.

Micah shook his head. "Don't bother. She knows what we each are. She doesn't care *who* we are. Beast affinities and empowered people don't play nice together."

I looked at Sianna. She nodded in agreement.

Well, that's awkward, I thought.

"What's going on?" Matilda asked, arriving with Jake.

"Charlie and Candy got in trouble for helping us in November. Last night, I tried to get them out of trouble. It only sort of worked. Next week, they're going to have a regroup and name me Peacekeeper. After that, everything will be fine," I explained.

"It's a little bit funny that Candy got in trouble for helping you, but not for blowing up your car." Noah laughed.

"It's not a funny kind of trouble," I said, hoping to head off a conversation about how Candy and I were no longer a couple.

Matilda looked at me, waiting for more information. I debated.

"What happened to Charlie, Luke?" she asked, not messing around. Charlie and Ellie were dear to Matilda in a way few people were.

"He and Candy are being held under a death sentence, but it's going to be fine. I can get them out of it," I said quickly, trying not to notice the ring of snow melting around Matty or the fact that the field was noticeably darker.

"Where is Eleanor?" Matilda asked slowly, rage burning in her voice.

"I don't know," I muttered. "She showed up last night, brought me to where Candy and Charlie were, then disappeared."

"My guess is that she is watching over Charlie," Sianna offered. "Her energy was there last night. I doubt she would leave him."

Matilda's glare shifted. "I've seen you before. You were in the bar the night I met Charlie."

Sianna nodded.

"I don't remember your name."

"I did not give it to you, Lady Light," Sianna murmured, eyes downturned. "We did not know who you were."

Micah blew out another gust of breath. "Sam and Addy are coming."

"Family training!" Sam yelled, laughing as he and Addy appeared in the center of the field. "We haven't all done this in a while. How is..." The words trailed off as he focused on Sianna.

"And here we go," Micah muttered.

"Walker. Mistress," Sianna greeted them, not looking particularly impressed or concerned.

"Sam?" I asked. He hadn't moved. I couldn't even see his breath.

"Wait," Adaline whispered.

We stood as a group, staring at my middle brother as he walked through time, looking for something.

This would be noteworthy in another family. It was just another day in my family.

"It's getting awkward," Noah muttered after a solid two minutes passed.

"Should we go about training until he's ready?" Will asked Adaline.

She shook her head. "I think that would be bad."

Noah plopped down on the ground, pulling Talise into his lap. Matilda started a fire that heated the field, despite not having any fuel.

"I really need to be here for this?" Adrian asked. "Ree and I were playing—"

Sam gasped, jumping back to the present with all of his Walker powers forward. The sky overhead cracked with lightning as the wind went nuts and Matilda's fire exploded. Gravity increased enough for it to feel like my joints were grinding together. As he stomped across the field toward Sianna, Sam's footsteps echoed—a dead giveaway that he had let his power go. He wasn't reigning anything in.

In one swift motion, he grabbed Sianna by the throat, lifting her from the ground. "Hear me now, Sianna Huntress, outcome of sacrifice and a true love's final gift, last of the Overlord's sane begotten: He is mine. Mine. I will come for you if you cross him. I will destroy every beast affinity and erase the knowledge of them from history if he is harmed. MINE."

He dropped her.

I think he intended for her to fall to the ground, but she landed squarely on her bare feet.

"Hear me, Walker of legend," she said directly into his face, voice quiet, despite the contempt. "The Peacekeeper is not a possession to be claimed. He exists by his own will, indifferent to your antics. I mean him no harm, nor will I allow harm to come to him. If you attempt to lay a hand on me again, I will rip it off."

Sam nodded, suddenly himself again. "Okay, thanks. That helps."

"Uh, Sam?" I asked.

He shrugged. "She'll either take your head or your heart. One makes her a sister. The other makes her an abject lesson for the ages. We'll see. I'm not entirely sure where we are right now."

I looked around, confused. "Isn't there some nice future where she stays for the week, we get Charlie and Candy back, and then she goes home?"

"No."

"I KNOW THAT'S NOT HOW TIME WORKS, SAM!" I yelled, genuinely panicked. I did not know or trust this woman.

Sam shrugged again. "No. The futures where she leaves aren't good for you. Go for broke."

"Fuck my life," I shouted at no one in particular.

Then, my power swallowed my panic and worry, as it was prone to do.

Oh, well. Death comes for us all. And, if we fall in love, we'll have fun kids.

I shook my head, laughing at the course of my own thoughts.

"Come on, lover boy," William taunted, walking to the center of the crowd. "Time to get beat up."

"Ugh. Can't we skip this today?" I wasn't whining. I couldn't whine. My voice was monotone. We'd go with that.

"Sam just told you someone would take your head, and you want to skip training?" Will asked. "You're not that stupid, right?"

"What is this?" Sianna asked. She was decidedly not amused.

"My brothers have been training me to physically defend myself as well as heal my injuries," I answered into the awkward silence.

"You can stop this now," she said to no one in particular. "It' is a waste of time."

"No, it's really not," Will disagreed. "We've had a few situations where the peace mojo didn't drop someone. He needs to defend himself, and he needs to know how to heal himself."

She glared at him. "I just finished saying I would not allow harm to come to him. Do you believe you are exempt, that I will not protect him from you? I would have killed you this morning if he had not claimed you as a brother."

The field was silent as Will and Sianna stared at each other. Will didn't deny that she could have killed him.

Eventually, she continued. "Healing himself from your energy is difficult and wrong. He will heal easily from my energy, as was also demonstrated this morning."

Will's gaze cut to Micah.

Micah shrugged. "I have no idea. I've never known a true peace pillar or a Peacekeeper."

They both turned to Sam. He smiled his little Sam smile. "I think we should test this."

"WHAT?" William asked, startled.

Micah nodded in agreement with Sam. "Charlie never demonstrated why Beast Lords should not be trifled with. I was hoping the Huntress would agree to a non-lethal sparring match."

Sianna grinned, genuine amusement showing in her eyes. "I can agree to those terms."

Sam cleared his throat.

"Non-lethal, no loss of limb," Micah amended.

The grin stayed on her face as she turned to Sam with a smirk. "It is good we understand each other."

He smiled back, the expression one of *otherness*. Sam was still holding his power close to the surface.

"You're going to spar, Sam?" I asked.

"I will not. I will referee," he murmured, his words echoing.

Sianna made chicken noises at him.

Off to the side, I heard Tali mutter to Noah. "I love her."

"How many of you?" Sianna asked.

Micah looked around. "Me. Fear. Loyalty."

She snorted.

"Hennessy is a trained military expert. He's tougher than you'd think, especially with his circle," Micah said, hiding a smile. "Also, Rage. Chaos, too."

"No," she objected. "No Chaos

"Really? Two former Navy SEALs, Micah, and indestructible

Rage are fine. But my schoolteacher brother is a deal-breaker?" I asked.

She nodded. "We agreed to non-lethal sparring. Madness can destroy me. I do not deny that. As your balance, he would never hurt you. I do not need to defend you from him."

"That's not my name," Matthew said, smiling at her to acknowledge her truth.

Sianna stared at him for a few moments in silence. "Pandemonium, lord of wild things, is perhaps an even greater risk."

"You told her!" Matthew yelled at me.

"I didn't. I didn't say a damn thing!" I objected.

"They're young," Micah murmured. "They don't know how you're doing that yet. Peace is closest to that talent, but not there yet."

"Last night, I watched him free Edgar," Sianna disagreed.

Micah turned, considering me. "I wouldn't have expected him to be able to do it yet. They've worn the names barely six months."

She shook her head. "The Peacekeeper does not belong to the Walker and Mistress. His power is not of the circle. If he took a name from them, he will return it before becoming Peacekeeper in truth."

"He will not," Sam and Micah said in unison.

She shrugged. "Sparring? Any of you, all of you, other than the Mistress, Pan, and Light are welcome."

"Why not me?" Matty asked, sounding almost affronted.

Sianna blinked. "I would no sooner harm Light than I would the Mistress. No, not even sparring, Lady."

Taking three short steps to meet Will in the center of the field, Sianna grinned. She looked back at me, pointing to the ground at her feet. "Sit."

I blinked.

"Sit. You are the goal. They will start at least five feet from you, and they will not touch you."

As I moved to obey, she sprouted a scaled hide over her skin. I paused.

"A beast affinity does not need to fully transform for battle. Do not forget that. Though, I will undoubtedly transform many times while sparring."

Will smiled, impressed, as he counted off five paces. "Sam?"

"Begin," Sam said calmly, stepping away from the center of the field.

For a moment, things happened too quickly to follow. Sianna went from a scaled hide to a roaring hunting cat and then a hissing snake in three fast heartbeats. William was down and not moving. Sianna stood in front of me, sparring at warp speed with Micah, the motions too fast to follow. As Micah seemed to get a hand on her, she shifted to a bird of prey, tearing one of his eyes from the socket as he screamed.

Hennessy was moving around the circle, trying to come upon me from behind only to meet the roaring lioness again. He paused, pulling back as she seemed to disappear. His one-second pause was long enough. He started screaming in pain, ripping at his clothes as a giant arachnid climbed out of his coat collar.

Back to human, she stood beside me, bare assed naked in the freezing cold.

"Anyone else?" she asked. The field was silent. A grin spread across Sianna's face as she met Talise's eyes. "That might work on another beast affinity, Lady Loch. You will find my lungs hard to fill. It is a good defense for you, though—worth practicing. If you were to pull the water from me, I would take the form of a poisonous desert lizard and kill you with a bite. You are not fast enough to kill me like that. Yet."

Turning to Adrian's girlfriend, Lucy, she continued. "Similarly, I can survive for some time without oxygen, Lady Wind. You could kill me with lightning. Probably. Unless I timed my transformation perfectly."

Looking at Beth, Sianna's eyes narrowed. "There is not much hope left to me. You are unlikely to slow me by playing with the positive emotions. You would be dead already if you faced me outside of sparring."

Beth frowned, seeming to shake her head. "Your mental defenses are excellent."

"My brain is not structured like yours," Sianna corrected. "Short of madness, you cannot play mind games with me."

Dismissing Beth, she smiled at Adrian. "Rage chooses to skip sparring?"

Adrian's answering smile was sad. "I do. There is so much rage and anger within you, I'd risk doing actual harm to you. I wouldn't harm someone fixated on keeping my brother safe."

She froze at his words, stunned. She seemed to consider him for a moment, then nodded. "Maybe," she allowed. "Physical sparring would have been fine, though."

"I'm no match for you, and I know it. You don't need to leave me in a broken heap for me to admit it." Adrian's smile warmed a bit.

Sianna smiled back, nodding her head at the compliment. Then, she turned back to me.

"Did anyone touch you?" she asked.

"No."

She nodded before punching me in the face hard enough to break my nose and knock me out for a moment.

I COULD HEAR Sam laughing as I came to. "Asshole," I muttered.

"Sit up," Sianna demanded, offering a hand. I glared at her, pushing myself up to sitting without her help.

"Pull the energy to heal your face from your circle," she said.

"I can't. It doesn't work."

She nodded.

"Pull the energy from Lord Micah. I'm guessing he's the easiest," she suggested.

I looked around. Sam nodded encouragingly. He knew something I didn't.

I found the binding to Micah and—

"You'd be dead by now," Sianna interrupted.

I glared at her.

She grinned, touching my face with one fingertip.

I could feel my nose crack back into place immediately, fully healed.

"You are Peacekeeper. I will keep you safe and well. This 'training' is pointless."

She began walking towards my house without another word.

11

———

*B*y the time I got back to the house, Sianna was gone again.

I guessed we weren't discussing her beating the shit out of my family (incredible!), Sam's prediction (horrifying!), or the fact that she could heal me (huh?).

After the bloody nose and sitting in the cold, I decided to take another shower, this one blissfully free of interruption.

Back in the kitchen, I realized it was barely noon. I took stew meat out of the freezer to defrost and began gathering vegetables.

"What are you doing?" Sianna asked ten minutes later.

"It's interesting that I don't feel you in my space. Usually, I can feel others, especially new people, in my space," I replied, not bothering to answer her question.

"You are Peacekeeper. I am of your... flock, I guess. I belong in your space." She said the words with confidence, but something in her mind wiggled unhappily. She was not at peace.

"Want to talk about it?" I asked.

"What are you doing?" she asked again.

I paused in my chopping and looked at her standing awkwardly in my kitchen. "I'm chopping vegetables. Beef stew tonight?"

"I told you I would prepare your meals."

"And I told you I would cook for myself. You're not my serv—"

She shook her head. "I am, in fact, your servant. All beast affinities await your pleasure."

"That's creepy. Also, I like to cook."

"It is a fact," she retorted. "Did the cat not make this clear?"

"Candy? No, she did not wait on me. I had no expectation of it. We dated. She's a slob. I like to cook and clean. It worked for us."

"Past tense?"

I went back to chopping.

"Passion said she blew up your car. The guard last night asked if you had a new car. She injured you? Your possessions?"

Warning bells went off in my brain. "No, she did not harm me. The car was a joke—kind of. We broke up. She put on a show to help me save face in front of my family. She helped me."

"But you claimed her?" Sianna asked, confused.

"I did. I will not see her 'claimed' against her will."

She nodded. "Nor would I. It is a terrible thing. Barbaric." The words were clear and truthful, but the unhappy, unsettled part of her mind was raging.

I sighed, setting my knife down and offering my hand. "May I help? You've helped me twice today. Allow me to help you in return?"

"You do not need my permission," she said, eyes narrowed.

"Nope, I don't," I confirmed, still holding out my hand.

She didn't take it, instead disappearing again. I went back to my chopping.

That wasn't an internal twinge of my power. My energy wasn't reacting to her absence. It wasn't.

Fucking Sam.

HOURS LATER, my stew simmered on the stove as I made music at my piano. Not in the mood to play anything in particular or work on anything, I just let my fingers flow, creating music without a thought.

The harmony wove around me, building my own personal cocoon of sound. I felt where my peace mingled with the tones, dancing within the shape of the music.

This was my own form of meditation. Everything stifled by my energy found a home in my music if I just let it happen.

Eyes closed, I let the music continue to roll. My mind wandered to Candy threatened and Charlie beaten. The music shifted to something darker, angrier. Slower.

I thought of Ellie in my living room, demanding my help. For a moment, I considered what Ellie would be without Charlie. I was reasonably confident I didn't want to know.

"You're going to break a key by slamming your hands like that," Sianna murmured from behind me.

I shrugged. I'd felt her come into the house.

"Do you always play with your eyes closed?"

"No. It's like therapy for me."

I could hear the smile in her words. "Therapy for the Peacekeeper!" She laughed then, truly delighted, her earlier unhappi-ness still there but buried deep.

"You're better?" I asked.

"I am."

"I would have helped." I wasn't offended that she'd refused me. I wasn't. I didn't even like this woman. I didn't trust her.

"You would have quieted my unease, not removed the source of it," she countered.

I nodded. That was true. I made people find peace and accep-tance with how things were. I didn't change reality.

"Talk about it?" I offered again.

"No, Peacekeeper."

"Sianna, you beat the snot out of my bully brother today. You can call me Luke."

"No, I cannot."

I stopped playing so I could turn and look at her.

"Don't turn around," she said quickly. "Prove my point."

I waited, frustrated by the games.

"What do I look like?" she asked.

"What?" I asked, now confused.

"What do I look like? The actual me. What do *I* look like?"

I thought about it for a moment. I didn't know the answer. Standing with her father the night before, she'd been short, not much taller than Matilda's five feet. She'd had dark hair and dark eyes with a smattering of freckles. Standing with Charlie, she'd been taller, maybe closer to five-eight, with blonde hair and blue eyes. Facing off with Sam, she'd been his height with short, light brown hair.

"I don't know," I admitted.

"I have very few friends. But friends know what I look like. We are not friends."

"Okay," I said, somehow sad.

"I will neither harm you nor be bound to you," she said, the words defiant. "Love has no place between us, regardless of the Walker's words. I want nothing from your heart. We will make beautifully strong children as allies and maybe friends. But I will be one of many. There will be no binding. It goes against everything I believe."

"No worries," I said, blowing out a sigh. "Love has no place with peace. I've learned that lesson a few times over."

She was gone again, lost in the sunset, when I glanced out the window after her.

I turned back to the piano, dusting my fingertips across the keys without making a sound. I waited for my mind to respond to the invitation.

This was part of my process. When I sat with a familiar instrument, my subconscious mind would eventually accept the invitation, eager to create sound.

But, that evening, the music wouldn't come.

*a*fter eating alone, I tried to play some guitar. When that didn't work, I picked up my e-reader and went to bed. I didn't remember falling asleep.

The beginning of the dream felt like reality.

I was at my piano, still blocked, unable to create new music. There was no sound, but I could feel the frustration coursing through me. I slammed the keys, punishing the instrument for my own failure, then stomped off to the kitchen. Walking through the doorway, though, I found myself in the barren fields outside the family compound—decidedly not in my kitchen. It was dark, but the moon was full, reflecting off the snow and creating enough ambient light to see by.

I looked around, confused. I was in my pajama pants and t-shirt, barefoot and alone, but not cold.

The black cougar that was Candy on the night of our battle in November walked toward me, head low.

"Candy?"

The cat's head lifted, meeting my eyes. Not Candy. Sianna.

Between one step and the next, she changed, standing before me in Candy's shape.

"You prefer this form?" Sianna-as-Candy asked, the voice a perfect replica.

"This is seriously fucked up," I said, now confident I was dreaming.

"No?" she asked as I stepped back from her.

She took another step toward me, and I was looking at Talise.

"This one?" she asked.

"Stop," I whispered, dumbstruck.

"Not this one," would-be-Talise acknowledged. "This one does not ignite your lust, just your affection. I wonder if the cat realizes she doesn't have *either* effect on you. Your time together has truly run its course, yet you still claimed her."

Talise's brows furrowed in confusion.

"Candy will always be a friend," I muttered, trying to will myself awake.

She changed again, back to the short brunette that stood with Nathaniel the previous night. "And she feels the same?"

I nodded.

Her frown deepened. "I would not be so quick to claim that one. She is selfish. Charlie is a good man. His selfishness comes from love. I have seen the bonds to the siphon. I know what is between them. His love for her outweighs his sense of obligation. Your cat is different—short-sighted and selfish."

"Because she won't create 'progeny' with random men?" I asked, annoyed. Candy was funny and sweet, wild, daring, sloppy... Many things, including selfish. But so was I.

Sianna shook her head. "No. There is history with that one.

I respect independence but don't tolerate selfishness. There is a difference."

"Is there?" I asked. "What looks like a selfish choice to you is likely independence from another perspective."

She shook her head again. "You did not come here to speak of this." Her form changed again, this time to a taller, shapely woman with golden blonde hair falling down her back in loose curls. She looked like a 1950s pin-up. My eyes just about bugged out of my head.

Did I mention she was naked?

She was naked, standing in front of me, without another creature around.

My body tingled in anticipation as I battled a purely physical response.

I took a step back again. "Why do you keep doing that? Don't be anyone but you! Animals, beast affinities, fine! Not humans like this. I can't process this."

"Peacekeeper, humans are animals. Those of us with the capacity can be anything or anyone, at least for a while. You have seen Charlie's preferred form and his true form. You know this."

I thought back to when I'd first seen Adonis Charlie in November. I had drained his binding to me, forcing him into his natural shape.

I tried to find bindings to Sianna. I couldn't seem to "turn on" the sight, then reminded myself this was a dream.

"This is the most fucked up dream of my life," I muttered.

She was pressed against me, kissing my neck, scraping her teeth against my skin. The (naked!) pin-up was rubbing her body against me.

"Okay, time to wake up. Wake up. Wake up!" I slapped myself. It seemed like the thing to do.

It didn't work.

Sianna chuckled, the sound throaty and low in my ear. The hair stood up on my arms.

"If we can't be friends, we certainly can't be fuck buddies!" I yelled. "Knock it off!"

She laughed again, pushing away from me as I bolted upright in bed.

"Holy shit!" I gasped, falling out of bed for the second night in a row.

A MINUTE LATER, there was pounding on the bathroom door.

"Peacekeeper are you ill?" her voice was all business.

It was a dream. I need to calm down. It was just a dream.

I looked down at myself.

I needed to calm down. It was a dream.

"I'm fine!" I yelled. My voice cracked.

I turned the shower on, setting the temperature to frigid, and stepped in without bothering to take off my pajamas.

"May I come in?" she yelled.

"NO!"

"Are you injured?"

Did blue balls count as an injury?

"No?" I called back.

"Why did that sound like a question?"

A swift kick later, the privacy lock on my bathroom door was busted. Sianna stood in my bathroom while I was in the shower.

I gasped. "WHAT THE FUCK?"

Sianna, the naked pin-up, stood in my bathroom. While I was in the shower. With my clothes on.

Shit.

"Are you ill?"

"What the fuck?" I yelled again.

"You broke the contact suddenly. Are you sick, Peacekeeper? Did you hurt yourself?"

I was beyond words, just bug-eyed staring, and confused.

Realizing I wasn't responding, she opened the shower door and grabbed my hand. "The water is freezing," she murmured, shutting it off.

"Towels?" She looked around. "Towels." A fresh towel from the linen closet wrapped around me.

"Get out of there." She tugged my hand, pulling me from the shower. "You have never dream walked before?"

I heard the words. Something in my memory twinged about dream walking. But I was still lost.

Her hands touched my face. "Breathe. You must breathe."

I gasped. She was right. I hadn't been breathing.

"Wha...?" I panted.

"Dream walking?" she asked. Her eyes were a dark blue. In the bathroom light, there were flecks of turquoise mixed in. Turquoise, like Charlie's eyes.

I shook my head. My teeth began to chatter.

"It's okay, Peacekeeper. All is well. You have that ability. I was resting when you came to me."

"D-d-d-dream?" I stuttered.

She nodded, touching my face again. "Please be calm. Please. Your... unease. It affects me. I cannot keep you safe like this. Please."

She was touching me. I didn't need to find a binding to drain away the energy that allowed her to transform. I pulled the energy from her in one pass and felt it go dry within her.

She gasped. "That is cheating," she muttered. "You learn quickly."

The curvy, soft-looking bits became less curvy, replaced by tight cords of muscle. Her face lost some roundness, her features becoming more angular.

Nothing else changed.

Sianna was maybe half a foot shorter than me with a muscular build and long, wavy golden blonde hair.

"Please don't do that again," I whispered. "It felt...wrong."

"Not too wrong," she muttered, pushing herself against my wet clothes and grinding her hips against mine.

Her lips lifted into a small smile as my body responded, cold, wet clothes be damned.

Her lips drifted to my neck. I felt her hot tongue touch before her teeth scraped my skin.

"I won't do this," I said. Back to myself, my teeth had stopped chattering. My voice was done warbling. Her energy seemed to steady me.

Her hips wiggled again. "I will put the curves back. I like them better too." Her voice was a purr, tickling my ear and giving me goosebumps.

"Sianna." It came out sharper than I'd intended.

She stepped back.

"Bonds and love may not be how you're built, but random fucking is not how I'm built."

She lifted her eyebrows with a smirk and then pointedly dropped her gaze below my waist.

"I don't care," I said. "I mean it. I won't do this. The harem nonsense associated with your Peacekeeper legends does not apply. Don't bother. I won't do it."

She laughed. "You will not be able to help yourself."

I stared at her, waiting for my resolution to sink into her head. "You said it yourself. We're not even friends. Why would you want this?"

"Aside from the physical pleasure?" she asked, still smirking. "The cat wasn't wrong. The sex will be fantastic."

I continued to stare, unamused and waiting.

She sighed. "Every generation removed from the Peacekeeper, those with affinities become more unstable. The Walker called me the last of the sane. He is not wrong about that. I am the last of my father's children with control of my mind. The six children before me were insane. The fifteen after me are also insane. Some never even understood what it meant to be human.

"We are not like the empowered of your circles, where the energy fades gracefully, leaving reasonably ordinary people in its wake. As our energy weakens, our ability to bear the mental burdens of affinities lessens. My father is a direct descendant of your predecessor, the last beast lord son of the Peacekeeper. Even he is unable to produce stable children now."

My eyes narrowed as I considered her words.

"You will usher in a new wave of affinities with stable minds. You will have many children."

"Get out."

13

I woke up Friday, ready to face the day, only to realize I had nothing to do. Sianna had rendered training pointless. For now, at least. I was pretty sure I'd pay for that after she was gone.

When she went away.

If she went away.

Thinking about it, there had been no discussion of the terms of her protection or how long it would last. I assumed just until Wednesday. Did anyone actually confirm that, though? And, had word spread about me? Were shifters looking for me even now?

Beast affinities I corrected myself in my head. Not shifters. Beast affinities. But "shifter" was so much easier to say. Maybe as their all-powerful Peacekeeper, I could talk them off that particular ledge.

Thinking over the previous evening, I was ashamed of myself for ripping away Sianna's mask. The woman was trying to help me. She answered my questions without any sense of hesitation or maliciousness. She didn't lie to me.

It didn't matter what face she wore. I didn't care

The pin-up flashed in my brain again.

Mostly, I didn't care. Mostly, I corrected myself again.

They weren't disguises. She wasn't hiding from me. I knew she wasn't Candy or Talise in the dream. I had recognized her as the same woman on the night I'd met her, even though she'd worn a few different faces. I hadn't even thought about it. I'd realized she was different, but I'd still known who she was. I wondered why.

Regardless, pulling her mask away last night felt like the height of rudeness.

Sure, I'd been freaked out. She'd been playing mind games. Maybe? Were they her mind games or mine? I wasn't sure how dream walking worked. Either way, I'd violated something she held dear.

I'd apologize.

My phone buzzed.

SAM: I'm awake whenever you want to talk about dream walking.

Well, that was a good idea that hadn't occurred to me yet.

SAM: I'm making waffles.

This situation was definitely improving.

SAM: Is the love binding there yet?

Ugh. Sam. Killjoy.

ADALINE OPENED the front door as I headed up the sidewalk. Their dog, McFly, ran out to greet me with an overly wagging tail and maybe a tiny bit of puppy pee.

"Better to do that outside, buddy. Preferably not on my shoes." I laughed, watching him jump up and run to pee on the bushes.

Addy narrowed her eyes. "Did he pee on your shoes?"

"I can't tell. I'm outside, where dog pee is allowed to be," I admitted. "But I don't think so."

"Shoes off."

My lips twitched. Adaline lived outdoors, alone for years, without running water. And she didn't wear shoes for most of that time.

"Shoes off. I love nature, but outside. It turns out heat is nice."

I kicked my shoes off quickly, bending to kiss the top of her head. "Good morning."

She smiled up at me. "Good morning." I could feel the stress radiating off her.

"Addy?" I asked. My energy was of no assistance to Adaline or Sam, but I still wanted to help.

"There's no binding," she said, voice quavering.

"No," I agreed, confused.

"There needs to be a binding," she said, wiping at tears. "He wasn't kidding, Luke. I made him show me."

"Addy," I said, folding her into a hug. "I'm fine. I swear I'm fine. No one's going to hurt me."

"I saw it, Luke. You will get hurt, and soon, without true love between you. She might do it, or one of her people might do it, but you will get hurt."

"Meh," Sam said, coming into the entryway. "I told you. I'm pretty sure it's going to be fine."

"Pretty sure?" I asked, eyebrows raised.

"You dream walked last night, right?" he asked.

The question surprised Adaline. He hadn't told her.

I nodded.

Adaline's eyes narrowed at Sam.

"I wasn't sure," he said defensively. "But I thought waffles and a discussion would be good. You like waffles!"

Her expression didn't change.

"McFly is pooping," he said quickly. "I'll just go pick it up." He grabbed the composting bags and closed the door behind him.

Escape by dog poop. That was a new one for me.

"You dream walked?" Adaline asked. "To where?"

"I think just to the fields behind the house."

"Outside the wards?"

Oh. Maybe McFly needed to drop another duce.

"Umm. Not on purpose."

She continued to glare.

"I guess I'm here for lessons on dream walking," I offered.

Addy turned back toward the kitchen, clearly displeased.

My phone buzzed. I pulled it out of my pocket.

SAM: She's gone, right?

Laughing, I opened the front door.

"I thought I saw her shadow move away, but I wasn't sure,"

he muttered. "Holy crap. I never would have shown her if I'd known she was going to freak out like this. You might be her favorite brother."

"Noah's my favorite!" Adaline yelled from the kitchen.

Sam patted my shoulder. "Hey, second favorite's not nothing."

We both turned, expecting a response from the kitchen. There was none.

"You didn't tell Mom, right?" I asked, experiencing a new blip of fear. Darla would go ballistic about the possibility of me being headless.

"Do I look stupid?" Sam asked.

"Do you want me to answer that?" I asked in return, looking at his yellow cat pajama pants and brown plaid sweatshirt.

"Same color families?"

I shook my head.

"Oh." Sam frowned at his clothes. "I thought this was better."

I shook my head again.

"I told Darla yesterday!" Adaline yelled from the kitchen.

"Oh shit," Sam and I muttered together.

"THIS MATCH NEEDS TO GET MADE! RIGHT NOW!" Adaline roared.

Sam and I shared a look before we ran out the front door together, headed for my house.

"HOLY SHIT!" I yelled. "She told Mom?!?" Few things panicked me like my mother.

"It's going to be fine. Calm down and let the peace roll. Tell me about the dream. Which one was it?" Sam asked hurriedly.

"What happened?" Sianna demanded, appearing from nowhere.

At my baffled expression, she rolled her eyes. "I came in the back. I heard you yelling."

"Addy told my mom you were going to behead me," I yelled, still panicked.

Now she looked confused. "I am not going to behead you."

"You might," Sam corrected her.

Her confusion turned to anger. "I will not behead him."

"This is pointless," Sam said, shaking his head. "Which walking dream was it?"

"Can you go back outside?" I asked Sianna.

She looked confused again. "I can still hear you outside."

"Logically, I know that. But it's easier to forget when you're not in the same room with me," I admitted.

"We're wasting precious moments. I can see her coming. She's at Will's driveway," Sam said, talking fast.

"Are you hiding from the Mistress?" Sianna asked.

"Yes," Sam and I said together.

"She's upset. She thinks you're going to behead me."

With another eye roll, Sianna walked out the front door at a normal speed, meeting Addy in the street. The two women spoke for a moment before turning back down the cul-de-sac toward Sam and Adaline's house.

"Oh. Okay," Sam said, surprised. "Hey, that can't be a bad thing."

"Sam, what the hell? Why would you show Addy?"

"She wanted to see!"

"You don't show her that kind of shit!" I yelled, hanging on to the anger. Adaline was horrifically powerful but also the gentlest soul imaginable.

"I don't hide things from her, but I admit I erred in this instance. Which dream walk was it?"

"We were in the field behind the houses..." My words trailed off. I didn't want to share details with my weirdest brother.

He sighed. "She was Candy, then Talise, then a few other variations."

I nodded.

"Did you have dream sex?"

"What?"

"Sex. Did you have dream sex? Dream walking is essentially a shared dream landscape. You were both mentally there, but not physically. So, did you have dream sex or not?" Sam demanded, all business.

"No!"

Sam exhaled hard. "Great. Okay. Did you see her? The real her?"

I nodded.

"Did she show you?"

I stared at him. I couldn't believe the precision of his questions.

"You took that from her?" he asked.

I nodded my head once, nauseated.

"That's not great," Sam admitted. "Could be worse. Dream sex would have been worse. It would confuse things between you."

"Sam, how do we get the future where Charlie and Candy are safe, and Sianna goes home, leaving me to my own little peaceful world? Because she's stated in no uncertain terms, there will be nothing between us."

His eyes narrowed. "No, she didn't. She told you there would be children but no bindings."

My stomach flipped. I stared, waiting.

"There has to be a binding for your head to stay where it is. She needs to know you and see you as *you*, not just Peacekeeper."

My response came out cooler than I intended. "You watched the world burn for thirty years, and it turned out that Adaline's forest just had to be cleared."

Sam's repeating visions of the future were usually correct. But sometimes, his interpretation left a lot to be desired.

"That vision wasn't wrong, Luke. We changed it. We shifted that reality."

"Well, we're going to shift this one too."

He pressed his lips together, thinking. "Can we shift it toward waffles? I was looking forward to that."

"ANY IDEA WHERE THE LADIES ARE?" I asked as we walked through Sam's front door.

"They're talking to Mom and Dad. I had the batter—"

"GAH!" I yelled, headed back to the door.

"No, this is better," Sam said, pulling on my arm. "Make me waffles. You're better at it. This works out better if Adaline and Sianna talk to Mom. When you're involved, there's a big argument. When you're not involved, Mom is fine and stays out of things until Sunday."

My mouth hung open. "If you knew that, why did you seem surprised when Sianna walked out to meet Addy?"

"Because I was surprised. I didn't look for the Mom angle

until then. But trust me. This works better. Make more batter, though. Talise and Noah are coming over."

I plugged in the waffle maker. "So, dream walking."

"It's awesome, right? Your mind goes, but your body stays."

I sighed.

"You sigh a lot."

"I know," I muttered. "The walking freaked me out last night."

"Did you know she could shift like that? Be anyone?" Sam asked, distracted.

"I did, but I didn't really think about it," I admitted. "She's worn several faces and bodies in the last few days. And I saw Charlie's natural form in November."

"I forgot about that," Sam confessed. "I didn't understand what was happening at first. I thought crazy shifter women were coming to get you. I almost woke William."

My eyes narrowed. "Were you *watching* me dream walk?"

"No," he said quickly, digging for the syrup in the fridge.

I waited. Sometimes I got more from Sam by not asking questions.

"You do the peace thing really well," he said. "Most people can't sit in silence with me."

I nodded, still waiting.

"I felt energy walking. I wondered if something had found a way past the wards. That happens sometimes. So, I did some looking. Then I realized it was you. I didn't realize you could do the dream walking thing, too, until you were actually doing it. I wonder if we can all do it?"

"I have no idea," I said, rubbing the dull pulsing ache at the back of my head. Another headache was beginning. "I didn't realize I could do it. I thought it was a regular dream until she showed up in my bathroom."

Sam's eyebrows lifted.

"No. I don't ask you about Adaline," I said coolly.

A true grin broke across his face. "This is good. Good progress for two days. You admit there's attraction and something similar to the relationship I have with Adaline forming."

"No, I don't. I just said I wasn't discussing it, similar to how we don't discuss—"

"Luke," Sam cut in. "I know you don't think the circle can heal you or that you can form the gold love bindings. You can actually do both things. I've seen you do both things in the future."

"Just because you've seen it doesn't mean it's true, though," I said, not sure why I was arguing. I would like those things to be true.

"Fair point. But the fact that I've seen it means you have the capacity for it. Something's blocking you, and I think it's you."

"Tell me how you really feel," I said, glaring.

"I'm trying to help," Sam muttered as he buttered the first waffle off the griddle.

"I know. I do understand that. I just don't know what to do here. I don't know her. I don't trust her."

That gave him pause. "What? What the fuck? Why don't you trust her? She would literally die for you."

I stared at him, back to waiting for more information.

He stared back. "What? There are several futures in which she offers her life to protect you. In many of them, she dies to ensure you live."

"SAM!"

"Okay, now tell me again how you don't know her and don't trust her," Sam said smugly.

Asshole.

"Just because I don't know her well doesn't mean I want her to die!"

"Great. We're in agreement. Her death would mean the loss of a truly awesome person. And, she is truly amazing, even if you haven't noticed yet. So, let's stop looking for futures where she goes home and leaves you alone next week. Because those futures all lead to her death and your subsequent self-destruction."

I groaned, rubbing my temples. My headache was getting worse. "I hate these conversations."

"I don't know why," Sam said innocently. "Sianna, he needs help again."

"What?" I asked, sure I'd misheard him.

The front door slammed open. "What happened?" Sianna called, headed our way.

"It's his head," Sam said conversationally.

She sighed at the sight of me. "You look terrible. Why don't you just ask for help?"

"What?" I asked again, confused. The room was spinning.

As she touched her hand to my forehead, gentle energy washed away the pounding headache.

"Why does that keep happening?" I asked.

"It's your version of overloaded," Sam replied, rescuing the waffle from the griddle while I caught my breath. "It's different than our circle overload."

Sianna nodded. "The Peacekeeper requires contact with beast affinities to stay well. We need your energy to stay balanced, and you need us to stay well."

"I didn't have this problem with Candy or Charlie," I muttered.

Her lips pressed together, her expression doubtful.

"Just ask," I prodded.

"How much time did you spend with Charlie?" Sianna replied quickly, like she already knew the answer.

"Not much," Sam interjected. "Two family dinners and that battle in November. Charlie did his best to stay away from him too. Almost no contact, as far away as he could get in the same room."

"And how often were you away from the cat for more than a day?" she asked.

I thought back. "Not often. We broke up the week before Christmas, though. I didn't get...."

I thought of the feeling of malaise before Christmas and the fatigue before New Year's.

Sianna's answering smile was sad. "I am not the cat. I have much more energy and use it more freely. I have never struggled with the energy, but it flows even faster here."

"This is where the harem thing comes from, Luke. I went back and looked. It wasn't that your predecessor had many lovers at once. He just *always* had someone with him. Always. It rotated to spread the extra power equally. It wasn't always a sex thing either. He just always had a powerful beast affinity with him."

"You will see. It will get easier," Sianna promised.

The front door opened again.

"Did I see the badass shifter come in here?" Noah called.

"There are waffles," Sam called back. "Or there will be waffles when Luke gets back to making them."

"Not shifter," Sianna admonished as Noah and Talise walked into the room. "Beast affinity."

"Shifter's easier to say," Noah replied without an apology.

"That is fine, assuming you do not want your knees to keep bending the way they currently do," Sianna offered with a sweet smile.

I scrunched up my face at Noah. "She's probably not one to fuck with."

"Noted," Noah said easily, watching Talise bury her head into my chest and wrap her arms around me. "It's been a long night. What's going on over here?"

"Tali," I murmured, gesturing for Noah to take over waffle duties. Sam was a useless cook. Noah was better equipped for waffle-mastery. "I'm fine. It's going to be fine." I added some peace to the words.

Talise's elemental water energy mixed with her life energy meant she was a strong empath, absorbing all emotions from around her. If Adaline had been upset all night, Talise had been feeling that unrest and amplifying it with her own fear. Before she'd had control of her energy, I was Tali's lifeline to calm her thoughts and her only insulation from the emotions of the world around her.

I missed the time we spent together but was glad for her control.

At my words, she broke into sobs against my shirt, despite the peace cocktail I was offering.

"Not fine," she muttered. "Not fine. Don't go back. On Wednesday, just don't go."

"They'll kill Charlie and sell Candy into servitude," Sam summarized.

"I don't care!" Talise yelled. "I know that's terrible, but I don't care."

"Talise!" I scolded, shocked.

"I'm sorry, but if I have to choose between you and them, I choose you!" she yelled at me, tears streaking down her face. "Don't go back. Don't do this. Send the badass beast lady away and just let it go."

"I agree," Sianna murmured. "About not going back, I agree."

Everyone in the room turned to stare.

"You do not want the rights and responsibilities of Peace-keeper. You have made that obvious. The Peacekeeper exists for his own purposes. You have made it clear you do not want your place in our society. You are not required to accept it. I will kill anyone who demands otherwise.

"I will stay to guard and protect you, as I promised. But you should not go back. You would not see the cat forcefully mated against her will. Why would you accept what being Peacekeeper will require of you?"

"I don't want them to die," I whispered.

"Everyone dies eventually," Sianna replied. "Charlie knew you did not want this. He did not want this for you against your will, either. Do not go back. My father will not attack this compound. He will go back to his preferred house in London after a few weeks. He does not actually believe what you are. Your disappearance makes things easier. Just do not go back. I will not force you to go."

"I don't want them to die," I said again, more clearly. "Not for me. No. I can't live with that."

"Do you truly believe the vampire will let them kill Charlie?" Sianna asked.

Everyone in the room stared at me.

"She will devour the entire compound before they take Charlie," Sianna added. "You do not have to do anything. Do not go back."

Talise's tears had dried. She nodded. "We're in agreement. Don't go back."

I looked at Sam's frown and wondered what it meant. He gave me a tiny head shake.

This wasn't a great time to discuss the idea.

14

---

*M*y phone buzzed on Friday afternoon as I was sitting down at my piano.

MICAH: Special family practice tomorrow at noon.

NOAH: On a Saturday?

MICAH: Is tomorrow Saturday?

NOAH: Yes.

MICAH: Then YES. Special Saturday practice at noon. Everyone is required.

JEN: Muhahahahaha

NOAH: Mind-Meld Saturday!

JEN: Not really.

JAKE: Oh, man. I was really looking forward to Noah getting a mind.

NOAH: Certainly can't get it from you.

NOAH: DID YOU JUST ZAP ME?

JAKE: Don't you forget who owns this family circle, jackass.

MATTY: Are you teaching us, Jen?

JEN: Huzzah!

WILLIAM: What are we learning?

MICAH: It's a surprise.

ETHAN: I know, and it's AWESOME.

MICAH: ...

ETHAN: AWESOME.

MICAH: Lording information over your family is beneath you.

ETHAN: No, it's not.

LUKE: Um. What about my visitor?

JEN: I've not seen the Huntress in a long time. Looking forward to it.

LUKE: Should I tell her?

SAM: Yes.

MICAH: It's up to you, Luke. She knows what Jen is.

JEN: No. You should not tell her.

SAM: YES, YOU SHOULD.

JEN: NO, HE SHOULD NOT.

SAM: Why?

JEN: Because I said so.

SAM: She'll be disturbed to see you as our ally without warning.

JEN: I know.

SAM: They need to fall in love. I thought I told you that?

JEN: You did. I told you it was a terrible idea.

SAM: Oh, yeah. I forgot. But you're wrong.

JEN: Practice tomorrow! I'll start by making Sam cry like a little girl, then squawk like a chicken. Get your phones ready.

SAM: I didn't mean it like that!

JEN: Too late.

SAM: This is your fault, Luke.

"WHAT'S WRONG?" Sianna asked, walking into the living room where I was staring at my phone.

"Nothing. Just family," I muttered, still watching Sam and Jen bicker at each other.

"You okay?"

"I'm wondering if I should tell you something," I admitted.

"If you're concerned about it, the answer is yes, you should tell me," she said easily, touching my hand to wash energy through me as she passed by on her way to the straight back chair in the corner.

I frowned. "Why? You don't tell me things that bother you."

She shrugged, then glanced at the piano. "Are you going to play?"

"I was thinking about it."

She lifted her eyebrows.

"Has anyone come here? Beast affinities?" I asked. "Have you had to scare anyone away?"

She nodded.

My mouth dropped open in shock. "When?"

"Mostly at night. Two this morning after I talked to your mother. Word spreads that I am here. They will stay away once a few examples are made. Thus far, no one has intended you harm. They are just curious. So, I sent them away."

My stomach dropped. "Should I just talk to them?"

Her face scrunched up, confused. I realized, at that moment, she was wearing her actual face. "Why would you talk to them?"

"If I can help them, I will," I said quietly. "I'm not up for the whole worshipful harem thing, but I don't mind the idea of helping others."

Her head tilted as she considered my words. We sat in companionable silence for a moment as she thought it through.

"Sianna?"

"Hmm?"

"What do you think?" I asked.

"I think you are unexpectedly kind and gentle. I also think you will change over time, and it makes me sad," she admitted, her smile sweet. "You are not what our legends say."

I shook my head. I knew that was true from my time with Candy.

"If some come that can be helped, we will see. The ones that are lost will not benefit from your gentleness," she finally agreed.

I nodded, deciding Sam was right. I didn't want to see Sianna shocked and on guard when Jen arrived.

"My family will practice tomorrow," I said, changing the subject.

She rolled her eyes. "Did I not prove that point yesterday?"

"You did, very thoroughly. Thank you. This is a different kind of practice. I'm not sure what. But a family friend is coming to help us learn."

I hesitated.

"Oh?" Sianna asked, watching me fidget for a second before my energy took the nerves away.

"The friend knows you. She said she hasn't seen you in years."

Sianna didn't move, just waited for me to get to the point.

"You see, she was the executive assistant for my family, but she was also sort of plotting the end of the world and—"

"Peacekeeper, who is coming to practice? Your nerves are grating against my brain. Calm yourself."

"Rajena Meeli," I blurted, happy to just get it over with. "Jen. She's a family friend."

There was no reaction.

"Sianna?"

Her tone was disbelieving. "The Queen of the Mind is coming for Saturday afternoon training?"

"It's at noon tomorrow. I guess that counts as afternoon?"

"What will she be teaching you?" Sianna asked, tone flat.

"I dunno," I said, confused by the utterly blank expression on her face.

She was decidedly not at peace. Her mind shifted and rolled with tactics for protection as if she was preparing for battle.

Wow, those thoughts are coming across loud and clear, I realized.

"Likely, she is coming to take your circle," she surmised.

I shook my head. "We've offered her a place. She won't stand with us."

"You have allowed the Queen of the Mind into your energy before now?"

I frowned. "No, not really. She doesn't join energy with us. She's protected us from mental attack, though. Si, I don't under—"

"Do not call me that," she snapped, furious with me. "You invite in a predator I cannot defend against and then try to call me by a pet name. No."

I blinked. "I apologize," I said slowly. "I didn't mean to take liberty with your name. It just came out that way."

"Hmm."

Then she was gone again.

I still hadn't apologized for pulling her energy away last night, forcing her to reveal her true form.

I sighed as I touched the piano keys, inviting music that I already knew wouldn't come.

"WHY IS THE DOOR LOCKED?" Sam asked, appearing next to my piano about a half-hour later.

"Holy fuck, Sam! Don't do that!" I yelled, thrown out of the music I was playing. Mozart made a good stand-in for my own meditative playing in a pinch.

"Sorry. I was going to knock, but the door is locked."

"She said I have to lock the door. Will put some kind of bio-fingerprint thing on the door. I bet it would let you in," I responded. "But you can still knock if the door is locked, Sam."

He shrugged. "My way is easier, but I wouldn't have bothered walking across the street if I'd known I'd end up Walking into your space anyway."

"Where's Adaline?"

"What are you making for dinner?" He ignored my question.

"Pizza," I replied slowly. "I didn't make enough crust for four people. You usually eat with Adrian on Friday."

Sam and Adaline rotated dinner plans among the family since neither of them enjoyed cooking. I was surprised he'd made waffle batter that morning, even if it was from a mix.

"Lucy and Linda are making oxtail soup. Soup is not Adaline's favorite."

I paused, reconsidering my own dinner plans.

Say what you will about using oxtails in cooking, but beef barley soup is a low-class, subpar cousin to oxtail soup.

Lucy, Adrian's girlfriend, cooked in restaurant-sized portions because Adrian ate enough food for six people. Lucy and her sister Linda cooked together because it took two people to manage those portions.

There would be enough for Sianna and me.

"No. You have dinner here with Sianna," Sam chided. "I'll ask Lucy to put aside a bowl for you."

I sighed. "Sam. I don't have the warm fuzzies for her. And I think she barely tolerates me."

"You are so full of shit, and you know it. Your colors were all kinds of lusty and admiring when she trampled William yesterday."

I didn't dignify that with a response.

"You're still Peacekeeper to her. You're not Luke. Not yet. You told her about Jen?"

I nodded. "Yes. It felt wrong not to."

"Good. Thank you." Sam exhaled in relief. "Before Addy wakes up, we need to talk about Wednesday. You have to go back."

"I knew you were going to say that."

"You were planning to go back anyway," Sam replied, smiling at my smug tone.

"I was. I won't leave Candy and Charlie to twist in the wind," I admitted. "Even if Sianna insists they'll be fine, no."

The expression dropped from Sam's face. "Sianna said *Charlie* would be fine. She didn't say anything about Candy. And I know you caught that."

I nodded again. There was no use in denying it.

"Anyway, you have to go back. If you don't go, if you don't fill the Peacekeeper role, the energy that comes with beast affinities will be lost. It's close to extinction now. When I follow the paths where you don't take your place among them, there are no more beast lords. Charlie will be the last."

"Does it matter, Sam? I've been thinking about this. Does it matter if the world no longer has people that can become animals?"

Sam paused, considering how to answer. "It matters as much as anything else does, Luke. It matters as much as Addy and me closing circles and being sane. It matters as much as growing enough food to feed the population. The world keeps spinning regardless, but existence is a whole lot harder.

"Energy is cycled and shared in many ways. The energy is all the same, whether someone empowered like you or me closes a circle or someone like Sianna transforms into another animal. It's the same power exercised differently. It's wrong and short-sighted to believe that our way of using the energy is the only way that matters."

"Okay," I mumbled, disappointed in myself for even asking the question. "So, I'm going to end up being some kind of beast god Peacekeeper with a harem of lovers? We should have built a bigger family compound."

Sam threw his head back, laughing in genuine amusement. "You have trouble figuring out what to do with one woman. Candy's breakup story was a work of art, and you sat there and told us because she'd kick your ass if you didn't. I'd love to see what you do with a harem. The ladies would absolutely be the boss of you."

"I like that you laugh as if we didn't run away from Adaline this morning," I said, miffed.

"Oh, I didn't say I wasn't whipped. My world absolutely turns on Addy's pleasure, and I'd have it no other way. I'm just saying that you're not capable of managing a group of ladies. You'd get too confused when given conflicting directions."

"True enough," I agreed.

"No. I told you. That harem nonsense wasn't really a thing. The Peacekeeper kept a powerful beast affinity with him at all times because it made it easier to disburse his energy.

"Much like our Sianna, the most powerful beast lords are usually women, which is ironic. It's a horrifically patriarchal society. The women rotated who guarded the Peacekeeper. People made assumptions. As far as I can tell, though, he only had one lover at a time. The Peacekeeper before the last one had a single mate and never took another lover after she died."

"Huh. The harem nonsense came from gossip?" I asked, confused how gossip could carry on for so long.

"Ech," Sam said, scrunching his face in distaste. "It's a patri-archal society. The man that's led for the last few centuries—is that Sianna's father?"

I nodded.

Sam pursed his lips, confused. "I'll look more. Anyway, the Overlord likes to sleep around. He claims his father had a harem. It makes his choices easier to defend."

I thought of Sianna talking about her twenty-plus siblings. I guessed it made sense. "Okay," I said again.

"So, you have to go back on Wednesday. You know that. I know that. I'm going to do some looking, then we'll plan. Let's not tell the ladies yet, though, okay?" Sam asked, eyes pleading.

I smiled, knowing he hated to hide things from Addy. He'd break before I did, and we both knew it.

"I won't tell," he said. "I won't. Addy loves you very much. Even the possibility of losing you terrified her. I won't scare her needlessly."

I nodded again, still smiling but for a different reason.

Once upon a time, we'd worried for Sam's sanity. I'd thought I was going to watch him starve and die horribly. I will be forever grateful that he found love.

Maybe a smidge jealous too, but mostly grateful.

15

"Sianna, what do you want on your pizza?" I asked, tone conversational even though she wasn't in the room or in the house.

"I will eat anything," she said quietly, coming in the back door without a sound.

"Huh. I thought that door was locked," I muttered.

"It was," she confirmed. "I opened it."

I decided I didn't want to know. I'd just assume William gave her a key.

Did he give me a key? I don't think I have keys to my own house, I realized.

"I have sausage, pepperoni, onion, sweet peppers, garlic, mushrooms… what would you like?"

She looked like she was trying not to laugh. "If I asked for a Hawaiian pizza with pineapple and barbecue sauce?"

I pulled a glare.

She laughed in truth, her smile making her eyes glitter in the kitchen lights.

"Do you really want that?" I asked.

"No. I am from Chicago. Sausage, mushroom, onion, peppers. Please tell me you have proper giardiniera if you are making pizza."

I raised my eyebrows, biting back my own smile. "I'm also from Chicago."

"You live more than an hour outside of Chicago."

"Still counts. But this is a recent thing. And I hate it." I did grin as I dug into the fridge.

"Did you make this giardiniera?" she asked, mouth hanging open in shock as she dug for a carrot.

"I told you that I like to cook. I like to eat too. Those things go together." I grimaced, remembering something.

"What's the face for?"

"Bah. It doesn't matter now. You're here!" I did a little cheer.

"What does not matter?" she asked, eyes narrowed.

"Will was making me workout—run and lift weights and stuff. I haven't done it in a few days. I just remembered, but you're here. I don't have to do that shit anymore."

"No, you still need to do that," she disagreed. "We will run in the morning. Then I will review your weight training."

My face fell. "What? Why?"

"You should be strong and fit, able to run for help if I am not nearby. No. I agree with him on this. You will do that work."

"No, I don't want to," I said, trying out a new, decisive, adult voice. She kept saying she awaited my pleasure. Working out did not please me.

"Too bad," she said easily, opening the package of ground

Italian sausage and dumping it in the cast iron skillet. "I'm going to put some pepper flakes in with this, okay?"

Fucking Sam. He's absolutely right. I couldn't manage a household of women.

"I put pepper flakes in the sauce, too," I warned.

She grinned, happiness radiating from her.

"PEACEKEEPER, that might have been some of the best pizza I have ever eaten."

We sat at my dining room table almost two hours later, the scraps of two large pizzas and assorted deep-fried things littered between us.

"Ate too much." I groaned.

"So good, though," she muttered, looking dozy.

"You know, there are four empty bedrooms here. You don't need to sleep outside."

"Hmm," she purred, eyes closed.

"Sianna, I suspect you're heavier than you look. I doubt I could carry you upstairs. Don't fall asleep there."

Her eyes opened to slits. "I am not sleeping. I am resting. At peace, like when you walked to me last night. And the only bed I will sleep in here is yours. I do not think you are offering that. Yet."

"You are correct," I said, voice chilly. "How did I dream walk to you last night?"

"I do not know the answer to that," she said lazily. "I cannot visit minds as you can. You came to my resting space. I thought you wanted me."

I shifted uncomfortably, my body reacting to her words. I'd deny what she said, but I'd be lying.

"I should tell you something," she said, sighing.

"Hmm," I asked, not quite able to form words.

"I can smell the change in your scent when you are aroused."

I sat bolt upright, suddenly mortified. "What?!"

She opened her eyes all the way to roll them at me.

"I-I-I didn't even know that had a scent." My face flushed scarlet in embarrassment. The embarrassment was profound enough to break through my natural peace as if it didn't exist.

"It does. You can deny your interest all you want. Your body does not lie. And, while your conscious mind might not be interested, your subconscious mind, your sleeping mind, sought me out last night."

"How do you do that? With the hearing and the sense of smell?"

"What do you mean?" she asked, confused at my topic change.

"How do you hear so well? Smell so much more?"

"Ah," she murmured.

After a moment of silence, I frowned in disappointment. "You won't tell me?"

"Of course, I will tell you." She disagreed. "I am thinking of how to explain it."

"Oh." I left her to her silence.

As I sat, waiting, a slight headache began between my eyes. Without even looking, she reached out to touch my hand.

"Thank you," I muttered, wondering what would happen if she wasn't there with me. Would I just not get the headaches, or would I be incapacitated by them?

She yawned, not bothering to respond to my thanks. Then, she held up her right hand, where four-inch-long claws suddenly appeared.

"I do not have to fully transform to take on the characteristics of an animal."

I nodded. I knew that.

"The trouble comes with maneuvering like this. These claws are not intended for human hands. I must cope with them or lose them."

I nodded again.

"It is the same with my hearing and sense of smell. I keep the senses of an elephant for smell. Their minds and instincts are amazing. I benefit greatly from carrying the traits with me. But I must make space in my mind. The human mind does not process elephant thought signatures."

"Candy talked about this as layers of psyches."

Sianna pulled a face. I don't think she realized she did it. "The cat is not wrong. But she copes with one family of signatures. I have adopted elephant for smell, bat for hearing, and… additional animals for other traits. It is difficult to do while maintaining my human mind.

"But it is why I am the Huntress. I have the sharpened instincts of predators and some of the strongest senses on the planet. Certainly, the strongest gathered in a single being. When something or someone must be hunted, or, in this case, protected, I will do it."

I stood to gather the remains of our feast. "You know what we need?"

"Sex?"

I sighed, even as tingles coursed through me. "Hot chocolate."

"Why not both? Melting marshmallows make for good sticky licking."

I couldn't breathe as my pants seemed to become three sizes too small. I sat down abruptly, flushing again.

She laughed, her own amusement catching her by surprise.

SHE SAT at the breakfast bar, waiting for me to finish futzing with the dinner dishes.

Thankfully, she had on clothes. As we left the dining room, I wondered if she'd continue to push the sexy-time talk.

I still couldn't decide if I was happy or sad that she'd dropped it. But there we were, in my kitchen, wearing clothes like civilized individuals.

I wasn't thinking of the pin-up physique. I wasn't. Those weren't appropriate kitchen thoughts.

I flushed red again as my brain combined sexy Sianna thoughts with my kitchen.

I glanced at her, wondering what her senses were picking up. She was calm, watching me, not pushing. She had on some sort of long, loose dress. She wasn't doing the naked temptress thing. The dress looked like the kind of thing that would come off quickly and not require undergarments.

I wasn't thinking about it.

What the fuck is wrong with me? I wondered.

I stomped my way across the kitchen, angry at my own thoughts as I pulled out a saucepan and the gallon of milk.

"If you tell me...." She stopped talking at the sight of my glare.

At a loss, I pulled my energy forward. The lusty thoughts

were out of control and out of character for me. The peace energy would settle things.

Sianna groaned, putting her head down on the counter and covering it with her arms.

"I'm sorry," I whispered, pulling the energy back. "I didn't mean to... I'm sorry. I'm struggling."

"You are struggling with the wrong things," she mumbled, her face still buried under her arms on the counter. "Sex is easy. Natural. Welcome. Needed, even."

I should have asked Sam for details on if sex was advisable. Dream sex confused things, but actual sex? I wondered.

I touched her arm so she'd look at me.

"I'm sorry I pulled your energy away last night. I'm sorry I made you show me your face. That was wrong of me."

She blinked. Whatever she had been expecting me to say, it wasn't that.

Reaching up, she touched the beard stubble on my face. "You are forgiven."

I went back to my milk steeping. "I have questions. About affinities. But, also about your... society."

"You are going back on Wednesday?" she asked. She didn't sound surprised.

I turned to meet her eyes. "I have to. I won't talk about it with Addy or Talise unless they force it. I don't want to upset them. But I have to go back."

"I will answer anything you ask," she murmured, sounding sad. "Understanding will only help you right now."

I nodded my thanks.

"How are you related to Charlie?" I asked after a few moments.

She nodded back at me, a small smile forming. "Very good.

Charlie's mother is several generations removed from my father's brother. You have met Edgar. Charlie is a several-times over great-grandson, making him a very distant cousin. Edgar's line has always been strong, but Charlie was a surprise to everyone. At first, many wondered if my father had relations with his mother."

I tried not to consider the oddness of that statement as I added chocolate to the hot milk and stirred.

"Actual chocolate? Not the powdered stuff?" she asked, pleased.

"Anything worth doing," I muttered.

"Your father was the final *son* of the Peacekeeper?" I asked, adding emphasis to the word.

She smiled again. "There were two daughters after him."

"Where are they?" I asked, already dreading the answer.

She shook her head. "Surely you have realized we are a patriarchal society."

"I have."

"My aunts each had several children. When their lines tended toward insanity, they were no longer needed."

I blinked, staring again.

She dropped her eyes to the mug I passed her.

"How many beast lords are there?" I asked.

"Sane?" she clarified.

I lifted my eyebrows.

"There are a few the elders refuse to admit are gone. There are ten now, depending on how you count. Edgar is the oldest. Then my father, four of my brothers who are sane, then two more brothers I doubt are truly balanced. Me. Charlie."

"Your father called Charlie his heir several times."

She nodded. "My brothers are not cunning. They can transform and maintain their human aspects, but they are not great thinkers. They do not have the capacity for as many forms. They do not have my ability to hold on to traits. My father intended Charlie to grow into the leadership role and for us to have children together."

This wasn't shocking news. I had guessed as much.

"Why does maintaining beast affinities matter? Why not let the power fade completely, deal with the mental illness, and let the traits die out?"

Sam had already answered this question and made me feel dumb in the process, but I wanted to know her thoughts on the subject.

She outright scowled at me.

"It's an honest question, Sianna. I'm not trying to be cruel. Empowered circles create and balance energy in the world. I don't understand what beast affinities bring."

Still frowning, she sipped hot chocolate. "What does humanity bring?"

I lifted my eyebrows, the *huh?* obvious on my face.

"What does humanity bring? Why does it matter if humans exist, grow, or evolve?"

"I didn't mean this to be a philosophical debate," I replied.

"Neither did I," she snapped. "It is an honest question. Humans are just one of many species on this planet."

"The energy created by our circles benefits all living things. Mistress Life feels all life, not just humanity."

Sianna gave a small snort. "She does not prioritize all living things equally. The beast affinities are more in tune with other creatures. I can communicate on some level with most creatures on the planet. Your mistress cannot do that, to my knowledge."

"How long has the Peacekeeper been gone from your society?" I asked.

"Many hundreds of years. Close to a millennium."

"Did you consider that your inability to maintain a mental balance with wildlife is due to the decline in wildlife rather than a decline in genetics?"

Her head tilted. She had not considered it.

"Our circles do not generate power in the same ways they used to. Micah insists circles once stood only at sunrise and sunset, too weak to form at any other time. The circles before Sam and Adaline and their predecessors were highly patriarchal. As women became more empowered, the Mistress became more empowered. Or the other way around—as the Mistress became more empowered, women began leading more."

"Your circle is still patriarchal," she muttered.

I laughed at that, startling her. "No, ma'am. Don't be fooled for a second. You saw Sam run and hide from Adaline today. Sam worships her and she absolutely drives that relationship. The women of my circle wait on no one."

"I had not considered the decline in wild things as part of our decline. It is an interesting thought. Regardless, there is a direct, undeniable correlation between being the offspring of the Peacekeeper and those maintaining the balance needed to survive. All of your children will have affinities."

"I caught that from Charlie. That's interesting."

She lifted her eyebrows, sipping her hot chocolate as if savoring it. I thought she might be rolling it around her mouth.

But I wasn't going to think about that, either.

"You know I'll make more if you want it, right?" I asked.

"More babies? I thought you were on some moral high ground." She grinned.

I rolled my eyes. I couldn't believe I'd stepped into that one.

"Why are beast affinity babies interesting?" she asked.

"I don't have a beast affinity."

She nodded in agreement.

"I just have energy."

She nodded again.

"Your energy heals me."

Another nod.

"Adaline's energy also heals me."

She didn't nod, but she didn't disagree, either.

"It's all the same energy," I surmised. "The energy of our circles, your beast affinities, the siphons, Jen's energies. It's all the same."

She nodded, lips turned up into a small smile. "I believe that to be true as well. My father disagrees."

"Next week, I'll meet the elders. Who are they?"

She sighed, putting down her mug. I topped it off, drawing another smile.

"There are eight elders: my father, Edgar, four of my brothers, and two remaining old ones, descended from the Peacekeeper before my grandfather. They no longer transform without risking themselves, but they can guide. Depending on the situation, I am also allowed to serve as an elder, voting on non-crucial affairs. I will not be included in discussions regarding your status, so I volunteered to be your guard instead."

"When you said your father needed five votes to sentence Charlie?" I nudged.

"Yes, five elder votes to test a beast lord and five votes to destroy one. I do not think my father expected me to vote against Charlie. I was supposed to be the hold-out. And I was, in the end."

"He didn't seem happy about it, though. He came close to shushing you when you said you would not vote," I prodded.

She hesitated. "I am not sure, but I think he wanted Charlie to be guilty and have a reason not to destroy him. I think there was supposed to be a bargaining where Charlie would agree to come back to us. It would not have worked."

"Why do you say that?"

Sianna gave me a look. "I told you. I have seen the bindings. He will not leave the siphon. And I doubt, very much, that Eleanor would let him go without a fight. I was waiting for an assault in the arena. I was shocked when she pulled you out of the woodwork."

"And that's today's lesson, kids," Eleanor called as she walked down the hallway and into the kitchen, startling us both. "No matter what, I will *always* be six steps ahead."

"Not two. Not four. *Six* steps ahead." She threw her arms out to her sides in a gesture of annoyance. "Where's my hot chocolate?"

I blinked, confused. "I'm six steps behind."

Ellie grinned.

"What are you doing here?" I asked, eyes darting between the ladies, unsure what to expect.

"She has come and gone several times since taking the car. She is watching you and Light closely," Sianna murmured.

"Okay, maybe only five steps ahead of this one. She's crafty," Ellie acknowledged, taking the other barstool. She clapped her hands in my face. "Luke! Hot chocolate. I like it more milk chocolate than dark chocolate."

I didn't move, my eyes still darting between them.

Sianna rolled her eyes. "You have welcomed her energy here before. I would only take her head if she threatened harm."

Ellie tsked. "You'd try."

They looked at each other.

"You'd try," Ellie said again with more confidence.

Sianna shrugged. "I hope to never test it."

"You attacked William!" I accused, stunned that Sianna had allowed Ellie to come and go. Ellie had been in my space, and I hadn't known it? How was that possible?

"He kicked down your door," Sianna replied placidly. "I did not kill him. But now we have an understanding."

"Woo, you took on He-man?" Ellie asked, eyeing Sianna.

"Mmmm," Sianna purred happily as I topped off her hot chocolate again before adding more milk for Ellie.

"She actually beat up Will, Hennessy, and Micah in under a minute," I murmured.

"Ha! I saw that. It made my day better. They needed a reminder of their place in the world." Ellie high-fived Sianna without looking.

"I'm so confused," I muttered, scratching my head. "I wouldn't have expected you to be friends."

Sianna's eyebrows lifted. "We are not."

"Not enemies either," Ellie agreed. "There's space between."

"I will take her head if she tries to injure you," Sianna said, still calm. It resonated like a vow.

"I have no intention of injuring Baby Trellis. Stop it." Ellie tsked again. "Charlie would take that badly too."

Sianna nodded, accepting that truth.

"What's with the taking of heads?" I asked. "Sam said that shit too."

"Separating the head from the body and destroying the remains is one of the most effective ways to ensure a creature is dead," Sianna answered, surprised I didn't know. "It's the easiest way to kill a near-immortal creature like the siphon. Or you. Or me, for that matter."

"Gross," I muttered, grabbing the saucepan to wash it.

Ellie snorted. "You can't leave the dirty dishes, can you? Matty told me about this. I thought she was exaggerating until I actually saw your house."

I glared at her.

"What is this?" Sianna asked, brow furrowed.

"He has this thing about keeping everything neat and tidy. Everything has a place. It's part of his 'peace' thing. Everything must be at peace, even random dishes. I've been discretely moving things by a half-inch and then watching him come into the room to fix them. It's hilarious."

I glared harder.

Sianna rolled her eyes. "That has to be the energy overload. It will resolve itself."

I frowned. "I'm not overloaded."

There was another eye roll.

"Back to business!" Ellie yelled, gulping her hot chocolate. "Also, Luke, you will forever come to my house and make me hot chocolate when I've had a bad day. This doesn't even need liquor."

Sianna glared at her. "He is not your servant."

Ellie snorted. "I'd bet you would say that about Charlie too, but even he would disagree. The world bows to my pleasure. Anyway, Charlie and Candy are doing fine. Candy remains untouched. They won't let Charlie shift. He's not having a great time of it, but he'll be fine. They've been moved into the house. Sianna, I need you to allow me into the house."

Sianna's eyebrows shot up. "You are joking, right?"

Ellie scrunched up her face. "No. I can get in but can't take form. I have next to no power there. If shit hits the fan, I won't be able to help them."

"Why would you expect me to let you into that home's energy?"

"Because you love Charlie. Candy too. They're your friends. Well, Charlie's a friend. You loathe Candy now, but whatever. Once upon a time, she wasn't so bad. Besides, they're the only people I care about. I've no interest in the home otherwise. Rescind the invitation after they're free. I don't care."

"No," Sianna said with finality. "That home belongs to the Overlord. Even if I could open it to you, I would not."

"Actually," I said, cutting in. "I think that house belongs to me. It's a Peacekeeper domain, right?"

"Ah! I forgot about that. I don't know if it'll work, but we can try it!" Ellie did a little happy dance on her barstool.

"Ellie, I welcome you to any property, home, or building that is mine to share with you," I said easily. "But stop moving stuff around. That's annoying."

Sianna was off her stool screaming about my foolishness.

"Thank you, Baby Trellis! We'll see if that does it!" Ellie yelled to me as she headed out of the kitchen.

"I'm not the baby!" I yelled back.

"Ha! Beth was born an adult. You're absolutely the baby!"

"YOU MORON!" Sianna shouted. "She is a parasite! She can live off the energy in your home for hundreds of years, slowly draining you dry of all happiness."

"Oh," I grunted, shrugging. "That's fine. Don't worry about it."

Her mouth dropped open in shock. "Do you think I am kidding?"

"No. Not at all."

"WHY DID YOU DO THAT?" she roared.

"Mostly because it's Ellie. But, otherwise, there's not much happiness in my home. Don't worry about it."

All expression dropped from her face. I could feel her confusion. My energy surged to soothe her without my permission.

I flushed but decided not to apologize for something I couldn't control. She knew how my energy worked—maybe better than I did.

I cleared my throat before I started speaking. "I don't do happiness or joy well. It's like anger and fear. Love too. It all gets swallowed by the peace in the end," I explained. "The other emotions don't hold up for me. So, Ellie would be feeding on a giant vat of sighs. Don't worry about it."

"Luke," she started.

I smiled, glad to hear my name from her lips.

She flushed at my expression, embarrassed by her slip up. "She is dangerous. Your home has many types of power in it, and she can take them all. You did not just open this home to her. You may have opened any dwelling you consider to be at least in part your own."

I shook my head. "She's always been welcome with my parents. With Matilda and Jake too. No one here would deny her entrance, Sianna. She's family to us."

She fell silent, staring at her hands.

"Ellie was Matilda's roommate in college. They've been besties for a long time. Micah had concerns too. Sam has searched. In every single future he has found, Ellie stands with Matty. She's on our side. Charlie too."

Sianna sighed. Her tone was quieter, more pleading. "The future shifts and changes, Peacekeeper. Letting her in without limitations is beyond dangerous. It borders on reckless stupidity. Please reconsider."

"It's going to be fine," I muttered, moving to offer her a hug.

She was gone before I touched her.

That was for the best.

I wasn't thinking of the pin-up.

I wasn't a pig.

I heard my phone buzz upstairs. Someone was texting or calling multiple times to bypass the do not disturb settings.

I ran upstairs, thinking something was happening.

ELEANOR: No sex, Baby Trellis! She is not your friend!
ELEANOR: No sex, Baby Trellis! She is not your friend!
ELEANOR: No sex, Baby Trellis! She is not your friend!
ELEANOR: Are you getting these texts?
ELEANOR: No sex, Baby Trellis! She is not your friend!
ELEANOR: No sex, Baby Trellis! She is not your friend!
ME: Good night, Ellie.
ELEANOR: I'm not kidding, Luke.

---

16

*W*hen I woke up, the sex was already in progress. I'd missed the foreplay.

Sprawled across the top of me, Sianna moved her hips, shifting her body around me.

"Holy shit," I breathed, trying to understand how this had happened.

Eyes glowing with power, face gleaming with a sheen of sweat, she pushed the base of her palm against the bottom of my chin, forcing my mouth closed. "Hush now, no more."

She did something that involved twisting her hips. I thought I was going to die. Or embarrass myself. Maybe both.

She eased her hand away from my mouth, testing my reaction.

I blinked, breathing hard as she moved again.

"Not like this. Not this time," I finally whispered.

I felt her despair as a part of her that wasn't at peace.

"Not the pin-up," I clarified. "You. If we're doing this, you. Please?"

Her eyes went wide in surprise as her form changed, her hips scooting just a bit to adjust.

I rolled her under me, kissing her long neck and tasting her jawbone as my arms braced around her. My body wasn't waiting for permission anymore.

"Let go," she whispered.

For a minute, I thought I'd grabbed her hair by accident in the darkness.

Legs wrapping around my hips, she moved with me, eyes focused on my face.

"Let go," she said again. "Let the energy go. You fight it back constantly. Let it go."

I felt her shiver. I groaned, beyond words.

"Let go," she whispered in my ear.

I shook my head. My energy could send Candy off into a spiral of orgasms that bordered on painful in intensity.

"I am not the kitty," Sianna said, monotone. "You will not hurt me. Let go."

There was a stab of anger through Sianna's mind as she said the words, decidedly pulling her out of sexy-time fun.

Lips back at her throat, kissing gently, I pushed a bit of power with my hip thrust.

Sianna exhaled, somehow stretching her body under me as she dug her fingers into the tense muscles on my back. "Let go, Luke. Please let go of it."

That did me in. The energy exploded through me, rocking into Sianna as our bodies moved faster, together—

"WHAT THE HELL?" Sianna roared, kicking open my bedroom door, sword in hand.

"HOLY FUCK!" I yelled, startled awake and falling out of bed. Again.

Her mouth dropped open in shock as she stared at me.

"Holy fuck, it was a dream," I realized. "Holy fuck."

"Your power rolled through the area like a giant tidal wave. I thought something happened," Sianna muttered, the sword now pointed down. "I thought I missed something. I thought something got through."

Well, she'd missed something, I thought, somehow ashamed of my dreaming self. *What the fuck, self?*

Then the pain hit.

I screamed in agony as my body tried to turn itself inside out. I reached for my power, trying to find acceptance of the pain.

The pain redoubled as my nose exploded with blood. "Oh, holy shit!" I screamed. "It's the energy!"

I vaguely realized Sianna was trying to get my attention. I tried to listen. I really did. But I couldn't stop screaming.

Her hands were on my arms, pulling them away from my face as my body convulsed on the floor.

"PEACEKEEPER!" she bellowed directly in my ear. "LET ME HELP."

I sobbed, my tears blending with the snot and blood on my face. I'd stopped screaming, having shredded my voice that quickly. The pain hadn't eased up, though.

"Let go," Sianna said calmly. "Let the energy go. You are okay. Let go."

"What's happening?" someone yelled. I thought it might have been Matthew or William.

Then, there was a distinct, "Oh." I knew it was Sam. There was no mistaking it, even in the throes of fucking agony. I heard his little sound and knew he was putting pieces together.

At that moment, I vowed to work out and learn to fight just so I could punch him in the head without breaking my fucking hand.

"Lucas," Sianna's voice called to me, laced with something new.

My eyes flicked to hers, confused.

"Let the energy go, Luke. You are killing yourself. Let it go before it kills you."

"I don't know how," I whimpered, no sound to the words.

"It usually involves fucking," Will supplied, laughing.

Sianna turned away from me for a second. I don't know what she did or said, but Will and Sam were both gone. Just gone.

I blinked, and when my eyes opened, I wasn't entirely sure Will or Sam had been there.

"Luke," Sianna said again, her voice melodic and inviting. "Let go."

Then her lips touched mine. My arms wrapped around her for dear life while the energy poured out of me.

I want to believe that the first kiss was sexy and hot. But there was no way. I had snot, blood, and tears on my face and in my hair. I could smell my own sickly sweat. When my senses came back, I was just glad I hadn't puked on her.

THE NEXT THING I RECALLED, I was in the shower with Sianna. I still had my arms wrapped around her in a death grip, holding her naked body to mine as she washed my hair.

"—almost done now," she was murmuring soothingly. "I can feel it settling." She reached for the showerhead, tipping my head back so she could rinse my hair without getting soap in my eyes.

She rinsed my ears well, making a slight sound of disapproval as she reached for more soap. "There is blood in your ears. In your ear canal," she said, voice still soothing. "It is almost over now, almost done now," she repeated as she washed my ears.

"Sianna?" I croaked, trying to relax my arms. My muscles were stiff.

Her eyes met mine. "There you are." She smiled as she lathered soap against my back, then down my arms.

I was so confused. And tired. So tired I thought I might fall.

"No. No," she said quietly when I tried to drop my arms from her. "Do not let go. After you are clean, you will sleep for a while. But do not break contact yet. There is still too much."

"Wha...?" I couldn't even form words.

"Shhh," she soothed. "Everything is fine. You cannot ignore the energy, Luke. You cannot force it back and out of shape forever. You were overloaded. I knew you were overloaded. I am sorry. I should have climbed into your bed and ignored your delicate sensibilities."

My head dropped, resting on her shoulder as she finished rinsing us both.

17

I woke on Saturday morning, wrapped up in bed with Sianna, with no idea how I'd gotten there. My body was naked and happy about it.

I felt Sianna's chuckle more than I heard it. She shifted, inviting a spectacular wake-up process. "Good morning to you too," she whispered in my ear, giving me goosebumps.

"Um," I said, in what was undoubtedly one the most articulate moments of my life.

I didn't know what to do.

My brain said morning sex only sounded like a good idea, and there would be consequences later. My body thought morning sex sounded like a good idea, full stop. It didn't care about consequences.

Usually, my head ruled the roost. But my body had taught me an excruciating lesson the night before. I didn't know if this was typical morning excitement or the energy demanding something.

She grinned at my indecision. "You are well. All is well. I will keep you safe." She kissed my cheek. "Come. We run this morning, and I want you to try something."

"I don't think I can run," I admitted. "That was horrible last night."

She'd climbed out of bed, her lovely bare ass directly in my line of sight. I looked away, drawing a chuckle from her. "Can you run if you are being chased by a tiger?"

"I THOUGHT YOU WERE FUCKING KIDDING ABOUT THE TIGER!" I yelled.

In case you're wondering, the instinct to run from a rampaging tiger is still a thing, even when you know the tiger is a friend.

Maybe. Maybe a friend. Maybe a girlfriend. Certainly, a wet dream.

She roared again, scaring the crap out of me—thankfully, not literally.

I picked up the pace.

I didn't know where we were going, but she was definitely steering me toward something.

After the fastest twenty-minute run of my life, I stood in a paved lot next to an abandoned gas station.

Behind me, Sianna had shifted back to herself, pulling on the dress that I'd carried in my backpack.

I should have seen the tiger thing coming when she'd packed extra clothes for herself along with water.

"Where are we?" I panted.

"It is an empty parking lot," Sianna replied, pulling a

confused expression. I caught the spark of amusement in her eyes.

"Because?"

"Because no one is here?" she suggested.

I sighed.

She burst out in giggles. "I am proud of that sigh. It means you are getting back to normal."

"You're downright playful this morning," I noted, eyebrows raised.

Her grin fell, turning into a more poignant, earnest smile. "I took in a huge amount of energy last night. It makes my mental barriers, or the layers of my psyche—however you prefer to think about it—easier to hold."

"My power overload helped you?" I asked, stunned.

She nodded, not moving her eyes from mine. "There is more separation and balance than I have ever had as an adult. It is easier this morning."

"What's easier?" I asked, trying to understand.

"Existing," she said, after considering for a moment.

That rocked me back on my heels.

"A family is coming to meet us. I expect them in about ten minutes, but I will tell you when I hear them approaching."

I lifted my eyebrows, surprised.

"You said you were willing to help. That is still true?"

"Of course," I said immediately.

She nodded. "The man—the father—came to the cornfields the night before last. I was surprised to see him. He is a strong affinity, part of a powerful sect of our population. I believed him to be well-balanced. We talked. He came to see for himself before talking to his wife. Their son is also a strong affinity, but his mind is not stable. He cannot find calm and sometimes acts as if he is an animal.

"The son is young, not even four years old. Such instability cannot be left unchecked. The child should be institutionalized before he hurts himself or someone else.

"Often, my father can help the young ones either settle the beast or strengthen the human. Nathaniel has not been able to help this one, and it hurts our relationship with the sect. I had thought the child was already gone. The father risks much by keeping the child with them at this point."

I could feel my anger but knew it wasn't visible.

Sianna still shook her head, responding to my emotion. "Do not judge us until you see the boy."

"Could Adaline help him?" I asked.

"It is his mind that is broken, his sense of self. Not his body. I think the Mistress can help the body. Can she also heal the mind?"

I didn't know. I'd have to ask her.

"Could Jen help him?"

The color drained from Sianna's face. "We would not burden the Queen of the Mind with our problems. You address her so casually. I still do not understand. I am amazed she has not taken her toll out of the flesh of your family."

I laughed. I knew Sianna's terror was real, and I even understood being afraid of Jen. But the thought of Jen taking a flesh toll was just too much.

Sianna was frowning as she turned to look down the road. "They approach. Pull your power forward, please, so they know it is safe. I do not believe the father trusts me. Nathaniel would kill him for keeping the boy at this point."

"He's three years old! He might get better with practice and age," I argued, even as I pulled the peace forward. I stumbled a bit; there was more energy in me now.

She shook her head again. "Not in our experience. The boy will get worse if we cannot offer aid. He will be a danger to all around him. Helping him, though, would be a boon for you. It would demonstrate what you are in advance of Wednesday."

I felt her unease at the mention of Wednesday. "Sianna, I felt that. Why are you worried about Wednesday?"

Her eyes flicked to mine. "We will discuss this later. They are here."

I could just make out the SUV in the distance.

THE MAN HAD to be a bear shifter. He just looked like a bear, even in human form. A few inches taller than my six-two, he had to weigh close to three hundred pounds, and not much of it was fat. Big, burly, and hairy, I was confident in my bear diagnosis.

So, when my energy touched him as he got out of the car, I yelled, "You've gotta be kidding me!"

It wasn't my finest moment.

Sianna sighed, not even bothering to look at me.

"He's a ferret!" I muttered. "Look at him! How does that turn into one single ferret?"

She still wasn't looking at me, but I could tell she was trying not to laugh. "I turn into a five-hundred-pound tiger and also a four-ounce spider," she murmured, not moving her lips. "Stop it. She has good hearing."

My energy said she was some kind of bird of prey, maybe an

owl. *How did an owl and a ferret fall in love? It had to be a story for the ages!*

I was fascinated.

No wonder the kid was a mess.

"Peacekeeper," the man breathed, coming closer, gesturing for his wife to get out of the car. "I didn't dare hope."

That was true, and it knocked all the humor out of me. This man came here expecting to be executed this morning. I could feel his fear of death as a part of him that wasn't at peace.

"My name is Luke," I said, voice light. "I don't think I'm actually Peacekeeper yet, but I'll help if I can."

The man nodded, not meeting my eyes.

"He is Joe; she is Deanna. Their son is Owen," Sianna supplied as the woman joined her husband, five feet in front of me. The child stayed in the car.

I extended my hand. "It's nice to meet you."

Joe took my hand out of pure instinct, a force of habit, without considering who I was. When my peace rolled through him, he landed on his ass in the parking lot.

"No one here's going to hurt your family, Joe. You can stop waiting for death now," I coached, helping him back to his feet.

Deanna also accepted my handshake, but she was ready for the wave of calm. She also came ready to fight if she had to, which was interesting.

"I couldn't even touch the Huntress," she said with a little smile. "But I'd gladly try for Nate's eyes before I met my end."

At my startled expression, she laughed.

"He does not understand what he is," Sianna said, smiling. "You were touching her, Peacekeeper. She can sense your emotions as easily as you can sense hers."

"Huh," I said, looking at Sianna. "You can do that too?"

She raised her eyebrows, waiting for me to process.

"Yes. Yes, you can. You've done it without touching me," I realized.

She nodded. "The boy waits in the car."

"I know," I said easily.

"Are you going to help him?" she asked.

"I will in a minute. I can feel his mind warring with itself. He's falling asleep right now. Once he's out, I'll go see what I see."

"He doesn't sleep much," Deanna blurted, head turning from me to the car.

I nodded. "I have a brother like that, too. We'll see. I can definitely make Owen sleep. I want him good and out before I go over there, though. He was terrified when you pulled in."

Deanna let out a slight sound, almost a sob, before she covered her mouth. "Please?" she asked, her eyes filling with tears. "He is my only child and was well until about eight months ago. Please."

Without thinking, I tugged her toward me for a hug, dropping her into a twilight sense of relaxation. "All will be well. You'll see." I handed her to Joe for support. "Be right back."

Sianna walked with me toward the car. "Luke?"

My lips twitched. *Luke, not Peacekeeper. We're friends, even if she can be terrifying.*

"Are you okay?" she asked. "You don't sound like yourself."

"I'm good," I said. "I know what to do. It's like with Edgar."

I could feel the utter wrongness in the child as we got closer. It called to me, begging for help. He was not at peace and fought desperately to hang on to reality.

"Poor Owen," I muttered, looking at his bindings. There was a giant, knotted snarl right in the middle of his life energy.

"How does this happen?" I asked. "I've seen other mentally ill people before. They don't look like this. Usually, the part not at peace is actually in the mind itself. Not this. This is a knot in his life energy, like he tried to..." My voice trailed off as I figured it out.

"Tried to what?" Sianna asked, still beside me.

"It's like he tried to twist his life energy into something else and got stuck. I'm guessing he tried to transform without understanding what he was doing."

She was frowning. I could tell without looking at her.

Taking Owen's tiny hand in mine, I felt the healthy bindings shift out of my way again, leaving room for my will to unknot the root issue. Owen's tiny little mind and body knew things weren't right. He was just waiting for someone to fix it. It took me less than a minute.

"It's done," I called to Joe and Deanna. Looking back to Sianna, I asked, "There are more children like this? Where are they? Let's get this done."

Her mouth dropped open in shock. "It's done? Just like that?"

"It's done," I said confidently. "It was kind of like Edgar, but not really. Edgar had a bad tie from outside. Poor Owen just got stuck. Where are the other kids? We should go there."

Her eyes were huge. "Truly? You helped him?"

Owen was stirring awake in the car. "Mama?" he asked, looking around.

"Hi, Owen! Mama's coming. Everything's good, buddy," I said, smiling at the kiddo.

He smiled back, uncertain. He didn't know me.

"Boo!" he said, pointing to the sky.

"Yep," I confirmed, "the sky is blue."

Sianna's energy rolled crazily around us: fear, pride, hope, despair, joy, happiness... victory. More than anything else, she was filled with a sense of victory. She had a way for her people to survive, even thrive, going forward.

"Owen? Owen!" Deanna wailed, crawling into the back seat with the kiddo. "Baby!" she cried, sobbing as she touched his sweet little hands and kissed his cheeks.

Joe stood, dumbstruck, watching. When words came, they were low and monotone. "It took both of us to wrestle him into the car. He raked his nails down her face when she tried to hold him to buckle the belt. He tried to chew through the seatbelt as we drove."

"That makes sense." I nodded. "His energy was knotted like he'd tried to shi-transform before he knew what he was doing." I caught myself, hoping Joe overlooked my faux pas.

"You call it whatever the fuck you want, Peacekeeper. We will bow to your whim and await your pleasure for all eternity if you can make our children well," Joe said, the words a promise.

I clapped my hands, trying to break up the awkward, trailing silence. "Great. Sianna! Let's go see the kids!"

"We cannot," she said.

At the same time, Joe said, "You can't."

I looked between them, confused.

"Not yet," Joe explained. "Not until you're recognized as Peacekeeper. If you start now, there will be fighting between us, arguments over favoritism. You can't do it until after Wednesday. I'll start quietly spreading the word. We'll start a list. The families will come to you, Peacekeeper."

I scrunched up my face. "Probably easier if I go to them. I have the means to do it. It's not a big deal."

Joe stared at Sianna. She sighed again. "This is who he is. I tried to explain."

She turned back to me, "It does not matter. You cannot help until after Wednesday without causing strife, Peacekeeper. Whether you go to them or they come to you, there will be an order in which you help."

"How many kids are we talking about?" I asked, feeling a little sick that kids were stuck waiting on politicking.

"Hundreds?" Joe asked. "Maybe a thousand around the world. They'll all be young. Most children like Owen don't survive into puberty."

I sighed. "Make the list. I'll talk to Addy and Sam too. I bet they can do this. We'll get it right."

18

"That was amazing," Sianna praised me. "My father often sits for hours, sometimes days, with the children like Owen who have true promise. We don't want to give up our most gifted but often can't help."

"Well," I said, drawing out the word, trying to decide if I should mention it.

"Say it," she prompted. "I know what you're going to say. I've wondered it for my entire adult life."

"I'm pretty sure your dad screwed over Edgar. That tie snapped and hurt your dad. I'm no expert, but I think that means your dad was benefiting from the tie that held Edgar."

Sianna nodded. "Edgar was Overlord for a great number of years and did not show signs of losing his abilities when he…."

She wasn't sure how to describe it.

"Got stuck?" I offered. The phrase fit.

She nodded. "It was before I was born. With Edgar unable to help himself, my father took over."

I nodded, having guessed as much.

"Could Edgar have fixed Owen?" I asked, looking for ways to speed up the process of helping a thousand children out of that kind of pain.

"I don't know," Sianna said. "He couldn't last week. I have no idea how he's doing now. While you are safe with your family at training, I will go to see Edgar. I have questions. And I want to check on Charlie."

We were walking back to the fields, away from the empty gas station. "You don't want to hang with Jen? She'll be disappointed to miss you."

Sianna grinned. "I will wait until after she arrives. I'm certain she has words for me if she is as close to your family as you say. I wouldn't dream of upsetting her by not showing up. But then I will go to my uncle and my father."

She started reaching for the hem of her dress.

"No! Wait! We can walk, right? I just did something nice. I don't need to run five-minute miles! SHIT!" I yelled, already running as Sianna transformed into a wolf with mighty large fangs.

It said something that my immediate reaction to a beautiful woman taking off her clothes was, "No, wait."

I'd made an error in priorities or judgment somewhere in my life choices.

I'd also dropped her dress. I wasn't sorry. She could get it later.

SIANNA and I had just joined the rest of my family on the curb when Jen pulled up.

She was glaring at me before she was even out of the car. I could feel it.

Stepping on the sidewalk, she greeted Hank and Darla with hugs and kisses before looking at us. I was working hard to ignore the glare.

"Lucas!" Her voice cracked like a whip. "Come here."

So much for ignoring her. I walked over to where Jen stood, chatting with my parents.

"Where's my hug and kiss?" she asked.

Oh, okay. This is normal Jen!

As I bent to give her a kiss, she whacked me with her purse.

"Ow!" I yelled as she whacked me again. "Did you put rocks in that thing?"

"Didn't I tell you not to play with the shifters? Didn't I? Didn't we have that conversation not two weeks ago over Christmas?" Jen yelled, whacking me again. "Now, look at you," she barked, "boinking the strongest shifter on the fucking planet!" *Whack!*

To be fair, Jen did tell me not to date any more shifters after Candy and I broke up. I was told in no uncertain terms it wouldn't be good for my health.

"We're not boinking!" I yelled, louder than intended.

"Sorry! Sorry!" I yelled, dodging whacks from my mother. "Jen's word, not mine!" I attempted the duck and cover strategy, but both Jen and my mother were short. It didn't help me.

"You're this far in. You might as well go for the fucking too, you moron!" Jen yelled, whacking me again.

"Sorry!" I yelled again for good measure. I wasn't even sure what I'd done.

Eventually, the whacking stopped.

"What the fuck?" Will yelled at Sianna. "I ran up his stairs to check on him, and you almost took my head off. But Jen gets to beat the shit out of him?"

Sianna nodded, unrepentant.

"Why?" Will demanded.

"She is scarier than you," Sianna admitted, not looking at Jen.

"She knows I'll snap her brain like a rubber band if she interferes," Jen called. "You! Come here. Now."

Sianna walked to my side, head high and shoulders even. I'm pretty sure only William and I knew she was terrified.

"Why are you here, among my *family*?" Jen asked, stressing the last word.

Sianna's mouth opened and closed twice before words came out. "He needed a protector. He declared himself Peacekeeper in front of my father and demonstrated his power. I offered myself as guard."

"Mmhmm," Jen said, looking at me again. "She has absolute control of her body, Lucas. If you go for the fucking, there will be babies. Multiple. There's no timing it. Ain't no condom in the world going to keep you from being a daddy. Absolute control.

"That's what she intended when she volunteered—she was going to be the first mate of the Peacekeeper. Now, she's on the fence about the whole Peacekeeper thing."

That startled me. "You don't think I'm the Peacekeeper?" I asked, turning to look at Sianna.

I would process the baby thing later. Much later. Maybe never.

Sianna didn't meet my gaze.

Jen whacked me again while I was distracted. "Of course, you're the Peacekeeper, and she knows it. The problem is that you're now also Luke, who doesn't want a harem of lovers and hordes of children.

"Okay. We're all on the same page. I thought there was some Nathaniel bullshit wrapped up in this, but Luke really is this stupid." Jen looked at Sianna again. "My family. If you bring harm to any of them, you will answer to me."

"I already threatened her. She didn't care," Sam called.

"YOU! COME HERE!" Jen bellowed.

"I didn't do it!" Sam yelled back, trying to hide behind William.

"Don't make me walk over there," Jen growled.

Sam dragged his feet across the sidewalk to stand in front of Jen. I could tell he was trying to brace himself to be whacked.

"What's the binding nonsense?" Jen asked, voice seemingly calm.

"They need a binding. I need there to be a love binding. They take his head without one. I need one. It's changed a little bit. *She* doesn't take his head. But I still need the binding."

Jen's eyes narrowed at Sam before she turned and whacked me again.

"Luke, you are my least favorite Trellis right now," she growled. "Let's go do this training thing. Sianna, go back to your father and your uncle. I'll await your return and information before I go. Move it, boys!"

Jen turned and walked to the other cluster of family.

"Bye, kids. I'm going inside," my mom called. "Jen has things under control. It's cold out here."

"Cribbage?" my dad asked, eliciting happy sounds from my mom. Cribbage in front of a winter fire was a favorite Darla pastime.

"Let me kiss the baby bump," Jen squealed with joy, jogging ahead to walk with William and Emma.

"So, that's Jen," I said lightly to Sianna, who was staring off into the distance.

She touched my hand to heal the bruises before she walked toward my house without a word.

"Well, okay," I muttered, turning to walk with Sam.

"What happens to her clothes when she shifts?"

"She'll leave her clothes on my back porch before flying off," I muttered.

"FLYING?! SHE CAN FLY? LIKE A BIRD?" Sam pulled out an actual fanboy squeal.

I was exhausted long before training actually started.

19

"So, we thought—" Micah started.

"Nope," Jen interrupted. "Close a circle. I want to see it."

"The family circle is up," Jake said, confused. "Can't you feel it?"

She glared at him. "Of course, I can feel it. You keep pulling me into it. No, I want an actual circle. Stand one up so I can see it, Addy."

My siblings and I looked around, confused. Jen was seriously pissed about something.

"What's wrong?" Will asked.

"I think your circle is fucked up," Jen said without preamble. "You can't feel it coming off him?"

She turned to glare at me again. I looked behind me, just to make sure no one else was back there.

"What did I do?" I asked, utterly lost.

"I don't know. What did you do to your power?" Jen asked.

"There is exponentially more power radiating off you now than there was two weeks ago. What did you do?"

"I don't...." I thought about my nose and ears bleeding. "Last night, my power went wonky. I don't know. She said I was overloaded."

"I had a dream last night," Will muttered. "You were rolling around on the floor with the mother of all hard-ons, screaming in pain."

"Oh," Sam muttered.

I flushed so red, I was likely purple.

"Close the circle," Jen said, staring at me. "A circle of ascendence is different than your family circle. I don't know if it'll close with him now."

I looked at Micah, hoping for some sort of contradiction. He wouldn't even look at me.

We each took our regular circle positions in complete silence as Addy made her loop to close the energy. It closed, but it didn't feel right. It was lopsided. I stared at William, directly across from me.

He shook his head. "Would it be better with different corners or more people? Does Luke need to hold a corner?"

"No," Jen muttered. "Either the cardinal positions, not the corners, will grow in power to match him, or he'll leave the circle. That's how this goes. I've never heard of a single person being Peace in an empowered circle and Peacekeeper to the beast affinities. I don't know if you can be both, Luke. I do know that giving up your Name in this circle will kill you.

"The circles that allow pillars to give up names are sickly and generally already falling to pieces. This circle is not sickly. Don't give up your name."

"I agree," Micah murmured. "I told you I've never known a

Peacekeeper. Beast affinities and empowered people do not play well together."

"You're not leaving the fucking circle," Will growled. "You've stood a circle longer than the rest of the family. I don't care how bad-ass the woman is—"

"SHE FLIES!" Sam interjected.

"—you're not leaving the circle. Figure your shit out." William finished.

I shot a glance at Matthew. He stared straight ahead, chewing his lip. He was thinking through something.

"I don't know what to do or say," I mumbled, looking around the circle for help. "I don't know how this happened. I didn't... Nothing changed. We didn't. We aren't. It was a dream."

"Was it a dream-dream or dream-walking?" Sam asked, serious.

"Regular dream. She came charging into my room, thinking I was being attacked or something. Said my power rolled like a tidal wave through here. And then I lost some time. It felt like my body was trying to turn itself inside out."

"Did you ask her?" William asked, his tone implying I was a moron.

"No, there wasn't time this morning. She chased me and then Owen—"

"She chased you?" Matthew asked, eyebrows raised.

"Yeah." I glared at William. "Turns out she disapproves of you beating the shit out of me, but she's all for the cardio. She turned into a fucking tiger and chased my ass all over the cornfields."

There were muffled snorts of laughter from all around me.

"Oh, shut up. Trust me. You know it's her. Logically, you

know it. But when she roars and charges, your ass is running at top speed. Full-on hindbrain action because a fucking *tiger* is chasing you."

No one was hiding the laughter now, not even Jen.

"The wolf form on the way home was less terrifying right up until she bit my ass!"

"Some guys like that," Noah called.

"Not me!" I called back, turning red.

"Poor Persnickety—" William started.

"This is not helpful!" I yelled to no one in particular.

I'd already lost them. My family had divided into little clusters of jokes, mostly at my expense. They didn't know how to help. This was how we dealt with stress.

I sighed, turning to avoid Will's mocking laughter, and unexpectedly met Adaline's worried eyes.

"I'm okay," I mouthed to her, knowing she wouldn't hear me over the banter.

"*You could stand the center of the circle with Sam and me. We would share the center, Luke. Don't leave us,*" she said into my mind as she blinked quickly, trying and failing to hide her tears.

"*I remain the most underappreciated Trellis,*" I teased back, mentally sharing the thought with her, hoping to draw a smile. It didn't work.

"We love you," she said aloud, the words lost to the silly laughter and wind around us.

Breaking the circle, I went to hug her.

"It's going to be fine," I whispered in her ear. "Promise."

"Training!" Jen hollered over the nonsense.

"THERE'S ACTUAL TRAINING?" Adrian asked, grinning. "This wasn't just an excuse to pick on Luke?"

Micah rolled his eyes. "There is actual training, and you'll like this training. You've asked before, and I've avoided the question."

Ethan did a little cheer.

This was going to be good. I could tell.

Micah and Jen shared a look.

"Go ahead," Jen said with a wave. "I'll watch."

"Okay," Micah said with a shrug. "Everyone watch me. Are you looking? You have to be looking. Ready? Set."

And then he was gone.

"YO!" He yelled from about a hundred meters away, in the opposite direction from the houses.

He jumped twice more before coming back to his starting place, not even a bit winded. "It's time to learn how to travel without the energy of the Mistress and Walker. You've been fortunate. The Walker doesn't typically use his control over space to be of assistance to others. I've never known a Mistress to have the ability." He paused, looking at Jen.

"Nope," she agreed. "Sam and Addy are unique as far as I know."

Nodding, Micah continued. "Usually, the Walker takes himself, maybe his Mistress, and leaves everyone else to hoof it. To that end, those with the energy to do so have learned to jump through space.

"Unlike the Walker, we must have some sort of anchoring energy, known as a marker, to guide us. A marker is a small piece of your own energy, left somewhere to sustain itself until your return. Typically, we leave markers with non-sentient,

living things—usually trees, but grass, shrubs, and other living
things work too."

"Why non-sentient?" Matthew asked. "Why can't I anchor
to Miranda to be able to always find her?"

Micah sighed at Matthew. It was a familiar sigh. It made me
laugh. It meant Matthew had jumped right over the lesson plans
and asked the question that was meant to be answered at
the end.

"You have a binding to Miranda. It's solid and sure. It can
serve as a marker for you without any additional effort. Bound
pairs can usually jump to each other when needed. It's a matter
of finding the binding and following it.

"But, otherwise, if you try to place a marker within a person,
even a loved one, you'll be merging your energy with someone
else's. Imagine having to carry around a lively, active chunk of
Noah's energy on the off chance he wants to visit? It'd feel
strange and wrong.

"We generally choose large plant life because the plant's
natural energy doesn't war with ours any more than it would
war with the rain that lands on it or the animals that walk by it.
The larger, the better; it makes it less likely someone will chop
it down. I walked my ass over there and created a marker to a
patch of grass for today's demonstration. The grass is dormant
with the snow. My energy will be disbursed by spring when the
new grass comes in."

Matthew nodded.

"How do we do it?" William asked, focused and eager.

Jen smiled. "You're so fucking sweet. He's thinking about
getting home in a hurry when Emma goes into labor."

"I-I am thinking no such thing!" Will objected, flushing, as we all cooed at him. "I am thinking about the strategic importance—"

"It's all bullshit!" Hennessy yelled, laughing. "He's thinking about babies."

"Now he's thinking about scaring the hell out of the kids' future boyfriends." Jen giggled, grinning with the rest of us.

"Why you gotta out me like that?" Will faux-whined at her. "I'm your favorite. Why be mean to me?"

"Noah's my favorite, and you know it."

"Fine, I'm your second favorite. Why Jen? Why?" Will grinned.

Jen reached up, touching a finger to his right dimple. "Love and Fear, William. Always. You're not mine, but I love you all the same."

"OH! Oh!" Sam yelled, smacking himself in the head. He turned to me. "You have to make that binding to her. I need it. You need it. I mean, we might not need it, but we might really need it. Make with the sexy time and the binding!"

I threw my arms up in frustration. "She's not even here, Sam. I'll drop trou and get on that just as soon as she's back, though."

"Great," he said, not sensing my sarcasm, which made it funnier for Matthew and me.

"Oh my God," Matthew muttered, shaking with laughter, "how is this your life? How did this happen?"

"I don't know." I wasn't whining. I wasn't. I was Peace. I couldn't whine.

"So, to jump, you place your energy marker. That's the first step, and I can show you that," Micah called, trying to bring us back to the topic at hand. "Getting the hang of actually forcing your presence from one place to another is a trick of the mind, though. In my experience, it involves a lot of trial and error. Ethan's been trying for three days and can't do it."

Ethan pulled a face at Micah for snitching. Just the sight of Ethan teasing made me grin. Like standing with Emma, who embodied love, or Beth, who embodied hope, just being with Ethan and his joy made you feel better about life.

I used to be like that, I realized. *My power used to have that sort of effect. Have I lost that?*

As if in answer to my question, Talise threaded her fingers through mine, resting her head on my right shoulder. "Hi, you."

I smiled, turning to kiss the top of her head. For as much as Noah annoyed me, I'd dance for joy at their eventual wedding, glad to have Tali as a sister. "Hi. You're better?"

"Now that we've agreed you're not going to get your head chopped off? Yes, I'm better."

We watched as William tried to create a marker. He was making a constipated face, kind of squatting and bouncing at the same time. I pulled my phone out of my pocket and snapped a picture without him realizing it. A moment forever captured.

Priceless.

I felt Tali shake with laughter as she stood quietly, leaning on me.

I wrapped an arm around her waist, offering a hug. "Gonna tell me what's wrong?"

"Hmm." She chewed on her bottom lip. "Addy and I think we're the only ones who caught it. Who's Owen?"

"Oh." I thought back over the conversation in the field. I'd mentioned him when I had talked about running this morning. "He's a little boy, a shifter. He was... unstable. I helped straighten his energy this morning. I'm going to talk to Addy about it. Other kids like him need help."

"Mmm," she said, still leaning. "Tell Addy. Let Addy help them, Luke. Stay away from the shifters. Please?"

"Tali," I murmured, voice chiding. "I won't leave kids to suffer. I'm just not cruel enough for that."

"It turns out I am, Luke." Her voice was cold, unlike any tone I'd heard from her before. "They don't get to take you. You belong with us. I'll flood their lungs with their own fluids and kill them all before they get to touch you."

"Talise." I gasped, at a loss. I could feel the resolution in her words. She was at peace about this. The thought didn't bother her in the least. "Tali—"

"No, Lucas. You kept me sane, healthy, and reasonably happy for most of a decade. You made my life livable and were my only friend. You brought your family to me. They fixed me and took me in as one of their own.

"Matilda plays with fire, Miranda with earthquakes, Lucy with lightning. I will drown them all without a backward glance. They wouldn't even see it coming. And I'll tell that woman as much. If they think they're just playing with Peace, they're in for a rude awakening. She should know that." There was enough scorn in Talise's voice, I wondered if someone had shifted to take on her appearance.

"Tali," I muttered, offering my peace through our joined hands. As she took it, the same water and life energy that made up Talise cycled through me. This was Tali—my sweet Tali.

"I can feel your shock and horror," she murmured.

I flinched at the reminder. She was touching me. There was no hiding my emotions from her.

She was silent for a moment, considering her words. "I feel the best and worst of people, Luke. Every day, all day long, their emotions wash through me. The minute I leave these wards, I feel exactly what humanity is. But there's nothing hard or ugly about who you are. You wouldn't even defend yourself in a fight."

She squeezed my fingers again. "I am not so soft."

I nodded, lacking anything productive or meaningful to add.

We chuckled again, watching William fall flat on his face.

"Are you going to try this jumping thing?" she asked.

"Pfft. No. Matthew will figure it out and then explain it to me."

As if on cue, William started bellowing. "How'd you fucking do that?"

Ten seconds later, Matthew was running from Will. Just as Will got up to speed, charging after him, Matthew jumped back to the starting point, in the opposite direction Will was running.

"This isn't going to get old," Talise said, genuinely laughing at William's hissy fit.

"I got this," Matthew said with a chuckle as he jogged past, touching the few trees within reach.

"Fucking asshole," William muttered, walking back to Micah. "I'm never going to catch him now."

Adaline came to stand on my other side, assuming Tali's relaxed posture of leaning against me.

"I'm surrounded by beautiful women," I said lightly, hugging Adaline in the same way I hugged Talise.

"I already told him," Tali said to Adaline. "It's done."

"Mmm," Adaline responded, watching Matthew try to explain jumping by actually jumping in place. "This is why we burned my forest."

I nodded.

We'd burned Adaline's family's forested lands and their

restaurant in Dallas to the ground in November. It made conceptual sense when we did it. Now that the logistics of jumping were clear, we knew the destruction was necessary. It'd taken Matthew five minutes to figure out how to jump. Adaline's lands would have been a feeding ground for centuries if we hadn't removed all the energy ties and markers wrapped up in the forest.

"I'll call them out to her, Luke. I'll point out the living shifters for Tali to finish off. I'll do it without doing any injury to myself," Adaline said, serene in her acceptance. "We don't trust that you'll stay home on Wednesday. You must know what you risk by going. We will kill them all if they take you from us. We will kill them all with or without Sam's help."

Taking a calming breath, I pulled my peace energy forward to cover my own emotions.

Both ladies sighed, relaxing into the feeling.

I clung to my own peaceful energy as realization dawned and goosebumps of fear washed over me.

My energy had never affected Adaline before.

20

"Alright, I've had enough silly for the weekend," Jen called. "Lucas, walk back to the car with me."

Sam wandered over to take Adaline from me. She was almost sleeping, though she was still standing.

"She hasn't been resting well," Sam offered, concerned eyes staring at me. He knew what had happened.

"Did you see this?" I muttered softly, trying not to disturb the calm.

His head gave a little shake. "I wasn't looking for it."

"What did I do? Can you see what happened?"

He pressed his lips together, hesitating.

"Sam?"

Adaline sighed contentedly as Sam pulled her into a hug, away from me. "My Sam," she murmured. "Love you."

Sam kissed her forehead, whispering something too softly for me to hear. Whatever it was, Addy liked it. She snuggled into his chest and let him support her weight.

"You didn't take your name from us, Luke. Over the summer, you took the name of Peace before Adaline and I took the names of Mistress and Walker. I don't think your power is limited to our circle."

I stared, dumbstruck. He was right. When my family discovered our unique ties to emotions and elements, we each took responsibility for what we were by claiming the name of our power. I had unwittingly taken the name of Peace before anyone else took their names. The rest of our family had taken their names after Sam and Addy, tying their powers specifically to Sam and Addy's circle.

I hadn't.

"I'll look," Sam mumbled. "But we're going home now."

And then they were gone in true Walker fashion. There one moment, gone the next. If you blinked, you missed it.

Talise kissed my cheek. She stumbled toward Noah, ushering him to their home without so much as a goodbye.

"Let's walk, Luke," Jen said quietly, wrapping her arm with mine. "You're getting more sturdy, like if I fall on my ass in the snow, you can pick me up."

My lips twitched. "William."

"William," she agreed, smiling as we watched Will twirl a very pregnant Emma in the snow. "So fierce in his love, as it should be."

"I thought you were going to wait for Sianna's return?"

"She's been back for more than an hour," Jen replied, surprised. "I got what I wanted from her mind before William faceplanted in the mud. You didn't feel her?"

I thought about it for a minute, only then realizing that I *could* feel her on the opposite side of the houses in hawk form, watching. "That's new," I mumbled.

"Is it? Did you try it before?"

"No," I admitted.

Jen nodded. "Let's both remember that she can hear every word we're saying. Still, I will say this: I'm sorry I told you her original intentions to lure you into bed and have children. She's ashamed of those plans now, realizing that family means something different to you than to her. So, I'm truly sorry if that affected the way you see her. She's always intended to keep you safe, regardless of the secondary motivations."

I shook my head. "Charlie warned me as much on Wednesday night. Not in so many words, but he made it clear. And every conversation I've had with Ellie has ended with some form of 'No sex for you!' I was surprised that she could control her body to that extent, not surprised that she planned for progeny."

There was more snark than I intended in that last word.

Jen laughed. "You *have* talked to Nathaniel."

I nodded, pulling a sheepish smile.

"He's a disgusting person. Absolutely horrible. His mind has always tended toward power and domination. I imagine he's not happy to have a Peacekeeper to steal his thunder."

"I'm not sure he's sane," I admitted. "He looked calm, but his mind was not at peace while we talked."

"That's not new. Even as a young man, he was a sociopath, focused on aligning others to his whims. Three of the sons are the same or worse—their minds are bent toward domination rather than leadership. The fourth son is different, but nowhere near as powerful.

"I'll 'reconnect' with Nate now that I've resurfaced. Empowered circles and beast affinities don't get along, but no one denies me," she said in the same even tone. Jen might as well have been discussing the weather. It made me glad she was on our side.

"Back to the girl, though. She will not bind to you, Lucas. I know she told you that. I know Sam keeps insisting. You'll need to find another way. In their culture, a binding like Sam wants, would make her subservient. If ever there was a man worthy of her, it would be one of you silly Trellis boys, but she's fought hard to maintain her independence. I mean that literally. Even as a young one, she fought those that would claim her. She is fast and strong out of necessity. She will not forge the type of bond Sam wants in a week. Maybe in time, but not so quickly. Find another way." Jen stared at me as we paused beside her car, like she was willing me to understand something.

I shrugged. "My energy doesn't play nice with the lovey-dovey stuff, Jen. You've seen it yourself. Even if she was willing to form the bond Sam wanted, I don't think it'd stick to me."

She smacked me again. "You're a moron."

I grinned. I couldn't help it. "Love you," I murmured, kissing the top of her head.

"Yeah, I know," she muttered back. "Keep your head attached, Lucas. I don't need Sam's foresight to know shit will go badly if you lose it."

AFTER JEN PULLED AWAY, I went "grocery shopping" in my family members' refrigerators. I wasn't about to go out in public, and I had failed to order groceries. My fresh produce pickings were getting slim. At times like this, it was nice to be able to pilfer food from eleven other houses.

I'd rejected eight dinner invitations, including my parents', before I got to Sam's house.

Sam met me at his front door with a bag of squash and zucchini. "Addy's sleeping. Don't come in. Stay home for dinner tonight. There are things you need to talk about."

I nodded, surprised. "I thought I'd be stealing bread from you. Since when do you have zucchini?"

"Make the vegetable chicken pasta in lemon white wine sauce with fresh bread," he said. "She'll like it."

"Sam?" I asked, eyebrows raised.

"I bought the vegetables just now."

"You Walked to a public place, where people could see you?" My eyebrows were trying to join my hairline now.

Sam was so paranoid about bending space with his mental teleportation, he bought a condo in the building across from his office. He Walked to the condo with everyone going to work that day. Then, they drove a car around the block and parked it in the office parking garage. He wanted it to seem like they commuted every morning.

"Good luck," he mumbled before closing the door in my face.

I wasn't taking that as an ominous sign. I wasn't. I couldn't do the love binding thing, and I knew it. Still, a solemn Sam was unsettling.

"Sianna?" I called, walking through my front door. I knew she wasn't in the house but also knew she'd hear me and answer.

After I unloaded the groceries, she still hadn't appeared. "I'm not upset," I called. "Are you okay?"

She still didn't appear. I actually considered screaming in terror to make her come running but decided against it. It was only three o'clock in the afternoon, too early to start dinner. So, I set the bread for its first rise, then sat down at my piano.

The melody that came out of me was soft and soothing, almost a lullaby. The accompanying harmony was subdued.

I felt her, her shame and her stubborn pride, as she entered the house. I didn't stop playing. She liked the music, liked the calm, even though she'd never voluntarily accepted the peace I'd offered her. So, I played, letting the sound fill my mind and my house, letting it drain the tension and fear from me.

"If that music had a voice, it would be an apology," she said at last. "I do not know what you have to apologize for when I am the one who has behaved so poorly."

I didn't know what to say to that, so I didn't respond other than shifting the music to something more playful.

She sat on the bench next to me, straight-backed and stiff. Something rolled through her that I couldn't identify at first. Then, the feeling of Talise resting on my shoulder came to me.

Shifting my arm behind her, I pulled Sianna close, tucking her head against my shoulder as I continued to play with one arm behind her back.

She sighed. "You are getting better at that."

"Nah, I've always been good at shifting the music around obstacles." I smiled so she'd know I was teasing.

"I cannot be bound to you, Luke. She is right about that. It is not a moral thing for me. It is survival. Once bound and mated, I am only as useful as the offspring I produce, only valuable so long as I keep producing."

I shrugged. "I'm not worried about it."

"The Walker insists—"

"The Walker insists brown plaid goes with yellow cat pajama pants. Sam's perspective is often flawed. There are many types of bindings, Sianna. I think Sam discounts a lot of them. And, I have never inspired the shiny gold bonds of true love he's looking for. Never. I don't think love like that can co-exist with the peace energy. I think love, in and of itself, brings uncertainty and a lack of peace. They don't play nicely together. So, you and I will be what we are—friends."

She shifted uncomfortably. "You are truly not angry with me. I can tell."

I nodded. "There's nothing to be angry about. Whatever you intended initially, you haven't pushed an agenda. You haven't done anything but try to help me."

"There should be sex and children between us," she muttered. "I am not wrong about that. There is no downside."

It was my turn to sigh. I closed the key lid and made my way into the kitchen to futz with food preparation.

"This is what you do all day?" she asked, smiling to herself. "Play music and cook food?"

I shrugged. "Some portion of every day is spent with my family—usually Matthew. During the school year, I teach music in after-school programs, but they're still on winter break until the week after next."

"You have a cleaning schedule." She was trying not to laugh at me.

"Don't judge." I grinned at her.

"You cook, clean, teach the children, and make the music. You'd make an excellent wife." She was pushing, trying to goad me into an argument, but I couldn't tell why.

"You carry a sword, beat up my brothers, and chase me around for better cardio," I replied, eyebrows raised.

"You're suggesting we have reversed roles?"

"I'm suggesting that roles have nothing to do with gender," I replied, voice neutral, still unsure where this was going. "Can I ask you a rude question?"

"You are welcome to ask me anything, Peacekeeper," she said immediately. I resisted the urge to sigh. Back to *Peacekeeper,* no longer *Luke.*

"How old are you?"

She nodded like she had expected the question at some point.

She answered my question with a question. "You are young, correct? Your circle is new?"

I nodded.

"How old are you?" she asked.

"I'll turn twenty-five in two weeks."

She hesitated. "I am older."

"I know," I said easily. "I guessed as much. I just wonder how much older."

"Older."

"Fifty years older? Five hundred years older? A thousand years older?"

That got a smile.

"You laugh, but Micah lives three doors that way." I pointed to the left.

"Fair point." She grinned at me.

"You don't look older. Your father looks older. Edgar looks older. How does aging work with beast affinities? Candy is around my age, right? Charlie a little older?"

The humor left Sianna's face. "Candy is in her early thirties. Charlie will turn fifty in a few months."

"Charlie is fifty?" I blurted, shocked. "He was in a college bar when he met Ellie and Matty!"

"And Ellie is older still," Sianna muttered. "Older than me."

"Huh. I don't think Matilda knows that."

"Our level of affinity influences our growth and aging. Those of us with a strong affinity can decide how old we wish to appear. Even your cat can do this to some extent, though she will not live as long as Charlie or me. She'll have a more human lifespan. I'm curious what sort of affinity Owen will end up having. I've wondered if our strongest are lost as children. You truly believe he tried to transform?"

"I do. I can't imagine how else life energy would get tangled like that."

"Does my energy shift as I transform?"

"I don't know. You transform faster than I can track with my eyes."

She smiled a bit again.

"You won't tell me your age?"

"I am one hundred thirty-four years old, Peacekeeper. Many times your current lifespan, but you will outlive me. I am confident of that."

"Do you have children?" I asked.

"Do you?" she asked back, irritated.

"No."

"Why?"

I stared at her.

"I ask honestly. Why do you not have children?" she asked again.

"Because I don't have a love. I will not have a family without a partner," I murmured. She already knew this. I finished rolling the bread dough for its final rise, throwing a towel over the metal bowl as I bent to grab the pot for making pasta.

"It is similar for me," she said after a moment. "There is no mate for me that is not an immediate relative. I will not give up my place in our society. My place is not perfect, but I can effect some change and keep things level.

"I adore Charlie. But for all my father's griping, we were always friends—not great lovers. We would have had children, but not your type of family."

She watched as I washed and then began chopping the vegetables.

"A hundred some odd years is a long time to be alone," I muttered.

She nodded. "These last few days are the longest I've spent with anyone besides my father. Consecutively, at least. I don't stay in the same place long."

I snorted. "You don't stay here long, either. You sit on my roof all night!"

"I would nest in your bed if you would welcome me." She grinned, obviously teasing. "You were lost this morning, but I was quite happy with the state of things."

"I was scared," I admitted. "I don't understand what happened to my energy. My circle is lopsided."

Sianna nodded again. "There is no denying it now. It radiates from you. You *are* Peacekeeper, whether my father accepts it or not. What did you do to awaken it?"

I flushed red, unable to look at her. Her eyes didn't move and I felt them on me.

Her voice was calm, matter of fact. "You tried to take me last night."

I dropped my knife and the pepper I had been chopping. "What?"

"This morning, I thought you had reconciled yourself and changed your mind about our partnership." She raised her eyebrows. "You do not remember?"

"No," I barked, somehow even more horrified. "After the pain?"

Her lovely features scrunched in confusion. "I heard you sleeping before the pain. Before the energy."

"I was," I muttered, knowing I was backing myself into a corner. I met her eyes, waiting for it to sink in.

Eventually, she nodded.

"What happened?" I asked, my voice shaking.

I was absolutely terrified. I'd once made fun of William for being afraid of someone else controlling his mind. I would never laugh at him for it again. I couldn't fathom forcing myself on someone.

"Lucas," Sianna said, tone gentle. "I have access to a giant sword and turn into many varieties of dangerous animals."

I continued to stare, waiting for the worst.

"I should not have told you."

"Sianna, please?" I whispered. "What happened?"

She tried to smile. "I know this offends your sensibilities. I can sense your terror. But truly, I did not mind. You were exploding with power. Your eyes were glowing. Do you remember?"

I shook my head. "I remember screaming until I couldn't scream anymore. I remember you pinning me."

She nodded. "You were ripping the skin off your face. Then energy started seeping into me a little bit where our skin touched. I told you to let it go and pressed my body to yours, my lips to yours, trying to draw the energy free. It seemed to work for a moment. Your eyes lit, glowing in the darkness, and then we rolled."

I continued to stare, digging through my memories for any remaining fragments.

"You were not yourself. Your voice was different. Your energy was different. I did not war with the power, but I did not allow more than playful touching—nothing more intimate."

She paused, shrugging a bit as she pulled a smirk. "I also touched. Rubbed too. You did not mind."

My cheeks flushed again.

"You seemed to come back to yourself for a while. I took you to the shower and cleaned you up. You talked to me in the shower."

"I remember a little bit of the shower. I was so tired," I mumbled.

She smiled, coming around the counter to turn the flame off on the stove. "You'll burn dinner, and I am hungry."

I didn't know what to say. *"I'm sorry"* seemed wholly inadequate.

"After the shower, I put you to bed. You asked me to stay. You remember?"

I shook my head again. "I remember leaning on you in the shower and then waking up this morning."

"Oh," she murmured. A crease of disappointment formed between her eyebrows and spiked through her mind. "I had hoped that was you."

Her hand covered my mouth before I could apologize. "You leaned on me in the shower. You may lean on me, Peacekeeper. You may lean on me and trust me, despite my original intentions. I will not let anyone hurt you, even you.

"I'm glad to be with you, glad for your power, and glad for your company. I had lost hope for my people before you appeared in the arena last week."

I nodded, blinking quickly. It could have been so much worse.

She smiled again, a slight, teasing grin. "There should be sex and children between us, but not yet. Not until you agree. I will not play those games. I know family is dear to you."

I yanked her into a hug, holding on tightly before she could run away. "Thank you."

She chuckled before smacking my ass. "Make me dinner, man-wife. I like sea salt on my Italian bread."

"As you wish, woman-warrior," I muttered, laughing with her.

*I*t was snowing on Sunday morning. I woke alone in bed, watching the snow outside. Eventually, I climbed out of bed like a functional adult and headed for the bathroom. I silently applauded myself for not falling out of bed that morning.

Immediate needs attended to, I wandered back into my bedroom, considering what to do with myself. Then, the smells of breakfast broke through my morning haze. Coffee and bacon beckoned.

Downstairs, I blinked in the bright kitchen, the daylight reflecting off the fresh snow outside and through my kitchen windows. "Good morning," I murmured, my voice scratchy and gravely with sleep.

"Good morning," Sianna replied, looking at me. "You slept well."

"I did," I agreed. "I don't remember being awake at all during the night."

She nodded in confirmation, a small smile on her lips.

"Huh?" I asked at her amusement, scrubbing my hand across my face and through my hair.

She shook her head, still smiling. "Coffee?"

I nodded as she reached for a mug.

"Do you sleep?" I asked.

She glanced over her shoulder, smirking at me. "You've visited my dreams."

"I mean, really sleep, deep sleep."

She shook her head. "Not when I have a goal, like now. And not when I am around others with affinities. Sometimes, if I'm alone. I don't require that sort of sleep. It is a luxury."

I scrunched up my face. "Why not around other affinities?"

She opened the oven door, checking something that smelled like cinnamon and vanilla.

"What did you make?" I asked, distracted.

She put the plate of bacon in front of me with my coffee. I sipped—a dash of cream, no sugar, as I preferred. I wondered how she knew that.

"I can smell it," she said, answering my unspoken question.

I nodded vaguely. *Wow.*

"What did you make?" I asked again.

"A bread pudding of sorts with the leftover bread from last night. It will be good. You made good bread, and your pantry is well stocked."

I smiled. "Thank you for cooking."

She smiled back, peeking at me over her coffee cup. Her hair was dark, almost black, and straight, pulled up in a messy bun. Her eyes were a deep brown with hazel flecks. She stood at maybe five and a half feet tall in a navy-blue knee-length dress with tiny white flowers on it.

"Not feeling yourself today?" I asked, bemused by her choices.

Her smile stayed. "It does not matter to you unless I'm the curvy one. I can match my clothing."

I laughed at the idea of changing bodies to match clothes rather than the other way around. "You're not wrong. You're always you, regardless of the shape. Even the curvy one."

"The curvy one is your favorite." She grinned.

"The curvy one is every man's favorite," I countered, unrepentant.

She shook her head. "Some men prefer this." Her shape changed to a six-foot-tall leggy blonde so close in appearance to my brother's ex-girlfriend, I literally shuddered.

She blinked, shocked by my repulsion, as she morphed back to her previous form. "You do not like that one." It was a statement.

"I don't like that one. Please don't ever do that one again unless you want to throw Jake and Matilda for a loop."

Her eyebrows lifted in surprise before she turned to pull her pudding out of the oven.

Already laughing, I decided to spend breakfast telling Sianna the story of how Jake and Matilda met, knowing the story would lead to how we had all ended up empowered.

She didn't laugh as much as I'd anticipated.

"Your power was tied?" Her voice was cold and flat.

"I couldn't control it, Sianna. I needed that help," I replied, realizing I'd triggered her protectiveness.

"You needed a beast affinity. You did not need an empowered circle. You needed an affinity."

I shrugged. "I didn't have one available. The circle helped me."

"They restrained you and taught you poor habits," she countered.

"What poor habits?" I asked, sorry I'd brought it up.

"You hold your power away and yank it around like tug-of-war. It should not be so. It is natural. It is a part of you. You treat it like it is separate, like it's not part of your fundamental makeup. You struggle with it because it has been forced into a space it does not fit."

"I'm not going to walk around forcing my energy on people, Sianna," I countered.

"That is my point, Luke. You should not be forcing the power at all. It should be no different than breathing. It is part of your being. Trying to control it like you do is like dieting all week and binge eating on the weekends—counterproductive to someone who needs to make a lifestyle change. And you do not see it because you do not know how it is supposed to be."

I sighed, climbing to my feet. "Thank you for making breakfast," I said again, taking my dishes to the sink and opening the dishwasher.

"This is what I mean. Leave the dishes!" she yelled, truly upset now. "The dishes have no sense of peace. You fidget with things all day, trying to make the energy calm. That is *not* right!"

I stared, unsure what to say.

She took a deep breath, considering her words. "My energy stays within me, ready to answer my call at any time. It responds quickly, and I move with speed because I have trained it to be so. I have given it bounds in which to exist and be natural on my terms.

"You only allow your power to exist when you tug it forward or when you stand in a circle, so it wars with you. It is an untrained puppy tugging on the leash and destroying the house while you're away. If you accept its nature and give it boundaries, it will not be so destructive!"

"It's not destructive, Sianna," I offered, wondering if I should douse her with the peace to calm her down. Somehow, I suspected that would just prove her point.

"You do not sustain feelings of joy or happiness. You do not believe you can love. You cannot be easy if there are dishes in the sink. I wonder at your definition of 'destructive,' Luke.

"The energy in you is so overloaded and uncontrolled, it holds your life hostage. It has been this way for so long, you do not even recognize it as a problem. I should not be surprised to learn it was tied when you were younger."

My mouth was hanging open. I had no idea what to say.

"Get out of the way," she barked. "I will clean up. Go get dressed. Your hair is sticking up in funny directions, and you are all rumpled. It was adorable at first, like your energy was calm enough for you to relax. Now it just adds to my irritation. Go away. I am sure you need to iron your undershirts, dust the attic, or do something equally as useless based on whatever schedule you have created in your mind."

Wow, Sianna. Tell me how you really feel. I shuffled out of the kitchen, lost and wondering about dust in my attic.

SHORTLY BEFORE FIVE, I got dressed for Sunday dinner.

I hadn't seen Sianna since breakfast, but I knew she was mad at me. She'd moved everything in the kitchen around just enough to be obnoxious. The salt and pepper had changed places. The napkin holder was empty. The paper towels were backward.

I drew the line at the toilet paper rolls going the opposite direction but left the rest of it.

As I was tying my tie, she walked into the bathroom behind me in the same dress and body she'd worn earlier.

"Does the rest of your family wear ties?" she asked.

"You look lovely," I tried.

She sighed.

Once I was done, she looked me over. "You're done?"

"Yep."

"Feel good?"

I nodded, looking myself over, wondering if she saw something I didn't.

"Great." She reached up to rake her hands through my hair, pulling large chunks of it out of place, so it stood straight up. Then she kissed my cheek. I could feel the lipstick smear.

"Leave it," she dared me.

I opened my mouth to object.

"Leave. It. Control the energy."

I scrunched up my face. "Lipstick makes my skin itch."

It wasn't true. I knew I wouldn't be able to handle the lipstick smear. I think she knew it, but she humored me by wiping it off. "Leave your hair alone."

I swallowed.

She smiled sweetly. "Let's go."

MY MOTHER'S head tipped to the side as she greeted us at the door. "Your hair?"

I shook my head, unable to form words. I'd instinctively tried to straighten it twice since leaving the house. Sianna had smacked my hand both times.

"I am proving a point," Sianna said, offering my mom a little smile.

"That he needs a haircut?" Darla asked.

"That he has no control over his energy," Sianna replied.

"Oh, well, that's true."

"Mom!" My voice cracked.

She glared at me. "Do you really want to talk about this and all the screwed-up things you do to be 'at peace?' Because I have a list."

"You're keeping a list?" I asked, suddenly wanting to avoid the topic.

"It's a family project." She smirked.

"Oh shit."

"Do not touch it!" Sianna barked again, whacking at my hand.

I sighed, lacing my fingers together behind my back. "Sorry."

My mom nodded, then unbuttoned my second shirt button. "There we go. This is great!"

I looked at the button, panicking.

My mom's eyes darted to Sianna. "This isn't going to break his brain, right?"

"His brain is already broken," Sianna muttered, glaring at my mother. "Where is your middle child? I am going to make him squeal like a pig."

Mom looked at me. I shrugged.

"It's going to be a great dinner. I can tell," she said, laughing. "Sam and Addy are always last to arrive. Everyone else is in the big room. I think it's just us this week."

Mom and I watched as Sianna stalked down the hall into the big room. "You okay?" she whispered.

"Please fix the button. Please?"

"No. Don't be a baby. She's right about that. But otherwise, you're okay? She's not going to cut your head off, right?"

"I CAN HEAR YOU," Sianna roared from the other room.

"I forgot about that," Darla breathed, making her way down the hall.

"Hi, Sianna," my dad said cheerfully.

Every female in the room turned to stare at him.

"I would call her 'sweetheart' too, but I don't think she'd like it," Hank said defensively.

Sianna nodded in agreement. "I am not your sweetheart."

She jumped in surprise when we all yelled "boo" in unison.

Sianna glared at me.

"I didn't do it! That's the universal sign of family disapproval! Boo! Dad calls the ladies, and sometimes Hennessy and Micah, 'sweetheart.'"

"I am not your lady. There is no bond. There will be no bond." Sianna bit out. "There will be sex and children and no bonds."

"Babies?" Darla's ears perked up.

"No, nope." Matilda shook her head. "We were Hank's sweethearts before we were involved with the boys. Relationship status has nothing to do with it. It's about being adopted into the herd."

"I'm not part of 'the herd,' either," Sianna said, face scrunched in disapproval.

"Okay, poor word choice. Part of the family. Part of the group. Expected for Sunday dinner," Matilda clarified. "You're a sweetheart. Accept it."

"You allow him to call you 'sweetheart,' Lady Light? You, who may dump the world into darkness and burn civilization to the ground. You'll allow the endearment to debase your power?" Sianna asked, clearly angry.

The room was silent as everyone stared.

My dad shared a look with my mom.

"We might have some work to do with this one," he muttered.

Darla nodded in agreement. "But can we go back to the babies part? Babies?"

"No babies." I groaned.

"Why no babies?" Darla yelled.

"She just got done saying there would be no relationship or love between us. You're really asking this?" I demanded, affronted.

"Yes," Darla said easily.

I scrunched up my face, covering my head with my hands. "I'm not going to sit. I'm just going to go now," I said, heading toward the door.

"Can I ask about the hair first?" Talise blurted, breaking out into giggles. "What happened?"

"And the button," Lucy breathed. "What happened to Luke?"

My family was laughing at me again. As I stood there, I wondered why I attended Sunday dinners.

"What's so funny?" Sam asked, appearing in the middle of the room.

"YOU!" Sianna roared.

I think Sam tried to run, forgetting that he could just disappear. She had him in a headlock, twisting his ear as he screamed.

"What'd I do? What'd I do? I didn't do it!" he yelled, panicked.

"Did you or did you not burn a tie in his brain?" Sianna growled.

"Oh. I did that, but this really hurts!" He tried wiggling away from her.

"Sam," William murmured. "You control time and space, man."

Sam went still again before he disappeared and then reappeared behind me. "Okay, I did that, but there was a reason!" he yelled.

"Is it gone?" Sianna demanded. "Completely gone?"

That gave Sam pause. "Of course."

Sianna turned to Adaline. "You've checked?"

Adaline frowned, shaking her head. "I didn't think to check."

"Ben checked," I muttered. Ben was a Harbor circle elder, highly skilled in mind energies.

"He was a part of the tie, yes?" Sianna asked.

I shared a frown with Adaline. I hadn't considered that the tie could still be there in some form. "They wouldn't leave it there, Sianna."

"Come here, Luke," Addy murmured, already reaching for my head. "What happened to your hair?"

No one laughed this time as we all waited for Adaline's confirmation.

"There is no tie," Adaline confirmed. "His energy is not centered in his mind, though. Not like Sam's or mine. Come here, Noah."

"Why me?" Noah asked, looking around.

201

"Because I asked," Adaline muttered, rolling her eyes as she walked to him. "Noah's energy is centered. Jess?"

Adaline's sister looked at me with her all-sight. "He's always looked like this. The energy's always been concentrated where the tie was. He's megawatt bright now, though. And she's kidding herself about the bindings. They are friends, partners, even. Those bindings will flip. She's not even been here a week."

"They will not," Sianna vowed. "Some part of me must accept a binding of love and mating, and I will not do that."

"I want to yell 'boo' to that, but it doesn't seem like 'boo' is strong enough," Jake complained.

I shook my head. "This has gone wildly off course. No love bindings, no babies, no more twisting Sam's ear. But thanks for that. It was oddly satisfying. Mom, what's for—"

"Hush," Sianna said, hand to my mouth. Then she was gone.

"What's this?" Mom asked.

"She does this," I muttered. "Either she heard something or is done talking to me for a while."

I followed after her as I heard the front door slam open but not closed. "Be right back."

I reached the entryway just in time to hear the lion roar a challenge.

"HOLY SHIT!"

"Gary?" I called.

"HOLY SHIT!" he yelled again.

Oh, shit. How was I going to explain a fucking lion in my parent's house?

"Um, um," I stuttered, slightly panicked. "Here, kitty, kitty?"

"Luke, are you fucking insane?" Gary bellowed, not taking his eyes off the cat. "Are you really fucking yelling 'here, kitty, kitty' to the Huntress?"

"Huh?" My mouth dropped open in shock.

"I brought quiche," Gary called. "Maybe you could vouch for me before she fucking eats me?"

"Sianna, he's a family friend," I said, not bothering to yell. "Adrian's best friend since kindergarten. He was one of Sam's first investors and employees. He has an open dinner invitation."

She growled at him again, showing her teeth.

Assuming she'd lost her temper with all the family antics, I loosed my energy. Gary staggered, as if losing his balance. Sianna roared in anger when the peace hit her, then walked back to me, sitting at my side while I heard my mom move into the entryway. Micah and Will wouldn't be far behind.

"Uh, Gary," I called, voice calm. "Something you want to talk about?"

"Yeah, Luke. Yeah. Damn right there is. You're the fucking Peacekeeper, and I'm a fox affinity. Let's chat."

22

"Holy shit," Gary breathed in the entryway, handing the quiche to Darla with shaking hands. "I should have called. I gotta check my fucking underwear. Do I smell? Did I shit myself?"

Darla's eyes flicked around the entryway, taking in the confusion, even as she smacked Gary upside the head. "I'm going to go put a show on in the game room for the kids. Maybe some adult time in the big room?"

I grabbed Sianna's dress, tossing it out the front door toward her before closing out the winter wind.

"You're a shifter?" I breathed. "Does Adrian know?"

Gary shook his head. "I don't have that much affinity. I don't transform."

"He is weak," Sianna muttered, coming in the front door. "And one of the last I expected to see here to test you."

"I'm not! I wouldn't!" Gary objected, looking uncomfortable. "I've known him since literally the day he was born."

"Hey, is that Gary?" Adrian yelled from the big room, voice coming closer.

"Then why are you here?" Sianna asked, hackles still raised.

Adrian was in the entryway now, glaring at Sianna. "My friend is always welcome here. Tone down the crazy in front of company."

"Adrian," Gary breathed, horrified. "She'll eat your fucking face. Don't."

I made shooing motions with my hands. "Everyone into the big room."

My mom walked through the door right after us, so I closed the big room door behind her, staring at the back of her head. My senses had to be screwed up. My mother did not just ping my Peacekeeper radar. She was normal.

"So, it turns out Gary's a shifter," I said, getting back on point.

"Beast affinity," Sianna and Gary corrected together.

Adrian lifted an eyebrow. "Huh?"

"Oh, fine," Gary muttered, glaring at Adrian. "You're Rage, Will is Fear, Sam is the Walker, Addy is Mistress Life, Noah is Lust, and Luke is the fucking Peacekeeper. Did I miss anyone?"

Will nodded. "More than half the room. Doesn't matter."

"You knew what we were?" Sam asked, frowning.

Gary nodded, his voice snarky. "Yeah, Sam. So, when the guy who waltzes through time asked me to make an investment with him, I jumped at the opportunity. Thanks for making me millions, buddy."

"Why didn't you tell me?" Sam asked, still frowning.

"I didn't think you'd care that I can talk to foxes," Gary said, throwing his hands up.

"That's not what I mean!" Sam yelled. "Why didn't you tell ME what I was?"

"Oh." That gave Gary pause. "I thought you knew. But, looking back, maybe not."

"Decidedly not," Sam said, still irritated. "You could have told me."

"Sorry," Gary muttered, looking around. "Anyway, I figured you all didn't care about my weird animal shit any more than I cared about your weird energy shit."

"Do you really shit like an animal?" Adrian asked, side-tracked.

William burst out laughing.

Gary glared at his best friend. "I'll give you a blood and urine sample later. It'll be a new level of gross in our friendship. I draw the line at shit, though."

"Why are you here?" Sianna demanded again. "It has been reasonably quiet. If you have brought danger—"

"No, Huntress. I've not told anyone. Joe is a cousin," Gary said, watching me again.

"Oh. They're doing okay?" I asked.

"Yeah, Luke. They're great. You fixed their kid's mind yesterday. They're on cloud nine and telling everyone they can find that they met the damn Peacekeeper. I drove all the way the fuck out here to make sure he was talking about some other moron named Luke in some other fucking cornfield. But obviously not. What is happening? Why would you do this? You don't want this!"

Sianna slapped my hand. "LEAVE YOUR HAIR ALONE!"

"It's my hair! I'll do what I want!" I yelled back at her. "This is too fucking much!"

I stomped out of the room to find a hairbrush.

I SAT in my spot at the dining room table, glaring at my mother.

"I don't want to hear it," she growled.

"She's not my girlfriend!" I yelled again.

"There was talk of babies! I heard Jen! I made lasagna," Darla yelled back.

"I am so confused right now," Gary muttered to Adrian.

"Remember Bella, Jake's old girlfriend?" Adrian asked.

Gary snorted, looking at Jake and Matilda, still holding hands at the table. Jake pretended not to notice the snort.

"She refused to eat Darla's lasagna. After they broke up, we made a family pact that if a girlfriend doesn't eat the lasagna, we get to vote on whether she's allowed back to Sunday dinner," Adrian summarized.

"Okay, so it's normal family bullshit," Gary said, blowing off the antics. He paused again when everyone at the table leaned away from him. "What's this?"

"We can't swear at the table," Jake muttered.

"Oh." Gary's eyes went big. "How do you function?"

"I try to not talk," Jake admitted.

"Moving on," Will prodded. "Why doesn't he want this Peacekeeper thing?"

Gary shifted uncomfortably. "There is a lot of politics involved—"

"He is Peacekeeper," Sianna disagreed. "There is no politics. He is above all others."

"Well, okay. More accurately, his presence shifts the politics, and there is a lot of it. A lot of silly customs and rules to the different... types... of what we are," Gary said, eyeing the kids warily. "There are a lot of people that will try to manipulate you."

"Sounds a lot like being wealthy," Sam muttered. "And don't worry about the kids. They ask questions when they want to know."

"Do you answer the questions?" Gary grinned at Sam.

Sam's little smile appeared. "I do."

"I bet that's just so helpful. *You* don't even know what you're talking about half the time," Gary mocked.

"I'm second favorite uncle, behind Ethan," Sam acknowledged. "The Peacekeeper thing is similar to how things change with money?"

"It is," Gary agreed. "But worse. 'Keeping the peace'—do you know what that is?"

"My peace energy?" I asked.

"There is more to it," Sianna interjected. "It will be fine. Uncomfortable at first, but fine."

Gary fidgeted again. "I don't want her to kill me. Just so we're clear on this. And she will. She is a lethal, unforgiving enforcer among us. You brought a death-bringer to Sunday dinner."

Micah laughed with genuine amusement. "She is one of many deadly things at this table. I still maintain Darla is more dangerous than the rest of us."

"Anyway," Gary continued, ignoring Micah. "If you could help me avoid a future where she slaughters me and then leaves me to decay in an out-of-the-way place, I'd appreciate it. Luke, she's skating over some big implications to the Peacekeeper thing."

I raised my eyebrows. "The harem thing? No thanks. Not for me."

Gary shook his head. "It's an exchange of energy, Luke. You will give peace, and every shifter you touch will return the favor by offering a bit of their own special energy. It's happening now. You knew what I was outside, even before I told you. You didn't know before tonight, right?"

I continued staring, trying to process what he meant.

"I told you yesterday," Sianna muttered, "there is no denying it now. You awoke that part of your brain. You are Peacekeeper. You will adjust to the sharing of energy."

"I guess I don't understand," I said. "It didn't irk me at all when I realized what you were. Why is this sharing of energy thing bad? Sounds like a circle."

"Luke, I'm one guy. This thing on Wednesday, this event they're having, there will be hundreds of affinities. Hundreds of bits of energy are going to besiege your mind. That's the test of the Peacekeeper."

"He's not going," Tali interjected. "We've agreed he's not doing this."

Gary looked between us, unsure what to say.

Somehow, Sianna glared at the whole table at once. "It will be fine. I will not let anyone hurt him. I've talked to Edgar and my father both. They intend nothing more than to present you as Peacekeeper and then honor you if the crowd accepts."

"If the crowd accepts?" William asked, eyebrows raised.

"If the energy doesn't cycle as it should, the crowd will reject him. Charlie and Candy will face the punishment for their crimes, and Luke will answer for his deception. However, there *is* no deception. There is no denying what he is. This is a pointless conversation. Even if he wanted to walk away, I do not think he could do so now."

"We decided you're not going," Tali said again, sharing a look with Adaline.

"Charlie and Candy?" Gary asked. "Hapner?"

Sadness flashed through Sianna as she nodded at Gary. "They were recorded transforming in front of a crowd."

Gary sat back, subdued and silent.

"You're not going," Tali said again, this time nothing but stubbornness in her tone. "I won't let you go. Adaline and I won't let you go. No."

23

By some sort of unspoken agreement, the family moved past the woo-woo of my shifter issues and onto plain old silly after Gary finished his doom and gloom warnings. I left shortly after Adrian and Gary started teaching the kids how to hang spoons from their noses.

There would be a lot of beer and laughter throughout the night. While Gary didn't make it to the cornfields often, he would undoubtedly make the most of the visit by staying overnight with someone and skipping work on Monday morning.

He and I weren't close. I didn't feel the need to stay around for the party.

Sianna and I walked back toward my house side by side, not speaking. It was still snowing. We'd gotten at least four inches of fresh powder through the day and there had to be close to a foot of snow on the ground.

"Luke?"

"Hm?" I asked, startled by the break in our silence. I had been close to a meditative state, actually listening to the snow gather and play in the wind.

"You did well tonight. You fixed your hair but forgot all about the button your mother undid."

I paused in our walk. I had forgotten.

"The tie is gone," she said, going back to our earlier conversation with Sam and Adaline. "You do not need to keep the energy confined as you do."

I shook my head, walking again. "I don't know how to move it. I'm not even convinced I should. It requires so much for me to maintain the internal triggers now. I'm not sure the energy needs more space to influence."

"I do not know," she admitted. "But it seems like it would be easier to manage with your whole mind, rather than a small piece of it. There is nothing in the stories about my grandfather requiring tidiness. Edgar says he was not a particularly clean person. The hair truly bothered you."

It wasn't a question, but I answered anyway. "Yes, I couldn't think straight. You didn't tell me about the sharing of energy."

She nodded. "There is nothing to do to prepare for it. I will help funnel it, but there is no doubt what you are, Peacekeeper."

"Fuck," I whispered, annoyed.

"It bothers you?" she asked, surprised.

"Yeah, it does. I thought we were past the 'Peacekeeper' shit. Why do you keep going back to it? I'm Luke!"

She laughed, stopping in our stroll to bend at the waist and laugh at me.

"I'm not joking!" I complained.

She kept laughing.

I grabbed a handful of snow and threw it at her. Bent as she was, a chunk of it fell down the back of her dress.

"Luke. My name is Luke!" I yelled, as she hopped around, shaking the snow away.

Her eyes went to slits. It wasn't until then I considered the implications of starting a snow fight with someone much faster and stronger than me.

I was pummeled with snow and laying on my back in fresh powder, having been tossed five feet through the air before I could even apologize.

I shrugged to myself, laughing at my stupidity, as I started moving my arms and legs.

"What are you doing?" Sianna asked, starting to laugh again.

"Making a snow angel. I'm in the middle of fresh powder with no footsteps around me. It'll confuse Matthew and entertain everyone else."

She grinned. "I understand where your concept of family comes from. You think of them all the time."

"Yup," I said, staring at the cloudy sky overhead.

A bird flew over me before I heard Sianna drop to the ground a few feet away.

"Are you making a naked snow angel?" I asked, laughing.

"Yup," she said, almost giggling.

"Make sure there's a clear ass print," I coached, laughing harder.

She threw snow in my general direction, laughing with me.

I climbed to my feet, admiring my work before glancing at Sianna. I'd seen her naked form several times now. I'd just intended to glance. But I was caught off guard by her laughter, the smile on her face that reached her eyes, and the joy radiating from her.

Her grin turned a bit. "I have never done this before."

"Naked snow angels? I should hope not." I pretended to shiver.

She transformed back to the bird, back in her clothes in a flash. "Played in the snow."

That gave me pause, but just for a minute. Then I scooped a double handful of snow and threw it at her face. "Get the full experience!" I yelled, running in the other direction, away from our angels.

She laughed, chasing me through the snow. She was faster and stronger, but I had more practice. It worked, right up until she transformed into a polar bear, making me run for the front door.

We fell in the front door together, having fought with the new biometric locks for a moment, both laughing hysterically as chunks of snow fell from us and melted.

In the entryway, she pulled a bit of ice from her hair and stuffed it down the back of my shirt and coat.

"Gah!" I yelled, wiggling out of my coat and trying to shake it free while still laughing.

My senses pinged as I looked at the wet, muddy floor.

"Do not do it," Sianna muttered. "Leave it. The floor can be wet."

"Someone might slip—" I started, already reaching for the mop in the closet.

Her lips were on mine, urgent and insistent, distracting, before I could finish the thought.

I froze as my energy surged, pouring through both of us. It felt like a bubble of sinus pressure releasing, the headache I hadn't recognized was dissipating.

I nudged her, stepping back.

"Okay," she said. Nothing else. Just an acknowledgment of my rejection and an indication that we were still okay.

Something in me gave way as I looked at her, messy blonde hair spilling down her naked back, eyes alight with flecks of turquoise. I was looking at Sianna as she truly was. She stood before me in her own form, and she wasn't smiling or laughing anymore. My world was a bit darker for the absence.

Fingers lacing through her hair, I tipped her face up and dropped my mouth to hers.

I DON'T KNOW how long we stood there, tasting and exploring each other's mouths, but there was no rush, no escalation.

"Okay?" I asked after a while, my forehead resting on hers, my eyes closed. I knew Sianna was uneasy, not at peace, but I wasn't sure what that meant.

"Look at me," she demanded.

I stepped back, opening my eyes.

She exhaled. I felt relief wash through her.

"There is power, but you are still you," she murmured, stepping back into my arms.

"Oh," I flushed red. "Sianna, I'm so sorry—"

"Hush," she interrupted, her lips brushing against mine. "I told you. I did not mind the power, Peacekeeper. I disliked that you did not remember."

My lips covered hers again, enjoying the feel of her at leisure as her own internal peace rolled against my energy. I sighed in contentment, pulling her closer as my fingers played with the ends of her long hair.

I was a bit lightheaded, a sense of euphoria rolling through me.

She pulled away from me again, a slight smile playing at the corners of her mouth. Her words came as a whisper so as not to jar me. "This is peace, Luke. It is not the absence of other feelings. It is the calm acceptance of life." She pulled another cycle of energy through us. "This is your energy. It is not meant to be caged."

Eyes at half-mast, my mouth closed over hers as my hands ran up her back, from hips to shoulders. Her eyes closed as she leaned back into my hands, giving me access to her lovely neck.

The next thing I clearly remember, I was lying in bed, Sianna astride me, her right hand holding my chin, forcing my eyes to hers.

I blinked, looking around.

"There you are," she whispered, letting go of my face. "I can tell now. I know now."

"I'm so—"

Her hand covered my mouth gently. "No. It is not your fault there is no balance. But I will not do this without *you*."

I kissed her hand, grateful for so many things. But, at that moment, it was her patience that stole my breath.

"Do you want this?" she asked.

Pushing myself up on an elbow, I pulled her mouth to mine, kissing her again as I rolled us.

"Stay with me," she murmured. "I will stop you if I must."

Kissing down her jaw, I bit her earlobe. She shivered with pleasure as my tongue traced her ear.

She lifted her body, threading her legs with mine and inviting more.

I had no idea what time it was, but I guessed we'd been at

this a while. I'd missed some of the fun. I gave a quiet chuckle, mouth and tongue drifting down her body, kissing and nibbling as my free hand snaked between us.

"Luke." Sianna sighed, as if things were getting boring.

I lifted my head from her breast, eyebrows raised as I pushed a wave of power into her. She moaned, panting.

I was not prepared for that energy to pour back into me. I shouted in surprise, my entire body tensing with pleasure.

We rolled again. My distraction cost control.

As her lips met mine, Sianna slowly pressed her body down, joining us bit by bit.

Tipping her head back, she sighed again, otherwise still around me.

She quirked an eyebrow, smiling. "Want to try that again?"

I accepted that challenge, moving myself inside her, letting my power pulse in matching waves as my hands held her hips, fingers digging into the flesh of her ass as we moved together toward oblivion.

An eternity later, we lay sprawled across each other, somewhere between asleep and awake.

"Daylight soon," she murmured in my ear.

"Not running." I groaned.

"It will make you stronger. You will run."

"I will," I agreed, shifting to snuggle my head on her chest, enjoying the music of her heartbeat and breathing. "But not today."

She pulled my hair. "Lazy Luke."

My lips tipped up. "Mmm. Like that."

She smiled. "Lazy, Lavish, Loving Luke."

"You're much better at this than the rest of my family," I muttered, dozing off to sleep again.

2 4

I woke up alone close to noon. My phone was buzzing… somewhere.

My pants were on the stairs.

Huh. Didn't bother me at all, I thought. *That's not where pants go, and I slept right through it.*

I shrugged, calling for Sianna as I dug out my phone.

SAM: Don't come to the circle tonight. You'll freak everyone out.

My mouth dropped open. I wasn't welcome in Harbor anymore?

SAM: Oh, stop it. I can feel your angst all the way across the street. Just not this week. Stay home until the Peacekeeper thing is worked out.

He was probably right.

I typed a quick response, agreeing with him, then went in search of a shower and clean clothes.

When I headed back down the stairs, fresh and clean, I actually laughed at the dried mud smeared all over the entryway. I wasn't sure what had happened as we'd gone upstairs last night, but it looked like it was fun.

My energy wasn't pinging like mad. There were clothes on the floor and the entryway was a mess, but I didn't *need* to clean it. I could leave it as it was if I wanted to. I didn't want to leave a mess, but I could.

"Sianna?" I said again, more loudly. There was no response. I frowned.

After cleaning up the mess, I warmed up leftover stew for lunch and then sat at my piano, debating. I wanted to talk to Matthew, but I also wanted to make sure Sianna was okay. I couldn't feel her in my range.

The music that came out of the piano felt like a question. *Where are you? Are you upset?* I played for almost an hour, calling for her twice more. There was no response.

I walked around the outside of the house, around the ward line, trying to sense her. There was nothing. I didn't even have a phone number to call her. I debated walking through the cornfields to look for her but knew it was a bad idea to do that alone.

The sidewalks were clear as I made my way to Sam and Adaline's house. Jake and Matty must have done their snow trick. I grinned at the snow angel with the perfect form of an ass crack, wondering how she'd done that.

Adaline opened the front door as I approached.

"Can you feel her?" I asked in greeting.

She frowned, confused.

"She's not answering me. I'm not sure if she's seriously pissed or if something is wrong," I admitted.

Adaline's eyes went vacant for a minute. "She is well— talking with an old man about how to help you understand the energy that Gary spoke of."

"Oh. She's not in trouble, right?" I asked, somehow hurt that she'd left without telling me.

"No," Adaline said, narrowing her eyes at me. "She's not in trouble, nor is she upset with you. Why would she be upset with you? Come in."

I shook my head. "If she's okay, I want to talk with Matthew. Thank you for checking." I kissed the top of Adaline's head.

Adaline grabbed my arm. "There is sex between you now. I see it in your colors. But still no binding? You care for her. I know it. Please, Luke. Please let the binding hold."

"Addy." I sighed. "I think it's like healing from the circle. I don't think people can form those bindings with me. I don't think I can form those bindings with others."

"Sam saw the bindings!" she insisted, actually stomping her foot. "Stop saying it can't be done. It can. Please!"

I hugged her, pushing peace at her. I knew it worked too, because her body relaxed in my arms. "I don't know why the binding won't hold, Addy, but it's going to be okay. She would not behead me. And, if she wants my heart, it's hers for the taking, okay? Sex, babies, family, love... whatever. I'll take what I can get."

She shook her head. "It's not like Candy."

"It's not like Candy," I agreed, not thinking too hard about that truth as I turned to walk away.

"Luke?" she called again.

I turned.

"Your front door is open. You didn't close your door."

For a minute, I thought she was talking about the zipper on my jeans. I looked down.

"Not your barn door, jackass," Sam yelled from inside the house. "Your front door! I can see it across the street!"

I walked away from the sound of Adaline's giggles. I knew they were laughing at me, but still, Mistress Life's laughter brought cheer. I was grinning like a fool as I closed my front door and made my way to Matthew's house.

I WALKED into Matthew's house without knocking. "Hello?" I yelled.

"Hi!" Miranda called. They were in the back of the house, tinkering with Miranda's plants.

Matthew rolled his eyes as I walked into the greenhouse room. "I'll wash my hands and meet you in the living room."

"Nah, I'm okay," I said with a shrug.

Matthew stared. "You're okay?"

Usually, the greenhouse triggered my senses. I could feel the plants that needed more water or less water and the rocks that were just a bit uneven in the bottom of the pots, the smears of mud on the worktable, even the bugs that my brain insisted did not belong inside a house.

"I'm fine," I said, shrugging again. "How are you both?"

"Is this like the hair? Are you testing yourself?" Miranda asked. She smeared a line of mud on my cheek.

I grimaced at her. "Gross."

"You don't like it, but you're not freaking out," she noticed.

221

"The energy's not pinging?"

"Nope."

"Hurrah for sex!" Matthew yelled, throwing his arms up in a cheer.

I glowered at him.

Miranda's face scrunched up. "We'd know there was sex even if you weren't all chill."

"Why?" I asked, drawing out the word.

"You pulsed crazy energy last night. For hours and hours. There's a betting pool going for whether you're *that* level of stud or if you just had crazy wet dreams again." Matthew grinned, enjoying my embarrassment.

"Pay up, woman!" he yelled to Miranda.

I flushed a deeper red as Miranda's cheeks turned pink.

"It was like four o'clock in the morning, Luke!" she objected, so embarrassed her ears were red. "HOURS! A girl gets tired!"

Matthew had his phone in his hand.

"Ugh. Please don't…" I stopped talking when my phone buzzed with a text. I knew it was the group thread. "I'm not even going to look."

"Stud!" Matthew laughed. "For the first time, I'm embracing this family subdivision lifestyle. I was very chill last night."

"It pulsed like Sam's energy?" I asked.

"Yep. Except Sam's energy is angry. Yours was very chill. And, for whatever reason, it was clear that sex was involved. So, if you were hoping that no one knew you were getting freaky with Sianna, that ship has sailed. Though I think the ass-print snow angel in your front yard was also a dead giveaway."

"Perfect ass cheeks, right? How'd she do that?" I laughed.

"I took a picture last night, just in case it melted this morning." Matthew grinned with me. "How do you feel?"

"Good. Calm. The energy's still there. I doused Addy a few minutes ago. But I also forgot to close my front door. And it doesn't bother me to be back here."

"You think you've been overloaded this whole time?" Matthew asked, eyebrows furrowed.

"I don't know," I admitted.

"This didn't happen with Candy," Miranda said, wiping the dirt smear from my cheek. "It wasn't bothering you, but it was making me crazy," she admitted sheepishly.

"Not like Candy," I agreed. "Not at all. Not to go into detail, but the energy flowed differently. It wasn't anything like other sex."

"There's no binding," Matthew murmured, "but I can feel the emotions. Did you acknowledge the emotions? There has to be some level of acceptance."

I blinked, not sure what he was talking about.

"You have to know and acknowledge you love her for there to be a binding, Luke," Matthew explained. "It has almost nothing to do with the physical."

"I know. I know that," I said defensively. "I care about her. Don't get me wrong. But she's made it clear that she will not bind to me. It'd mean giving up her place with the beast affinities and essentially becoming a broodmare. She won't do it."

"Okay," Matthew said slowly, "but that doesn't mean *you* can't bind to *her*. She won't bind to you. Fine. Sam didn't say he needed both bindings. He said he needs a binding. One. Singular. Make the binding."

"The emotions are there, Matthew. I really don't think I can form that binding. She doesn't want it anyway."

He sighed at me before making chicken noises.

"I'm not being difficult. It won't work. My shit doesn't work like that."

"I think your shit probably works like that if you allow it to, Luke. Have you tried pulling energy from the circle now that you're not overloaded?"

As I shook my head, Miranda slashed my hand with pruning shears. "What the fuck?" I asked.

"Try it," she suggested. "Can you do it now?"

I longed for the days when my family didn't randomly injure me.

Finding my bindings to the family circle, I tried to access the healing energy.

"No dice," Matthew muttered, frowning. "Can you pull from me without the chaos?"

"No!" Miranda objected. "You're not trying it in here. There are living things in here! Go try it somewhere else!"

"Hello?" Sianna called from the front of the house. "Are you bleeding?"

"Hi," I called. "I'm fine."

Sianna was in the greenhouse before I finished talking. She rolled her eyes at Miranda before touching my hand, healing the wound. "Healing is really not part of the Peacekeeper power. You just keep hurting him like this."

"Hi," I said again, shifting uneasily. "Everything okay?"

"Yes," she smiled. "Do you have another car? We need a car for tonight."

"We have the circle tonight," Miranda interjected.

"No," Sianna and I said at the same time, eyeing each other.

"Sam says I can't go back to the circle until after the Peacekeeper thing is done," I explained.

"We have other plans tonight, and maybe tomorrow night," Sianna said, smiling. "You will like this."

25

"*W*here are we going?" I asked for what felt like the eighty-fifth time.

Sianna grinned. "Just get in the car."

We paused awkwardly outside the driver's side door of Matthew's SUV.

"What is wrong?" she asked.

"I'll drive," I said, feeling strange.

"I will drive. I know where we are going."

"I... prefer to drive."

"Well, you are not driving this time," she said, frowning at me. "You are already overloaded again, aren't you?"

"No?"

"I can feel it, Luke," she disagreed.

"Can I drive?" I blurted. "I usually drive. I like to drive. You can tell me where to go."

Anger flashed through her. "No. You will not let the energy control you like this."

"Okay. Can we have sex before we go? Just... real quick?"

She smirked, biting back a smile.

"I'm kinda serious," I admitted.

"I know. That just makes it funnier. Get in the car."

"How long is this car ride?"

"Get. In. The. Car." She slammed the driver's side door closed as she started the engine.

"Oh. No." My stomach rolled as I got in the passenger side.

Sianna glared at me. "Don't you dare let the energy make you sick."

"I might not have a choice?" I suggested.

"Poor Puking Peace," she grated out, angrily. "Stop it. Center your energy properly and get over it."

"Can I please drive? Please?"

I knew it was useless.

She backed out of the driveway and flipped a wave to the security guard as we left the compound.

"Where are we going? Will you at least distract me with that?" I asked, swallowing the nasty salivating mouth feeling that came before puking. I didn't want to puke.

"We are going to see friends, including Edgar. They have strong affinities. Edgar and I agreed it would be good for you to know the feeling of being around many of us at once. There will only be twenty or so people, but it is a start. I do not know if it will help you with the overloaded feeling."

"Oh." This was not the fun date I was hoping for. "Want to go ice skating instead?"

She wasn't amused.

"Also, there will be some children. They are older than Owen. It does not seem like they can wait for the politics, so their families will bring them. Edgar says it will work out, but I still have my doubts."

"About whether I can help them?" I asked, subdued.

"No, about whether helping them now is wise. Many people will want your time and attention when you are honored. We choose favorites by doing this now."

"Okay," I snapped angrily. "How about this: the kiddies that are suffering get my time and attention first. The power-hungry adults can wait in line."

She sighed. "I understand your point. I honor you for it and appreciate the person you are. Truly. But that is not how our world works, Luke. You will see. As Peacekeeper, you will see. And I will mourn the loss of your principles over time."

"Sianna, this part of me is not going to change. Could you imagine Darla or Hank allowing me to be otherwise? No. Even if I lost all sense, my family would keep me in line."

"Time will tell," she muttered, her words laced with sadness.

"These are the same fucked up social customs that would treat you and Candy as broodmares. No. If I am above it all, I will rise above it and force it to change."

She pressed her lips together, eyes shining in the dashboard lights. She didn't look at me.

"It's a church," I muttered. We were parked at the very back of the half-full lot.

Sianna nodded. "Edgar's church. Most of those here tonight are of his line. We are trying to help you, Peacekeeper. You must remember that. If you tell my father of this, he will see these people punished."

"Why?" I asked, startled. And decidedly ignoring the fact that she was not using my name. Again.

"I told you. My father does not believe you are Peacekeeper. He will say this gathering helped you prepare a fiction for Wednesday as if your ability to share peace with the crowd could be faked. It cannot. There is no denying what you are. And you need us as much as we need you based on how over-loaded you are again. But he will still argue it."

"Why doesn't he want a Peacekeeper? I don't have any intention of interfering with his leadership. I want Charlie and Candy out of trouble. I want to help the kids...."

And I want you, I thought. I recognized the words in my brain, but I didn't say them aloud, knowing they would make her unhappy.

"I'm not going to interfere with anything," I said instead.

"Are you not?" she asked, eyebrows raised. "Not ten minutes ago, you shamed our society structure, suggesting it would change to your liking."

I sighed. I had done that, and I'd meant those words. If I could lift the beast affinities out of ancient practices, I would. But I had no intention of removing Nate from leadership. I didn't want to be in charge of these people.

"Let's go," she muttered, getting out of the car. "Tell me when you can feel them."

Five steps from the car, I paused. "I can feel them."

She blinked. "Could you feel them while we were in the car?"

"I don't know. I wasn't trying."

"Let's walk back. Tell me when you can no longer feel them."

We were outside the parking lot, across the busy four-lane street, behind the business on the other side of the road with nowhere else to go unless we climbed the fence at our backs. I could still feel the affinities in the church.

"And there are more in the houses behind us," I said. "Some sort of canine affinity there. A water creature of some sort over there," I pointed.

She nodded, no longer surprised. Something in her bearing shifted, becoming more formal. "Peacekeeper. Untrained Peace-keeper. Let's go back toward the church. They are waiting for us."

"PEACEKEEPER," Edgar greeted me in the vestibule, shaking my hand and taking the peace I offered. His eyes flicked to Sianna.

She shook her head. "He is already overloaded again. This will be difficult."

Edgar sighed. "There are more here than anticipated. More children too. They've been tranquilized for the time being. They are dangerous otherwise. Peacekeeper, can you feel the others in the church?"

I nodded.

"From all the way across the street. Once he picked up the sense, we could not find the edge of it," Sianna summarized.

"You hold the energy back now." Edgar wasn't asking a question, but I nodded in agreement anyway.

"You'll need to stop doing that eventually, but for now, it's for the best. When I shook your hand, I took some of the energy you offered and gave you some of my own. Did you feel it?"

"No," I said, surprised. "I felt you take a bit of peace, but I didn't feel anything come back to me."

My eyes dropped to Sianna, only then realizing she was the short brunette that hung out with Nate. "I felt you share energy back to me last night," I said.

Her face crinkled as she smiled. "That was different."

"Am I supposed to comment every time you change your hair? This is very confusing for me. I feel like I should notice and compliment appropriately, but I swear you looked different when we left the house."

Edgar laughed, amused.

"I was me when we left," Sianna admitted, grinning. "Most of these people know me in this form. It is less confusing for them if I look like this."

Edgar paused, his smile softening at her words. Hope drifted through his emotional profile, lifting his calm sense of self to something more unsettled. It took me a minute to realize that he understood the significance of Sianna being herself around me.

He patted my shoulder. "This will be different. Maybe uncomfortable. Worse for your overloaded energy, I think. But it will be fine. I swear it."

"What are we talking about?" I asked.

"It is as the fox said," Sianna replied. "As your energy reaches each person, some portion of their energy will come back to you. You will share peace. You can keep the peace they share with you. I know it doesn't make sense. You will under-stand in a minute."

"Let's go in," Edgar said. "Peacekeeper, you may let your

energy go."

"Not all the way," Sianna interjected quickly. "Don't let go completely. Just... a little bit."

Edgar frowned at her. She frowned back.

"The energy is not balanced," she explained. "Sometimes it takes over."

That gave Edgar pause.

"I'll pull it forward," I said. "It's what I did the night we met."

Edgar nodded, pulling open the main door for me.

THE NEXT THING I KNEW, I was lying on the floor of a church. "What happened?"

"Peacekeeper." Sianna said the word as a sigh. "Sit up."

"What happened?" I asked again.

"You shared a lot of peace quickly and got a lot of energy back," Sianna summarized. "I punched you, knocking you out cold when you started to glow. Do not pull it forward like that again. It is too much."

I looked around. There had to be fifty people in the church, all silent and staring.

"They're fine," Edgar murmured with a smile. "Perhaps concerned that our Huntress would lay hands on our Peacekeeper, but fine."

"Things get freaky when he glows!" Sianna yelled to the crowd. "Calm down. He is fine."

"I'm fine," I confirmed. "I just wish that hadn't happened."

"Let's try again," Edgar suggested.

WHEN I CAME TO AGAIN, Sianna was staring down at me.

"We should have had sex. I told you," I muttered, rubbing my face.

Edgar's laughter rolled through the church as other little sounds of humor were hidden behind hands.

"Again," Sianna growled, unamused. "Hang on to me. Do not give over to the energy, or I will kick you next time."

It was easier while holding her hand. "Okay. I can sense them all."

"Pull it forward a little bit," Sianna muttered.

I did as I was told, jumping a bit as those closest to us gasped. "It's fine."

"More," Sianna prodded.

In the end, I pushed my peace through the entire crowd without losing control of the power.

"Can you feel their energy?" Edgar asked.

I shrugged. "I feel their emotions, their affinities. Like that?"

"I don't know," he admitted. "My father always talked about it differently."

"I feel their energy," Sianna said. "It is there. He just does not know what it is. It is like sensing the church from the parking lot. Once he recognizes it, he will understand. But this works. He is fine."

"Let go of her hand," Edgar suggested.

I hesitated. Sianna didn't move either.

"It's better to know now, dear one," Edgar said, meeting her eyes.

She dropped my hand.

I made it about four minutes before vomiting. Happily, I was in a bathroom, not puking on strangers and making an ass of myself.

"We'll work on the overload," Sianna muttered to Edgar. "Where are the children?"

WE HEADED down a hallway into a secondary room that looked like a classroom. Eight children between the ages of five and ten were strapped into wheelchairs, restrained and mostly unconscious.

My stomach rolled in revulsion.

A pair of adults sat in the center of the room, chatting quietly.

"Why are they like this?" I demanded, more loudly than I'd intended. The two adults started guiltily, turning to stare before dropping their eyes in deference.

Sianna squeezed my fingers. "They are a danger to themselves and others. We warned you of this."

"They're trapped like this—mentally trapped in nightmares. Can't you feel it?"

She shook her head, eyes circling the room. "They appear to be resting, not quite fully asleep."

"They're terrified."

I walked to the eldest child, who radiated the most energy. She had the affinities of two different predator animals, though I couldn't tell which ones. Like Owen, her life energy was a tangled mess. Her mind was also disturbed. She couldn't identify reality anymore.

I unstrapped her arm, taking her hand gently. The healthy bindings were sluggish to respond to my touch and energy.

"They can't be like this. It's harder like this. Let them wake up."

Without a word, the pair of adults started circling among the children, injecting something into the intravenous ports I hadn't noticed. These kids were given so much medication, they had ports.

My stomach rolled again. I wondered if I was going to be sick.

"Is it the overload?" Sianna asked. "Harder to do this with the overload?"

I hadn't noticed that she kept in contact with me, even after I dropped her hand to approach the first child. She stood behind me, out of the way, her hand touching the bare skin of my neck.

"Thank you," I murmured, for her ears only. "I forgot."

She nodded, understanding. "I did not. Is your energy level making this harder? We can make the others leave the church. Most of the people here are related to the children and eager for some sort of news."

I shook my head. "I think it's the meds. With both Edgar and Owen, the healthy bindings moved out of my way, making space for me to work on the source of discord. Her bindings are sluggish. They still move, but I have to be more careful."

Rather than pulling at the knotted life energy, I started with the child's mind. After I encouraged acceptance of the past and assured her the nightmares weren't reality, the girl's eyes flickered and then focused on me.

"Hi," I said, smiling as I let the peaceful energy roam free. I didn't push her toward sleep, just calm.

She didn't speak. I wasn't sure she could use words with the way her energy was knotted. But she watched me.

I sat down on the floor in front of her, still holding her hand. It took me a minute to realize she was hanging on to me too.

I closed my eyes, focusing. I could hear her heartbeat and her breathing. I could feel the waves of my peace wash against her mind, keeping her calm.

Humming under my breath, I kept time with the girl's natural life rhythm as I began pulling her energy free of the knot. Slowly, careful not to touch the other bindings, my will untangled the mess of her power.

In the distance, I heard Sianna say something. I didn't respond. When the other children started pinging my senses, I pushed my peace out, pulling them all into my calm without losing my focus.

I felt the girl's natural energy and sense of self snap forward when it was done. If I hadn't been holding the beat steady, I might have lost her mind, then. It reeled away in shock and confusion, but I had the child snared in a web of calm meant just for her. As her mind spun, my power held her steady, giving her time to find equilibrium.

I knew it was done and the girl was safe when she dropped into a regular, restful sleep.

"Let her sleep," I murmured quietly. "It's done. She needs rest."

I crawled to the next child. I didn't want to risk dropping my web of calm focus by standing.

26

Sianna was stiff and silent as we made our way back to the car. She was not at peace, not even close.

"The children are harder to work with the longer they've been stuck," I said, breaking the silence.

She nodded. "You helped them all, though." She didn't sound happy about this.

"I'd like Adaline to visit the second boy. She might be able to help with the cognitive issues that were beyond me."

"He was born like that. He never had human instincts. There are others like him, more animal than human. I did not expect you to help him."

There was something she wasn't saying. I could feel it. Much like how I dealt with Sam, I gave Sianna time to find the words she wanted.

It took a solid ten minutes. We were on the expressway to home before she spoke again.

"The boy's parents are half-siblings. Some families believe

their affinities will be stronger if the parents share the same powers."

I wasn't incredibly surprised by this. The child's brain, his reasoning, was limited. His issues didn't seem to be a result of the energy, but a fundamental flaw with his physical makeup.

Still, I waited. I could feel the unease and horror creeping around in Sianna's brain.

"You are just going to sit in silence?" she snapped.

"I'm waiting for you to tell me whatever you have to tell me," I said, reaching for her hand. I offered peace. She didn't take it.

Exhaling, she pulled her hand away.

I frowned.

"I cannot touch you and talk about this. Tender affection and this knowledge do not fit," she explained, an apology somewhere in the words.

I wrapped the peace energy around myself, trying to keep it from her, as I prepared for whatever she was going to say.

"I have had many siblings."

I nodded. I knew that.

"Some of them came from family trees without enough branches."

I knew she was serious, but a laugh bubbled up at her explanation. I would have felt bad, except her lips twitched into a smile too. She used the words intentionally to break up the weighty topic.

"I have never dared to ask outright, but I have wondered if Nathaniel is truly my father."

That threw me. "Edgar?"

She made a so-so gesture. "I would like to believe it, but it would mean my mother had relations with him while he was part beast. I am not sure that would have been possible. And I doubt it now. The Walker called me the last of Nathaniel's sane begotten."

"You haven't asked? Maybe a drunken mother-daughter weekend of shopping. 'Hey, Mom, did you get freaky with Uncle Edgar when he looked like Bigfoot?' Something like that?"

"Nathaniel killed my mother shortly after my birth. They had a disagreement. She would not submit to his demands. I have never asked what the disagreement was about, but I have my suspicions."

"Whoa!" I wasn't expecting that. "His control is absolute? He can just kill someone like that?"

She chewed on her lip. "His power is absolute because he is the head of his family, not just because he is Overlord. A man may kill his mate as well as his daughters. Doing so causes no disruption to our norms, though he must still deal with the authorities."

"Mate and daughters. Not sons?" My words were quiet, but there was rage buried within me.

"There are questions about sons. If the child is young, fewer questions, but our sons are more carefully monitored."

She sighed, breathing deeply again. "This was not the point of our conversation, but you must understand. My father's command of my life is absolute. I am unmated with no children. He may take my life. I believe my position as Huntress and enforcer protects me somewhat, as does my power. I told you. I have no equal. If I had different anatomy, I would already be Overlord. But if he suspects that I have interfered with you and your ability to stand as Peacekeeper, he will kill me."

"He'll try."

She pressed her lips together. "I do not believe I would fight him. It would be pointless. My brothers would finish me if my father could not. This brings me back to the point.

"Two of my brothers are like that boy. They have limited reasoning skills. They are more animal than human and have been so for longer than I have been alive. They live because they are the Beast Overlord's sons."

She hesitated before continuing. "I feel strongly about this, but I have no evidence to back it up. Please, believe me, though."

"Okay," I murmured, touching her hand briefly, just to reassure her I was there. She was distraught, close to tears, expecting to argue.

"You pulled the older children into your peace. You pulled them in completely and held them in your power."

"I did."

"Do not do that if you are asked to help my brothers. Do not do that with adults and near adults. I worry they can attack your mind. I tried to stop you with the first girl. I felt you doing it and tried to stop you. You did not listen."

"I didn't hear you," I admitted. "I was focused."

"You were in a trance of sorts. It was like a meditative trance, like when you play music with your eyes closed. Do not do that so freely."

"Okay." I nodded.

"I don't know that they could hurt you, but I don't want to find out. I feel strongly about this," she said again.

"I said okay. I agree. I won't do it with adults and certainly not your brothers."

She sighed in relief. "Thank you."

I squeezed her fingers again as she turned onto the road that led to the compound. "Did you really think I would argue with you?"

"I do not know," she admitted. "It is hard to remember how you are, sometimes. As I said, I have spent most of my time with my father. He does not always accept my counsel, and I cannot argue the point if I am not given a vote."

"Do you have sisters?" I asked, already dreading the answer.

She nodded. "Three surviving sisters. They are similar to the cat in affinity and have each made many children. There are more than four dozen children among them."

She fell silent again as she pulled into Matthew's garage. "Until recently, I feared a sibling would produce a child of adequate power, and I would end up paired with a nephew."

She shuddered, seeming to gag.

I sighed, truly understanding then. "There will be sex and children between us."

She nodded.

"A binding would free you of your father, Sianna."

She met my eyes. "He would see a binding as a theft of a strong asset. He does not believe what you are, Peacekeeper."

I slammed the car door in frustration.

"YOU ARE ANGRY," Sianna muttered as we walked into my house.

"I'm not. Not really."

"Peacekeeper—"

"Sianna!" I yelled, temper flaring. "I'm not angry with you. I'm angry at the situation. But, for fuck's sake, we're standing in my house, just you and me. Can I be Luke while you're Sianna? I don't call you Huntress."

Sorrow flowed through her.

"I'm sorry," I said, meaning it in many ways. I was sorry for her fucked up family, sorry for the fucked up situation, sorry for my anger, and sorry for our likely future.

"Come Wednesday, you will be Peacekeeper. Always. I will miss Luke," she said softly, touching her hand to my face and taking the headache I hadn't realized was there.

"Sianna." I sighed her name, hugging her. She refused my peace, as always. "Sam went through this too. The empowered in our circle would only see him as Walker, only see the power, not the man. That has changed over time. They recognize the power in our circle and the power when he uses it. But, otherwise, he is Sam. I will hope for the same."

"In our culture, Luke, I think it would be wise to remain Peacekeeper. The Peacekeeper is above reproach, untouchable and sacred. He heals our children and keeps our sanity. I am afraid Luke would be another man and adversary, someone to be challenged and ranked in our pecking order. Do not give my father the option to see you as anything but Peacekeeper."

I turned away, frustrated again.

"Where are you going?" she called.

"To make a sandwich. I'm not especially hungry, but I haven't eaten since noon. Are you hungry?"

Sensing her hesitation, I turned to look at her. She fidgeted, playing with the ties on her dress for a moment.

"What, Sianna?"

"Will you make hot chocolate?"

I smiled then, walking back to brush a kiss against her lips.

"Maybe hot chocolate and cookies? That sounds better to me too."

"You have cookies?"

"Cookie dough balls are in the freezer in the basement," I said, laughing at her expression of wonder. "Molasses or chocolate chip?"

"Man-wife," she muttered, grinning.

WARM COOKIES and hot chocolate between us on the breakfast bar, I took Sianna's hand, toying with her fingers.

"You have questions," she said.

I grinned, causing laughter to bubble out of her.

"Why was I better with the affinities and shared energy while touching you?"

"I have no idea," she said, almost immediately.

The response was so quick, I knew she'd been thinking about it and likely had a theory. I raised my eyebrows, sipping while waiting.

"Your brother has said the Peacekeepers always had someone with them. Maybe I serve as a filter? Maybe I ground the energy for you? I do not know. But, on Wednesday, we will stay in contact. I will help keep you centered so the power does not take over."

"What if the power takes over on Wednesday?" I asked, smiling at the bit of cookie stuck in the corner of her mouth.

"I do not know that either," she admitted. "Part of me wonders if we should allow that to happen. You are very... authoritative when the power commands. Your demeanor changes. There is still peace, but there is no option to take or refuse it."

It took me a minute to realize which emotions were stirring within her, causing her lack of peace. "You're turned on by bossy me?" I asked, already laughing.

If she'd blushed in my presence before, I couldn't remember it. The rose color rising in her cheeks took me by surprise.

"The energy does things to me." She squirmed, trying not to laugh even as I chuckled. "You are proper and polite, patient and kind. When the energy takes you, you are also demanding."

I made some mental notes for later, taking in her rapid heartbeat and uneven breathing. Apparently, there was something to be said for "demanding."

My mind shifted to the Sianna-as-pin-up form. I did my own uncomfortable squirming, knowing my next question would dump cold water over both our libidos.

"You said earlier that you'd be Overlord if your anatomy was different. Don't you have the ability to change your anatomy as you choose?"

Her face scrunched up.

"I know. I'm sorry. It's an honest question, though," I said.

"I thought we were on our way to melted marshmallow kitchen sex a second ago, but now..." she sighed.

I sighed with her.

"There must be more sex," she blurted. "There must be more sex and balance before Wednesday, so your control is better. We have to try. Everything we can do to make the energy cycle properly before Wednesday, we should do it."

I sighed again, knowing she was avoiding my question.

She sighed back, knowing I wouldn't drop it.

My lips quirked at us sighing at each other.

"Yes, I can change my anatomy," Sianna agreed. "Our is not a patriarchal society because of penises, Luke. It is patriarchal because it has always been so, despite many of our strongest being women."

"Sam said that to me the other day," I interjected.

Sianna nodded. "Assuming the shape of a man would not cause our society to see me as a man. They would not honor me as such. It would be a fact but ignored. Plus, then I would be a man." She pulled a face. "I am not sure I could pretend to be that stupid."

I grinned, acknowledging the joke.

"You could be a woman, though," she allowed. "So in touch with your emotions, fond of cleanliness, and excellent at cooking."

I laughed again. "I told you. I am a modern man."

"Modern men are not this evolved. Most men struggle if their woman makes more money than them."

I shrugged. "I make no money. Sam made all the money. More accurately, Jake made all the money by doing what Sam told him to do. Jake and Gary and Dad made all the money. If we waited for Sam to do things, I'd have a normal job right now, and we wouldn't be in a compound. Anyway, I'll give you the money to do something with. It's lost on me."

"There is a box of money in your attic I have meant to ask about," she said, already laughing.

I shrugged. "Rainy day funds."

"It is a big box."

"I have a lot of money. What were you doing in my attic and is it really dusty?"

"Snooping." She grinned, unrepentant. "There is no dust

anywhere in this house. And I know you checked the attic for dust yesterday afternoon."

"You found the money in the attic but not the cookies in the basement freezer? I question your priorities."

"It was the first night, before I knew you. I was sorting through what lived here with you and trying to figure out why you were acting so strangely. One moment you were abrupt and rude, like the Peacekeeper. The next moment, you were too polite to sit quietly in the car. Now I know the truth."

I grinned, getting up to rinse the milk pot. "I have another question. I know you haven't lied to me. Please don't lie to me now?"

Her eyebrows lifted, a smile still playing around her lips.

"Will there be children from last night?"

The smile changed into a mischievous smirk. "Maybe. The energy rolled far and free. I do not believe your siblings could have missed it. They are all young and healthy. Maybe many babies will come from last night."

I flushed red, remembering that I still hadn't read the text thread from last night and today. "That's not what I mean."

"I know," she said, her smile fading. "No, Luke. I told you to trust and lean on me. I would not do that if it was not what you wanted. I intended to when I came here with you, before I knew you. I don't deny it. But not now. I thought this was clear after… Jen… left. There is sex between us now. Children will come in time."

I nodded, mostly relieved.

"What are you doing now?" Sianna asked, confused when I put the saucepan back on the stove and tossed butter in to melt.

"Making marshmallow sauce."

27

My phone buzzed before six o'clock in the morning. I ignored it on general principle.

SAM: Get up and meet us in the field. Sianna too. You can go back to having sex and sleeping in a little bit.
SAM: Are you reading this?
SAM: I can't tell if you're ignoring the phone or sleeping.
SAM: Hello?

"WAKE UP!" Sam yelled from the foot of my bed.

"For fuck's sake, Sam." I groaned. I knew my bare ass was on display, but if he didn't have the courtesy to knock, fuck him. He could look at my ass crack.

I heard the camera shutter on his phone.

I still didn't care. My naked ass looked fine since William forced me to run and do squats.

"Get up!" he yelled again. "We need to circle now. With

Sianna. Get up."

"I am not part of your circle," Sianna muttered, rolling over to snuggle closer.

"It will help his energy. It will help it balance. We will do one now, at sunrise, another at sunset, and one tomorrow as well. Wake up! This is going to help!" Sam was almost giddy. "Get up now, or I'll let William drag you out of bed. We're meeting in the field in five minutes."

"GET IN!" Sam called to Sianna. "You need to be in this one."

"I do not stand circles. You may not have my power," she said coldly.

Sam scrunched up his face, waving away her words. "I don't want your power. I want you to take his! Get in. I saw it. I saw it with the church last night. That worked. This will work. I know this will work. Get in."

"Did you follow us to the church last night, Sam? After you told me I couldn't stand in my own circle, did you follow us?"

"No," Sam replied, impatient. "I looked back when you kept us up all night fucking. Get in the circle, Sianna. Please? It's almost sunrise. This is going to work."

I looked around the circle guiltily. "Sorry," I muttered to my siblings.

Jake snorted. "No problem, man. You're my favorite sibling right now. Loving the sexy mojo! We didn't get this with Captain Passion over there."

I smirked at Noah; no words were needed as he sputtered, looking for a retort.

I stepped back to Sianna, taking her hand. "Please?"

She groaned, stepping inside the line of the circle. We weren't at my usual place, making my skin crawl, even before the circle was closed.

"Can we move?" William bitched. "This is all wrong."

"No, it's not. Just wait. We won't stay like this, I promise. But it'll help him," Sam said as he almost dragged Adaline around the outside of the circle in his haste to close it.

"Samuel," Micah's voice was deep, resonating through the field with raw power. "How could you? I didn't think you would ever... How could you do this without asking me?"

"I do what must be done," Samuel responded, the Walker energy suddenly forward. "You are my circle, and I demand it. Now."

Dead eyes stared at me from Micah's usually lively face. There was nothing in his expression now, no love of life, no devotion to his principles, no desire to do right. There was nothing to Micah but hate. Hate radiated off him, spilling through our circle.

"How?" Ethan breathed, eyes filling with tears. "Why? I won't forgive you if this hurts him."

"Micah of Rome, you will give my circle Hate," Samuel said, infusing the name with energy and ignoring Ethan.

"Holy shit," Adrian breathed as Micah's energy hit him.

"Rage will join Hate now, then Terror," Samuel demanded. "Light will give us Pain."

This was not our process. We were not controlling the energy, contributing in turns. Sam, who gleefully ran around the circle a moment ago, was braiding a circle of ugly human emotions. Combined, hate, fear, pain, and terror appeared as a glowing, hideous mustard yellow color.

"Lu-CAS," the Walker sang my name. "Bring my circle peace."

I knew it was coming. I knew he was going to ask it of me. He said this circle would help my energy. I pushed peace through the circle for all I was worth, enough power washing through me to make me light-headed.

The putrid yellow color remained unchanged.

Samuel nodded, unsurprised.

"Sianna Huntress, give my circle peace. Channel the power, as you did last night."

Her look was skeptical at best.

"I am the Walker of legend, Sianna Huntress. Would you have me break this circle and take *this* energy for myself?"

That was crap. If I couldn't drown the horrible energy in peace, I knew Jake would suck it up and make it something else. That's what Jake did. That was his role. He anchored our circle and cleaned up its energy for worldly consumption. I opened my mouth, intending to say as much until Sam turned to me, eyes glowing, as a storm formed overhead.

I felt Sianna pull on my energy.

"Let go," she whispered.

I did as I was told, letting go of my restraints. I stood with my family, all power forward as Lord Peace, Peacekeeper in truth.

"Well, that's freaky," Lucy muttered, staring, as her sister Linda nodded in agreement. "He even looks different."

Taking on an angel's glow of white light, Adaline faced me. "How do you feel? Your energy is centered in you, no longer hovering over where the tie was. Can you feel the difference?"

I shook my head. It didn't feel any different. "I feel the

energy loose. My mind is not as crowded. I'm not overloaded. But my sense of the power hasn't changed."

Sam nodded. "We will do it again at sunset. Sunrise or sunset, with this circle configuration, channels hate through Micah."

Adaline broke the silent, uncomfortable circle without another word, releasing us all to our day. Ethan and Micah were gone before I could say anything.

"They will remain angry with me, but they will come to help you." Sam's words were tight with shame and sadness. Ethan was his dearest brother and best friend.

"I'm sorry, Sam." I meant it.

He looked at me, eyebrows raised. "I broke that tie in your mind, causing you extreme pain. But I did it for a reason, just as I do this for a reason. I don't want to talk about breaking the tie anymore, Luke. If I could have saved you that pain, I would have. If I could force your energy to act right without Micah as Hate, I would do it. You must know control and balance to survive."

2 8

*T*uesday and most of Wednesday passed in a haze of circles, sex, and food. I remembered most of it and started to understand the feeling of my energy being centered in my mind.

Like most things, I didn't realize it was wrong until I felt it righted. I knew it was wrong now but didn't know how to fix it without Sianna pulling it with me. Practice would make perfect in time, I was sure.

But time was in short supply.

Wednesday afternoon, Talise and Adaline sat in my living room, watching me play the cello. They'd shown up earlier that morning and stayed.

"Are you two staying all day?"

"Yup," Talise said easily. "You're not going tonight."

"You know I have to go tonight," I countered, frowning.

"I know you think you have to go. But we're still going to

stay right here, reminding you why you shouldn't go," Talise argued.

"There is no love binding, Luke. You risk your life needlessly. Sianna even says it is so. Ellie will not let them kill Charlie. You should not take this risk."

"I have to go, Addy," I said calmly. We'd had several iterations of this same conversation already.

"You've never been interested in being Peacekeeper. That hasn't changed. I can tell you don't want this," Addy countered.

"I don't want this," I agreed. "But I still have to go."

"No, you do not," Talise yelled. "You have this weird fucking white-knight thing going on for a woman you broke up with! You don't have feelings for Candy. Just stay here. Be with Sianna. Make babies and have a family. She's great. But don't do this!"

I sighed. "There are children—"

"I will help the children," Adaline snapped. "We've been over this. They just need to ask for my assistance, and I will help."

"They won't ask, Addy."

"Then the children will die. All things die in time, Luke."

"Including me," I muttered.

Adaline's anger washed through the room. "You endanger us all and risk yourself by going. If you die at their mercy, there will be war."

"If I don't go, they will fade away, Addy. That energy will leave the world forever."

"I don't care," Talise said for the ninth time. "You keep saying that. I still don't care. Don't go."

I went back to my music. There was a plan for this. There

was a plan for each future Sam could find... except for the one where I lost my head.

Sianna appeared in the early evening. "Burgers tonight?" she asked.

I nodded in agreement.

It was timed perfectly, allowing us to avoid a conflict with Adaline, Talise, and my mother, who had joined in the "don't go" chorus after we'd eaten dinner.

It was a rather full table for Wednesday night, but I wasn't sorry for the company of my family before walking into what would likely be a dangerous meeting.

We'd just finished putting the dishes in the dishwasher when there was a boom from Matthew's house followed by the unmistakable sound of a roof collapsing.

We ran out the door after Talise and Adaline to check on Matthew and Miranda. I knew they were fine. I could feel them in the circle, just as I'd felt the spike of Matthew's power before the explosion.

While everyone was looking the other way, Sam pulled us through space.

"PLEASE DON'T MAKE me regret this," Sam begged Sianna.

We were in Candy's house, a short jaunt to the expressway that would lead us to the beast compound. Sam's car waited for us, along with some more sturdy clothing for Sianna and a variety of weapons, including her sword.

"Walker, I will not hurt him. They do not intend him harm. Edgar has confirmed this, and he would not lie. There is no ulterior motive here. The elders will feel his power and honor him as they should. All will be well."

Sam shook his head, chewing on his bottom lip. "Amber bindings. I don't know if that will work. I can't tell. But leave the sword with me."

Her expression dropped into a rage.

"No, that's not... No. Just leave the sword with me. You don't need it for this part. We're not on that path anymore. You might need it later, though," Sam muttered, obviously still coasting through time.

"What path are we on?" Sianna asked, looking morbidly curious.

"I can't tell you. It'll go wrong if you know it's coming." Sam shook his head, joining us in the present. "I don't know about the friendship binding, though. Luke, try. Please try?"

"Try what?" I asked, confused.

"Try changing the binding," Sam replied. "You care for her and want her to be well. Let that feeling grow."

"You want me to fall into true love right this moment because it'd make you happier?" I was dumbfounded.

"Please? I know it works with gold. It's risky like this. I think it'll work, but I'm not one hundred percent sure. It's not the type of bet I like."

I sighed at the absurdity. "Let's do this," I murmured to Sianna, grabbing the keys from Sam and tossing them to her.

I WAS doubtful of Sam's timing but decided it didn't matter. It was my party. They'd wait for me if traffic was terrible.

I should not have doubted him. We were right on time.

I could feel Sianna's affinity pressing heavily against her mind. "Sianna?"

"I am scared," she whispered. "I trust Edgar with my life, and yours too, but I am still scared. You will stay with me, touching me in some way, the entire time. I will help ground the energy and help you process it. Do not let go, okay?"

"I know. I won't let go of you," I promised, offering her my peace without forcing it on her.

She shook her head. "I will keep this fear. It makes me faster."

My eyebrows flew up toward my hairline. *Faster?*

She smiled, guessing my thoughts. "I am the fastest beast affinity alive, Peacekeeper, no matter my form. You have seen my normal speed so far. I can be faster."

I smiled but felt the wash of sorrow even through my peace —*Peacekeeper*, not Luke. I was destined to forever play a role without being a person. I wouldn't be Luke again.

"We both know I'm not that fast," I said, teasing. "Don't go too fast, or I won't be able to hang on."

Sianna's lips turned up as she touched my hand without taking her eyes off the road. I resisted the urge to sigh as raw energy cycled between us.

"All will be well," she murmured to herself.

IN-BETWEEN

I paused in my reflection, pulling my thoughts back to in-between, where I shared this story with some version of myself.

"That's the last you remember?" the other version of me asked.

"No," I mental projection whispered. "There's a little more."

"What's the problem?"

I stayed silent. If I'd had eyes, I think I would have been crying. I could feel the peace trying to wash away the sadness, but I held onto it.

"Oh," other me said, the thought projection somehow full of anticipation and excitement. "You should admit that."

"I should have said thank you. She risked everything for me and probably lost it all. I didn't trust her for half of our time together. I wasted some of our time. But she did everything she said she would, and more, to help me. I should have thanked her."

"That's it?"

The energy washed through me, taking the remorse.

"That's it."

Other me sighed again. "Not yet, but there's hope."

29

ianna pulled up to the gate and hit a series of buttons.

We both fidgeted as the gate opened.

"Do not," she whispered. "Do not hide it now. Like the first night, pull the peace forward without pushing it. You did very well that first night."

"Ellie told me what to do," I admitted. "I felt like an ass."

"Do you think she is here? Do you think giving her access worked?" Sianna asked.

"I haven't heard from her again," I said. "Why?"

"I would like to know if she is here somewhere. If something goes bad, there will be help," she muttered.

I watched as her form changed, her long blonde hair replaced by the short brown bob. Her body shrunk about six inches.

I raised my eyebrows.

"My father prefers this form," she said. "I would like to keep him happy. Besides, I told you. Most know me in this form."

I nodded, straightening my tie one more time.

A genuine smile lit her eyes. "Persnickety Peace."

I returned the smile, glad she was comfortable enough to tease. "Startling, Sexy, Savvy, Sianna."

Her smile touched her eyes for a moment.

"Time to do this," I muttered.

"Wait!" she blurted before I could open my door.

I turned back to her, still smiling from our teasing.

"Thank you for sharing your time with me this week. I know you are Peacekeeper, but I will also remember that you are you, no matter what comes."

A swell of emotion hit before my peace swallowed it. "Thank you."

She nodded, seeming to understand the energy wouldn't allow more.

IN-BETWEEN

There was a snort of amusement from other me.

"What?" I asked.

"Keep going," he said. "I'll tell you later."

30

*A*s we walked through the main house, Sianna visibly relaxed.

I squeezed the hand I was holding, asking for clarification without words.

She shook her head. "It worked. This is your abode."

It took me a minute to realize what she meant. "Backup," I breathed, not even mouthing the word.

Sianna smiled. "And more. The Walker uses all his pieces when he plays chess."

I raised my eyebrows.

"You'll see," she said, pushing open the back door to lead me across the grounds to the arena.

"Why do you have an arena?"

She grinned. "Beast affinity cage matches."

"You're lying." I laughed.

"No. When there are disputes, sometimes we allow them to be settled with tooth and nail. But it also serves as a place for a large number of us to gather. The arena seats several hundred when full."

"There weren't that many cars," I observed, hoping it wasn't a large crowd.

"There are other parking areas. There are close to a thousand people here, Peacekeeper. My hearing is affected by all the noise. Do not depend on my hearing tonight." She gripped my hand, a reminder to keep in contact with her.

My energy washed through me, taking my anxiety immediately.

I was just beginning to hear the sounds of the crowd when Sianna paused. "How far can you push the energy?"

My lips twitched into a bit of a smile. The whole point of holding hands was to make sure I managed the power properly. She wanted to play with it *now?*

"It is deafeningly loud to my senses. Make an entrance, Peacekeeper."

That made more sense.

"You will share energy with them all before long, anyway. Might as well see how it goes out here, where few are watching."

I tilted my head up to look at the January night sky. I accepted that the stars would keep shining and the world would keep turning no matter the outcome of this evening. In that simple acceptance, my peaceful energy grew, multiplying rapidly as the living energy around us flowed toward me, answering my call. Then, I pushed it out into the world.

This was different than sharing peace in a circle, with a person, or even with a group of people. I was sharing my peace with the world through a wide area.

I'd never done this before. It was an interesting feeling.

The faint sounds of the crowd in the distance faded rapidly. The arena went quiet.

"They are silent," she whispered. "But I am unaffected. How did you do that?"

I shot her a look. "I don't know. You told me you wanted to keep your emotions, your fear. So, I didn't push in your direction."

"Peacekeeper," Edgar muttered, bowing deeply. He'd been waiting outside the arena for us. "None can doubt what you are after that display of power."

"Uncle," Sianna murmured, stretching to kiss his cheek. "You look well. In fact, better each time I see you. Are you feeling better?"

He smiled fondly. "*I am well, dear one.*" Something passed between them at Edgar's emphasis on the word. I hadn't gotten the subtext. But Sianna had.

She nodded in understanding.

Edgar muttered something too low for me to hear.

Another nod. "Peacekeeper, my uncle wishes to know the feeling of flight again. Will you help him?"

I blinked, unsure what to do.

Edgar smiled. "Offer me your peace and hold mine for me. It's as easy as breathing, Peacekeeper. You don't even have to think about it. I don't worry about the transformation. It is coming back from it that gives me pause."

I looked at Sianna.

"Just offer him peace and pull him back to human when the time comes."

I nodded, understanding. It would be like what I did with Charlie and Candy during the November battle.

Edgar was out of his clothes and in the form of a giant hawk faster than my eye could follow.

"Wow," Sianna and I muttered at the same time.

"Uncle?" Sianna breathed, holding out her arm. Hawk-Edgar landed carefully, not piercing her skin. The human instincts were still in control. She exhaled in relief. "Your hand, Peacekeeper?"

I hesitated.

She glared at me.

"I'm about to bleed again, aren't I?"

I couldn't see it in the darkness, but I knew she rolled her eyes.

I held out my hand, waiting for a jab of pain that didn't come. I didn't feel the bird's beak break skin. Whatever injury there was seemed to close immediately.

"Well, now I feel dumb. I didn't even feel that. Candy bit my hand in November. It ached until Addy fixed it."

"Clumsy." Sianna sniffed with disapproval.

And then I felt it. Deep within her psyche, buried where I would typically miss it, I sensed the jealousy and anger she harbored toward Candy.

It pinged my senses as a part of Sianna, not at peace.

I rocked back on my heels, surprised despite my power being forward.

"Peacekeeper?" she asked, concerned.

I wondered if she realized the feelings were there, but decided it wasn't the right moment to discuss it. "I'm fine."

I pulled open the arena door for her. It was completely silent inside.

She glared at me.

Ah shit, I realized. *She was supposed to do this part.*

We traded places, swapping our joined hands as Edgar flew in before us, screeching to announce our arrival.

Through the web of peace I'd woven, I could feel the shock and recognition roll through the crowd before a roaring cheer shook the arena.

IN-BETWEEN

I fell silent again, thinking.

"Luke?" other me asked.

"I should have asked her then. I should have asked her about those feelings. The crowd would have waited for us."

"Why didn't you?"

"It didn't feel like the right time."

"Bah. Those moments should never be wasted, Luke."

"I might not get the chance now," I acknowledged, the thought riddled with remorse.

"What did you expect to come from those emotions?" other me prodded.

I hesitated. "I don't know."

"Yes, you do. Admit it here and now, just between us."

I hesitated again, thinking of Sianna laughing as we ran together, laughing as we fought in the snow.

"I wanted there to be real feelings," I projected, admitting it to myself as well as other me.

The landscape of in-between rocked around me. In the distance, I could hear another voice yelling in panic.

"Why?" other me asked.

"Hmm?" The yelling was distracting. I couldn't make it out.

"Why did you want her to have real feelings? Which feelings?"

"Do you hear the yelling?" I asked.

There was an annoyed sigh. "Finish the story."

"The yelling—"

"Finish the story," other me demanded, seeming disappointed. "We're almost out of time."

31

As I entered the building, I felt all the minds press against mine. I felt the combined power of the gathered beast affinities. As my energy circled the space, I could pick out the clusters.

Bears, canines, felines, reptiles, insects, sea creatures... Every animal imaginable and even some I couldn't identify washed against my senses.

My power roared out of me, unlike anything I'd ever released before. It seemed to acknowledge the beasts, welcome them to the energy, and... take raw power from them. I felt it in truth then, for the first time. *This* was what Sianna and Gary had been talking about.

I paused, wondering if Gary was in the arena somewhere. I wondered if Joe and Deanna were here, and I wondered how Owen was doing.

Nearly a thousand minds touched with beast awareness ran through my psyche. They begged for my permission to coexist within my energy, thanked me for my peace, and offered a more significant tithe of power than I had any idea what to do with. But it was there. It was mine if I wanted it, more open to me than a circle's energy.

I froze, trying to sort it out. Then, I realized Sianna's eyes were blazing a pure turquoise in the strange arena light. She pulled the extra energy from me, helping me to cycle power and stay balanced.

I stared at her, lost.

"Peacekeeper," she breathed before kissing the hand joined to hers. "Stay with me."

"Sianna." I almost groaned her name, stuck somewhere between indescribable joy and horrific pain. It was so much energy. I was sure it would have broken me if we had not done everything we could to fix my overload.

She squeezed my fingers again. "I can't do much more without transforming, and I won't do that. Not now."

I nodded, stumbling a bit as I started forward again.

We moved down the aisle, through the entryway, until Sianna and I stood together at the edge of the arena. Ten chairs sat in the center, facing a throne.

The chairs were filled.

The throne was empty.

I knew my ass was about to land in it and flushed red with embarrassment before my peace swallowed the emotion whole.

Nate sat in the center chair. Hawk-Edgar was to the right, followed by two older men I didn't know.

I stared at the last chair on the left.

Jen looked at me with pleasant indifference on her face, as if she'd never seen me before in her life.

"Lucas," Nate greeted, walking toward us. "There are many

here you do not know, and we are favored by additional guests as well. Please, will you take your seat?"

He stared meaningfully at the throne.

Fuck my life, I thought, hoping no one took a picture. I'd never hear the end of it from my brothers.

I walked across the arena, turning in place to nod at the crowd—a greeting of respect my power demanded. It was a show of thanks for the energy they'd gifted me.

The crowd roared again with joy as I sat.

"Daughter, welcome home. You may go," Nate said, dismissing Sianna with a hand wave.

"She will stay," I said, voice firm and commanding, the tone new to me. The crowd went utterly silent at the sound of it.

Sianna bowed her head, yanking her fingers free of my grasp. She glared at me from under her lashes.

Well, now what am I supposed to do? I wondered as the energy poured into me with no way to cycle itself out.

She knelt at my feet, her hands tucked behind her back with her fingers discreetly tucked under my suit pants and wrapped around my ankles.

Oh, holy hell. If mom ever sees a picture of this, she'll beat my ass with a serving spoon over Sunday dinner.

Adulthood didn't faze my mother when such things were at issue.

Nate stood before his daughter, staring at us both. Together.

He tilted her head up. Their eyes met. He smiled like the proud father he was, making my stomach turn in revulsion. "Are you with child?"

Sianna minutely shook her head.

"Not yet," Nate predicted before his eyes met mine. "You

honor my line, Lucas. May my daughter bring you many fine offspring."

I had the sudden urge to punch him in the head. I stayed quiet, not dignifying his words or presumption with a reply.

"Allow me to introduce my elder advisors as well as our guests." He turned back to the line of chairs in front of me. I made a point of not looking at Jen again.

"You know Edgar," Nate began. "I cannot question my elder brother's bravery, just his sense. To transform after being trapped for so long... I cannot imagine."

Just looking at Edgar made Nate's psyche scream in rage and pain in a way I didn't fully understand. Something was going on that was above my pay grade. But I could sense Nate's sense of self, his inner peace, roll tumultuously, threatening to splinter and crack, even with my power still flowing freely.

"Next to Edgar is Godwin, then John. Together, these three men make up the former beast lords more aged than me. I serve as Overlord as they can no longer *safely* transform."

Ah, that clarified the subtext. Edgar transformed, showing himself to be older and still in control of his power with me here. It was a political move. He was baiting Nate.

Sianna's fingers dug so hard into my ankles, I wondered if she was trying to draw blood. But no. I hadn't acknowledged the elders. They shifted uncomfortably, waiting for some sort of greeting from me.

I nodded. "Well met, Godwin and John."

Where did that come from? I've never used the phrase "well met" before in my life.

"On the far end, the Queen of the Mind honors us with her presence. Her telepathic power is unmatched by any creature on the planet. We are grateful for her presence and make her welcome." Nate's words were full of worship and wonder, but he was terrified of Jen.

I nodded my head, working not to smile. "Greetings, Majesty."

"You may call me Rajena, Lucas Peacekeeper," Jen said. Except, there was no sound. She'd projected the words through every mind in the arena.

I touched the medal around my neck, a gift from Jen that was supposed to block mental intrusion.

Her lips quirked as she fought off a smile. *"Mental intrusion from all but me, Baby Trellis."*

I cut my eyes away. Jen had picked Ellie's pet name for me directly from my thoughts. I hadn't even been thinking about it. But, after she used it, I was afraid the name was going to stick. I was *not* the youngest.

"The first chair on my right is held by my eldest son, who is also Nathaniel."

Of course, I thought, nodding a greeting.

"Then my younger sons Elias, Jordan, and Daniel."

Even with my peace roaming freely, I knew Elias and Jordan were mentally broken beyond repair. There was no peace at all within them, no logic remaining to repair. These were the elder brothers Sianna believed to be insane. She was right.

Through our contact, I felt a pulse of her terror, disturbing our balance. I offered her peace again. For the first time, she took it of her own accord.

"On the far end, we greet Lord Facet of the siphons," Nate finished, not entirely happy to introduce the last guest, but expecting me to place the name. It wasn't hard. I was looking at Ellie's relative.

"Her grandfather, Luke. He's a pompous ass. Make sure you call him Paul," Jen said directly to my mind.

"Nice to meet you, Paul," I said flippantly, decidedly not noticing Jen's muffled giggle.

"Lord Facet will see that his granddaughter stays out of our affairs."

The vampire's lips twitched. He was almost smiling. Almost. "I did intend to take Eleanor home, but I won't touch her here, Nathaniel." The words boomed through the arena with the same type of energy I'd seen Ellie exude.

Either Paul wasn't making an effort to hide his energy, or Ellie's control was just that much better.

Nate's eyes narrowed dangerously, silently asking for more information.

Ellie's grandpa pulled a mocking smile. "When trying to rid yourself of a siphon, I don't recommend giving her access to your threshold, home, or energy. She is welcome in these buildings. I will not remove her. She is also welcome with your Peacekeeper and has fed from him before."

"She is not welcome in my buildings," Nate breathed, staring at the siphon. "I rescind any invitation she may have."

"These are not your buildings."

It took me a full ten seconds to realize I had spoken. I didn't even recognize the voice. I was too focused on the flash of realization across Nate's face, followed by the wash of madness tearing at his mind. His beast nature wanted out of its lifelong cage.

"Ah, Lucas," he made a tsking noise at me. "Let us first discuss the Hapners."

Candy stood from the lowest tier of seating behind Nate's

274

chair and walked to the center of the arena, eyes focused straight ahead, refusing to look at me.

Well, that can't be good. Where's Charlie?

A moment later, Charlie was forcefully dragged in by four men in security uniforms. He still appeared severely beaten but in new and horrible ways. Parts of his skin were branded and burned. His face was sunken, and his eyes lacked all signs of intelligence... right up until they landed on me.

I think he would have dropped to the ground in relief if the guard had let him. Still bare assed naked, there wasn't a single stretch of skin that appeared undamaged.

Charlie had been tortured.

My rage overrode my peace. I ripped my energy from the crowd, using my words like a barbed whip. "By your own word, he was to be a guest, welcome in your home."

Surprised by my control of the energy and keeping a wary eye on Hawk-Edgar, Nate glanced at me. "He is a welcome guest in my home. I made no secret of my intention to separate our Beast Lord from the filthy siphon."

Looking back, I think Nate forgot Lord Facet sat behind him. When the siphon's energy cracked with anger, Nate jumped, looking caught.

"ELEANOR," Lord Facet called, each syllable of the name laced with more power.

From the back of the arena where only shadow existed, Eleanor called back. "Awww, you sound grumpy, Grandfather."

"You will leave the *filthy* animals to their sty and come home," he demanded.

"Nope, I won't," Ellie shrugged. "You can pull me out of my hidey-hole because I allow it. I won't move another finger at your command."

The two siphons stared at each other, unblinking.

"Are you ready for this confrontation?" Ellie sneered at her grandfather. "I am welcome here and welcome in his energy." She gestured to me. "You are not. I will meet you on these terms if you choose it."

I stared at Ellie, confused. What the hell was happening?

After another moment of staring at Ellie, Lord Facet seemed to shift and undulate, his body turning to smoke.

"I'll be seeing you soon, Grandfather," Ellie taunted before she turned back to Nate. "And I'll be taking my husband home. Now."

"You stand in my arena with nearly a thousand beast affinities, girl. I don't need your grandfather to kill you," Nate responded, looking to his eldest son.

Nate Junior stood, pulling a massive two-handed sword from a scabbard I hadn't noticed on the ground.

"Hmm," Jen purred. "The manners of those with affinities have slipped greatly since Edgar's reign. I am disappointed."

The word "disappointed" echoed through my head, reflecting her rage.

The crowd shifted uncomfortably. The Queen of the Mind had just talked smack about their leader's manners. To make things worse, the Peacekeeper of legend sat before them, enraged enough to withhold power from them.

I was rather proud of myself. This was the longest I'd held onto an emotion while my power was forward.

Everyone in the center of the arena took a step away from Jen. The men that had been seated stood and moved behind Nate Jr. Hawk-Edgar seemed unfazed and remained perched on the back of his chair, eyes shifting between Jen and me.

I wondered if he knew that Jen and I knew each other.

"I beg your pardon, Lady Rajena?" Nate said, not able to hide the insulted anger from his voice.

If my earlier words hit as a whip, Jen's response flayed. "You've held a 'guest' against his will and now threatened his wife. What is the reasoning?"

"I do not justify myself to you!" Nathaniel roared at Jen.

She didn't even blink. "You will explain yourself now, or I will return your brother to his position of power. Your people suffer under your leadership. Edgar may not be able to control his transformations. That remains to be seen now that he has returned to himself. Regardless, he can rule with a Peacekeeper and shift as needed. I can sleep comfortably with Edgar as Overlord. You make me uneasy, Nathaniel."

Nate's voice was flat. "Charles and Candace Hapner were recorded transforming into animal forms in front of humans."

"In front of my family," I corrected. "They transformed at my request to ensure my safety. Is it not my right as Peacekeeper to have beast affinity guards? Do you deny me that courtesy?"

Outrage rolled through the crowd at Nathaniel's actions. At least the gathered mob did not want to deny me an escort.

Nate froze, dumbstruck by the crowd. This was not going the way he'd anticipated.

Jen stepped into the awkward silence, somehow positioning herself as judge and jury in this strange drama. "Am I to understand you hold Charles Hapner as a prisoner and threaten his wife for nothing more than protecting the newly risen Peacekeeper? Half the minds in this room are utterly baffled. The other half are contemplating mutiny. Think quickly, Nathaniel, lesser son of Jude."

Hawk-Edgar screamed into *that* awkward silence, drawing attention just as Elias's sword flew toward him. The bird took to the air just before the sword strike chopped the Edgar's chair in half.

Where the fuck did the swords come from?!

The crowd was screaming in rage, pushing toward the arena floor, revolting against the inadequate security guards tasked with keeping the floor clear.

"LET US SPEAK TO THE PEACEKEEPER ISSUE!" Nate roared over the crowd, his veneer of sanity starting to slip. "He has put forward an impressive show, but he is not Peacekeeper!"

The crowd stilled for a moment.

"Nonsense," Godwin said, his deep, melodic voice easily overcoming the murmurs from the crowd. "His energy is undeniable, Nathaniel. Queen Meeli is correct. Your honor is lost."

Nate shook his head without even facing the elder. "Candace," he called. "Tell them."

"Lucas is not Peacekeeper," Candace's voice carried clearly through the arena. "He stands with the Mistress and Walker in the empowered circles as Lord Peace. He already wears a name, and it is not Peacekeeper."

3 2

"*L*ucas," Jen shouted in my mind, her panic evident, "*don't say a word. Stay seated on that ridiculous throne. It's too late. I already got a picture.*"

I snorted in disbelief. I couldn't believe she was making a joke.

"Charlie and I didn't claim him as Peacekeeper during our trial because we knew he was not what he seemed to be. It is not possible to be bound to the Walker and Mistress and also hold our peace," Candace finished, still not looking at me.

"You are mistaken," Sianna said, words laced with a threat. "You will take back your testimony now before I challenge you."

Candy blanched, backing away from Sianna, hiding behind the guys with swords. "I speak the truth. If I'm wrong, let him deny it."

Of course, she wasn't wrong. Of course, I wouldn't deny standing circles. But why would she tell these people I stood circles? Why would she do this? We were almost out of there!

"He holds Edgar's peace, even as we speak," Sianna countered.

"Daughter, come here," Nate growled in a low voice.

As she climbed to her feet, I had a bad moment. I thought she was about to leave me to my fate. I'd been completely blindsided by Candy speaking against me.

But bless Sianna and all of her beautiful bravery. She stood, moving to my side. "He is Peacekeeper," she said softly, meeting her father's eyes. "Lucas, give Edgar back his peace."

I didn't think about it. Standing from the throne, I spotted Edgar as he flew down from the rafters. Once he was safely on the ground, I pulled back the energy he'd passed through me earlier, returning him to human form.

The arena remained silent as Edgar walked toward us, of course, bare assed naked and not caring in the slightest.

"Peacekeeper," Edgar called, "Charles has been awake for five days and not allowed to transform. Share energy to allow him to change, heal, and defend you."

I didn't even have to see Charlie. I felt the tug on my energy and let it go. There was a growl before the giant wolf, which Charlie seemed to prefer, was standing by my side, opposite Sianna. The wolf then transformed to the largest lion I'd ever seen. It roared in challenge directly at Candy.

"I believe Charles objects to your testimony against the Peacekeeper, Candace," Sianna said calmly. "Do you prefer to meet his challenge or mine?"

In the time it took me to turn my head, Sianna was out of her clothes and had transformed to the black cougar Candace had been the night of our family battle in November.

"You know, I think getting out of your clothes that quickly is its own kind of superpower."

I don't know why I said it. It just came out of my mouth. If I'd known they would be among my last words, I might not have said them. Maybe.

"LUCAS! SIT!" Jen roared in my head.

Too late.

"Oh shit," I mumbled, feeling the sword slide through my neck.

IN-BETWEEN

"That's what happened," I finished, waiting for the snarky response from the other part of me.

Silence.

"Hello?" I asked.

"I'm here," the other voice said. "Lucas, what am I? Have you figured it out yet?"

"I had hoped you were the snarky part of my personality, but there has been a severe lack of commentary thus far."

"You're smarter than this. You know who, or more accurately, what I am."

"I didn't think I had something like you. I'd wondered if you were truly separate after this week, but I'd hoped it was just the overloaded power being strange."

"And what am I?" the voice asked again.

"Other Luke," I muttered.

"Hmm?" He seemed confused.

"Before my brother was the Walker, he would treat his power as a separate entity, Other Sam. You are Other Luke. You are Peace. You are the power within me. I'm like Sam now. I have so much power, it's taken on its own personality."

"Huh."

"What?" I asked, wondering if I'd gotten it wrong, if I'd misinterpreted things over the last few days.

"I don't know of another Walker that has recognized his power as a separate entity. You are not the first Peace to do so, but you are the youngest to reconcile the parts that make you whole."

"Sam is Sam. One Sam, now," I muttered, thinking through reconciling the parts.

"The Mistress helps him hold his humanity. They are unique."

"I've never fought my power. I've never denied you," I said, changing topics. "There is nothing to reconcile. The tie that held you is long gone. There's nothing left to reconcile."

"Lucas, you don't need to reconcile me. You need to reconcile yourself. And quickly. There is no more time."

He waited.

"I don't know what you're waiting for," I admitted.

"You left part of the end of your story out. Tell it now."

I didn't respond.

"Be brave, Lucas. Be brave and admit it, even though she might not feel it too. She's been so brave for you. Embrace that bit of your humanity, Luke. I don't take it from you; you refuse to claim it. Be brave and hang on to the binding, even if the love only flows in one direction."

Somewhere, far away, I could hear the yelling again. It was harder to project my thoughts. I was leaving in-between.

"I counted the steps as Sianna walked away to meet Candy. I counted them. Five steps."

"Why?" Other me asked, already exhaling in relief.

I thought of several reasons why. There were other valid reasons for me not to be separated from her. But, in the end, only one of the reasons mattered. If I couldn't admit it here, to myself, I was unworthy of her. If I couldn't admit it I was unworthy of the feeling.

"Because I love her. Because I don't like being apart from her."

With the admission, I felt the binding from me to Sianna snap into existence.

"—bleeding. Have to slow it!" Adaline was yelling. "I can't make it stop this fast!" Her voice cracked on a sob.

"THERE! THERE! GOLD! GIVE ME THE DAMN SWORD!" Sam screamed with all of the Walker's power.

"SAM, YOU FUCKING ASSHOLE!" William yelled. "LUCAS! STAY HERE!"

Far away, there was a crunch that I was pretty sure was my jaw breaking again.

"His heart's not beating. His heart stopped," Talise sobbed. "I can feel his blood sitting still. Please, Luke. Please. Please don't go."

My energy moved weakly toward Talise, offering peace one last time, trying to heal her broken heart. *I'm sorry, Talise. I'm so sorry.*

"Move," Adrian yelled, his tone sharp with a doctor's command.

There was a thumping noise in the distance.

CPR. Adrian was doing CPR, making my heart circulate blood in my absence.

How did I get here? I wondered.

33

SAM—TWO HOURS EARLIER

*A*daline's rage glowed around her in a red haze, visible to the naked eye.

"I love you?" I tried, even knowing it wouldn't work. Things would get worse before they got better.

"Bring him back. Now," she demanded.

"I can't," I admitted. It was true. I couldn't feel Lucas. He was beyond my reach.

"Why?"

"I can't feel him. I don't have any idea where he is to go get him. They left in a car."

Addy's eyes went unfocused as she searched her own bindings. Her rage redoubled. "HOW DARE YOU?"

"Uh, Addy," Adrian started, as the house shook around us, "let's take a calming breath. He doesn't...."

The words stopped when Addy's glare hit Adrian. He literally cowered, grabbing his head as he whimpered. "Too much, Addy. Too much power."

"Oh shit," Will muttered, putting his head between his knees. "We will never tell him if I puke, agreed?"

"Love," I tried addressing Addy again, "you're overloading the family circle."

"How dare you?" she whispered, eyes back to me, her words more terrifying for their lack of volume. "How dare you deny me?"

I felt the bonds between us stretch with her rage. She was about to pull apart the bonds that tied us in accordance as Mistress and Walker. I didn't think she realized it.

"Mistress Life," I barked, words heavy with my own power. "You are not yourself. Your fear and anger cloud your thoughts. I would not do this lightly."

She rocked back, realizing she'd tripped into my anger. Or at least she thought I was angry. I didn't smile.

Back to my normal voice, I tried again. "He had to go, Adaline. He has to do this. I was surprised Sianna appeared as quickly as she did. I wasn't expecting her for a while. But he has to be Peacekeeper to them."

"Why?" she asked, eyes narrowed.

"Without his energy, the beast affinities will be lost to madness. He's already told you this. Their balance in the world is already fading. We'd lose that entire.... scope of power," I said, looking for the right words.

"And if he dies?" Adrian asked, staring at me. I could tell he disagreed with my decision to help Luke do this.

I met his eyes coolly. "The result is the same. If he dies, I'll just speed up the process by hunting them. Regardless, he had to do this. It's bigger than Candy and Charlie. And I think it'll be fine."

"You *think*?" Adaline asked, voice still dangerously soft.

"We have a plan, and it ends perfectly. Most of the time. Unless it doesn't. But then there's a backup plan. And a backup plan to that plan. There's only one way this doesn't end well, and it'd require Candy to speak out of turn about things she doesn't understand as well as the binding not holding between them."

"The binding between Luke and Candy?" Addy clarified.

I shook my head.

"Luke and Sianna?" she tried again.

I nodded.

"There was no binding, Sam." Talise's voice was monotone as her terror washed through the room, over and over, even with William trying to soothe her.

Noah's teasing aside, there was no denying Luke was dear to Talise. Her emotions danced toward anguish and grief, already convinced the worst would come to pass.

"There is an amber binding. They each have a strong amber binding," I disagreed. "It might be enough. I think it's enough. He's great at friendship. If anyone could carry friendship to death's door, it's Luke."

All eyes around Lucas's living room went wide again.

"But that's not going to happen," I said immediately. "We would have to get to the eighth backup plan, and there's no way Candy would spill the beans about him. She was ready to die for him."

"What's with the sword, Sam?" Will asked. "You're not someone I want to see carrying a sword, just so we're clear."

"Cosplay?" I tried.

Will's lips twitched.

"It was a little bit funny," I muttered.

"Only if he doesn't die," Micah murmured. "Why are we here? And why do you have the Huntress's sword?"

"She might need me to bring it to her. And, if we end up on the eighth backup plan, I need you all. If we end up there, William will be pulled to Luke. Adaline will follow William and bring both of them back here."

"I can't follow anything," Adaline bit out. "You've closed off your power to me. I cannot Walk through space unless you allow it to be so."

My heart lurched in my chest. Closing Addy from my energy was the worst part about this. "Promise you won't Walk to him unless William does?"

"How would William walk to him?" Adaline asked.

"It's to do with the third backup plan." Will's words were an admission of guilt. He knew what I was doing and why. I needed him for plans three through eight. Love and Fear, always bound.

"Here, I'll get a piece of paper and sketch it out," I offered, trying to make amends to my wife.

"*I'm so sorry,*" I mentally projected to Adaline.

"*No, you're not. You'd do it again. I can tell.*"

"*I'm not sorry I did it. I'm sorry you're angry. I did what had to be done,*" I corrected the thought.

"*I can't stomach the idea of losing him, Sam.*" She was blinking quickly to hide tears.

"We won't lose him," I said aloud. "He's my brother. I won't lose him."

"Being your brother does not guarantee survival," Addy disagreed.

My power rolled of its own accord, making everyone shift uncomfortably. I was more nervous than I cared to admit.

"Go get the paper. Leave the sword with me," Micah muttered, pulling the sword out of my reach. "I dislike the idea of you with sharp, pointy objects."

34

WILLIAM

I yawned as Sam explained all of the plans in detail. I didn't care about any of the ones I wasn't a part of, and I was tired. Pip wasn't sleeping well this close to the end of the pregnancy. I'd gotten up and made her pancakes at three-thirteen in the morning—again—when sane people were asleep.

"Why is he so ridiculous?" Jen asked, laughing in my head. *"They just made him sit on an actual throne. He looked around like he expected Noah to jump out of the shadows and start giving him shit."*

I chuckled. I couldn't do the mental stuff as well as Adaline or Jen, but I knew she'd feel my humor.

"Holy hell. The girl just kneeled at his feet. He's horrified, thinking of your mother."

I laughed out loud at that. Mom would go ballistic if she found out. I laughed some more as Jen's commentary ran in my mind.

"Jen says it's plan one so far," I butted into Sam's explanation.

"Jen?" Micah asked, startled.

"We haven't gotten to those plans yet," Sam said, shooting me a glare for ruining his show and tell.

Whatever.

"Plan three," Jen said. *"Sam was right. The energy is speaking through him."*

Before I could get the words out, Jen was panicking in my brain. I felt her tug the bond that tied all Love and Fear pillars together, essentially inviting me to jump to her.

To make Sam's worst-case-scenario plan work, Jen agreed to carry around a small amount of my life energy, giving me a marker to jump to her if she needed me. Jen had once stood a circle as Lady Love before giving up the name. She and I shared some natural bindings, as Love always binds to Fear. It felt less awkward for her to carry part of my energy than it would for someone else.

I took her invitation to use that marker without a word, already reaching for my gun.

SAM TOLD me what to expect if Jen reached for me. He told me Lucas would be near death, bleeding profusely as a man tried to yank a sword free from what remained of Luke's neck.

Sam described it in graphic detail. Luke's head would mostly be detached, hanging on by a fragment of the spinal cord. Energy similar to Sianna's would be rolling around him. The people in the stands would be giving Luke chunks of their own life force. The healing would be started, but it would still look bad. Luke would be in real danger of dying. The energy from the crowd wouldn't be enough. If he didn't get help, Luke would die.

I knew it. Sam had told me. Logically, I was prepared. I knew what death looked like. I was as prepared as possible for this moment.

But, when I saw it, a little piece of my mind broke. My youngest brother lay before me, clinging to life. His blood was everywhere, spurting from the wound in waves, his eyes vacant and unseeing. The sight of it snapped part of my brain to pieces, allowing my fear and rage to roll through the goddamn stadium of people watching my little brother being executed.

A thousand fucking people turned and cowered, staring at me. I wasn't sorry. I amped up the terror for good measure.

I would rot in hell forever, but those I loved would be safe. Fuck everyone else for just standing there.

Pistol aimed, I fired three shots into the asshole who had just yanked the sword free—two shots to the chest, one to the head. Dumb ass brought a sword to a gunfight.

Before the body even fell, Sianna appeared from nowhere, grabbed the sword and decapitated the man I'd just shot.

"He would have survived," she shouted over the bedlam, trying to get a hand on Luke while dodging other sword wielding men.

What is with the fucking swords? I wondered.

Then I was diving for Luke. Hand wrapped around his wrist, I shoved my power through our brotherly bond, desperately trying to start the healing.

A lion roared at Sianna, trying to call her attention back to defense as the men closed in. I watched as she took a stab wound to the midsection. It didn't seem to faze her as she hung on to Luke.

"Where is Adaline?" Jen shouted in my mind. I couldn't find her in the crowd.

That can't be good, I realized.

The lion roared again, charging one of the men as he closed in on Luke and Sianna.

Candy? Was Candy the lion? No. Candy was on the other side of the battleline, face buried in her hands as she sobbed.

Plan eight. I was here because Candy had betrayed Luke.

She and I would discuss that later. If Luke lived. If not, well... Sam. God help all these people in the wake of Sam's savage rage and grief if Lucas perished.

"Go!" I shouted, watching helplessly, as Sianna tried to push energy into Luke at the same time she tried to defend herself. She'd just barely avoided being cut in half.

I was good with a gun. But I wasn't good enough to fire one-handed while lying on the ground, distracted. I'd risk shooting the wrong person.

Rage-filled eyes on me, Sianna all but growled. "Get him out of here. Keep him alive. There are too many for me to keep him safe and help him heal. Keep him alive. Please."

I nodded, even as she transformed to attack the closest guy with a sword.

A naked old man was running from the other end of the stadium, bellowing something at me. *What the fuck happened here?*

Adaline appeared, getting a hand on both Luke and me to take us back to Luke's house.

35

SAM

"He's lost so much blood," Adaline yelled. "The bleeding needs to stop."

Adrian, Micah, and Matthew were already getting hands on Luke, trying to help Adaline and William.

"Tali," Addy panted. "Water. Dehydration. I need him to have water to make more blood!"

Talise nodded, still sobbing as she grabbed hold of Luke's leg, out of everyone else's way.

The blood loss was going to kill Luke.

"THERE'S NO FUCKING BINDING!" I shouted, panicked. "THE AMBER BINDING DIDN'T HOLD! WHERE'S MY FUCKING GOLD BINDING? I NEED THE BINDING! THERE WAS SUPPOSED TO BE A GOLD BINDING FOR ME TO FOLLOW!"

Panting, I searched manically through time for a solution while also watching the nightmarish tableau play out in front of me. My baby brother was going to die.

I'd fucked up. I'd fucked up, and he was going to die.

"William! Can you get back to Jen?" I demanded, frantically looking for a future where that was possible. All I could find were the possibilities of a gold binding taking me to Sianna.

But there was no gold binding. There was nothing for me to hold on to.

The futures involving the binding shouldn't exist anymore. There was no binding.

"I can't do this," Addy sobbed. "Too much bleeding. Needs to stop!"

There was a flicker—just a flash, gone before I could react.

Then, newly forged and shining brightly, I saw it.

"THERE! THERE! GOLD! GIVE ME THE DAMN SWORD!" I screamed, my power already preparing for the battle ahead.

I dove for the sword and followed the binding to Lucas's love. To Sianna, who would be my sister.

She needed me.

TEETH BARED, Cougar-Sianna and Lion-Charlie stood with a glowing, misty Eleanor, facing three large men with swords.

The stadium was in chaos as the remnants of William's power ate at the control of every beast affinity in the building.

"I TOLD WILLIAM NOT TO DO THAT!" I yelled to no one in particular. "Now shit's all panicked."

Sianna, Charlie, and Ellie jumped, startled by my presence.

"SAM!" Eleanor yelled. "This is your fucking fault!"

Sianna's sword-wielding brothers didn't hesitate while the others were distracted, nor did I.

I folded them neatly between one second and the next,

ensuring they couldn't move but could understand what was happening.

"Those belonging to me will come to me," I bellowed, shaking the building with my power, staring directly at Candy. *"I'll tear this building apart if I must."*

Yanking the sword from my hands, Sianna was back to human and moving. I freed her brothers from time. They deserved a fighting chance, after all.

"CHARLIE!" I yelled, grabbing his mane and Ellie's not-quite-solid arm at the same time. "Need you!"

I yanked them back to Luke.

"POWER! HEAL!" I demanded before disappearing again.

There were more lost lambs to collect.

Back at the stadium, I caught a glimpse of Sianna doing battle with her brothers. I wasn't worried. I knew how that was going to end—the remaining insane one needed to go for the rest of the cards to play out. Now was the best time for that.

I ran for Candy, who was trying to hide from me.

Too late, Candace, I thought. I didn't like to move other people through space without a hand on them. I knew it could be done. I just wasn't that good at it yet. I didn't want to lose anyone outside the province of time and space. It'd end badly if I couldn't find them.

I closed the space around Candy, essentially trapping her. "I told you to come to where I was," I growled at her, grabbing her hair to drag her through space, back to Luke's house.

"Oh, my God, Luke," she wailed, unable to catch her breath.

She was lucky I'd taken Charlie back first. In the roughly ten seconds I was gone, Charlie's energy had already helped to stabilize Luke.

I dropped out of the now crowded living room again, going back to Sianna.

I surfaced just in time to see Sianna's batshit crazy brother's head go flying.

"And that makes two crazy ones toast!" I yelled. "Where's the naked hawk dude? We need him!"

"Walker!" a voice accused.

Oh. There he is.

I grabbed his arm, even as he tried to jerk free of me, then I touched Sianna's bare back as her sword fight continued with her remaining brothers. There was no sense in letting that continue. She couldn't take them both down, yet.

I looked around for Jen.

"GO!" Jen bellowed in my mind. *"I'm fine, Sam."*

I saw her then, on the ground ten feet away, blood flowing from her nose and ears. Being used as William's marker had hurt her, as I knew it would. There was no way I'd leave her to this mess.

I cheated. I jumped to Jen to grab her hand. My power to Walk through space didn't work here, but I could use the other bindings and markers to jump around. Jen wouldn't stand my circle. We were not bonded or mated. But I loved her. The familial bond was good enough to take me ten feet. If I'd been able to Walk, it would have been easier, but I took what I could get.

Come to think of it, I was surprised I'd been able to fold Sianna's brothers in time. I shrugged to myself. There was no avoiding time, I guessed.

Again, I used the binding between Sianna and Luke to land in his living room, dropping Jen to the floor.

I went back to the stadium once more, knowing I was pushing my luck.

But my luck held. Except for the part about Luke losing his head. That sucked.

I landed directly behind Sianna. Neither she nor the old dude had moved far. When I grabbed his arm and I touched her back again, I yanked them both through space, dumping them on the carpet in Luke's living room.

"Fix him!" I panted, beyond exhausted. But, it was done. Plan eight had worked.

"Luke," Sianna breathed, diving for him.

"He lives," the old guy exhaled, shoving power through the room, directly to Luke, without contact. As we watched, the neck wound closed, and Luke's breathing improved.

Adaline glared at me, moving to help Jen.

"There was a plan. It worked!" I said with way more cheer than I actually felt.

Her eyes softened as I looked around the room. My brothers were covered in blood, shellshocked with fear. Even Micah stared off into space, lost.

"Terrible fucking plan, Sam," Ellie growled, trying to get a hand on Charlie to help him.

Charlie had spent five days without rest, then fought a short battle, only to offer his remaining life energy to Luke. Without looking, Charlie pulled Ellie under his arm, hugging her tight and accepting her help. "Babe," he muttered, kissing the top of her head.

Still, he didn't take his other hand off Luke.

Talise and Candy were outright sobbing out their fear, remorse, and grief.

Sianna and the old man were completely oblivious, or maybe indifferent, to us. They were wholly focused on Luke.

Lucas. Luke. My little brother. Who'd almost died.

My stomach rolled as shivers took over my body.

Falling to my hands and knees, I vomited as my own sobs rocked through me.

36

SAM

*O*nce all the bleeding was done, and everyone was on the road to recovery, we went across the street to the house I shared with Adaline.

No one wanted to clean up the blood or puke in Luke's living room.

Plus, it'd be funny to watch him freak out. Later. When he was better.

"That did not go according to plan," William muttered.

"I beg your pardon?" I asked. "It went *exactly* according to plan. It was just Plan Eight, the worst possible outcome."

"For the rest of eternity, let's just assume it will always be the worst possible outcome," Adrian said, staring at Luke's chest as it rose and fell.

I resented the implication but didn't feel like this was a great time to argue it.

"He is healing," Sianna murmured to Adrian, squeezing Luke's hand. She had not let go of him, even when pulling on clothes. "He is not pulling as much power from me now, just resting."

"I started CPR on my little brother tonight," Adrian whispered, eyes glassy.

"I wouldn't have been able to save him," Adaline added. "Even with William, Micah, Matthew, Adrian, and Talise. I was losing that battle."

"It worked," I muttered, feeling sick again.

"Why the binding?" Will asked me. "Why didn't you come when Adaline followed me?"

"Wards," Adaline answered, knowing I would be sick if I opened my mouth at that moment. "There were wards that prohibited the Walker and Mistress from using our energy to get in the building. You followed a binding to Jen, not using power like ours. I followed my binding to you. But Sam and I couldn't be there at the same moment. Even for the few seconds I was there, I felt the energy of the building fighting my presence. We are not welcome there."

I risked speaking. "I followed my binding to Luke and his to Sianna. Strong and new, it lit the way for me and held strong for multiple trips."

"My father never trusted the Walker or Mistress. More than once, the Walker tried to take us from the Peacekeeper. I'm amazed the wards still hold so much power," Edgar murmured.

"James?" Micah asked, surprised. "James tried to interfere with the Peacekeeper?"

Edgar shook his head with a dismissive flick of his hand. "I don't know what his name was. What is it you intend to do now?"

"We won't talk about this in present company," Charlie said, voice cold, eyes on his sister.

Adrian's rage roamed through the room, stoking tempers.

"No," I muttered. "Selfish, not traitorous."

"Your life is forfeit just as soon as I get a free minute, traitor," Sianna said to Candy, ignoring me.

Candy stared at the ground. When her words finally came, her voice was resigned. "My period showed up this morning. They knew I wasn't pregnant."

"You are both selfish and a traitor," Sianna summarized.

Candy didn't react. "Nathaniel came to me saying Elias would claim me, allowing me to bring honor to my line by mating with him. I argued that I had been claimed by the Peacekeeper. He said Luke was not the Peacekeeper. He knew that Luke stood in Harbor and belonged to the Walker and the Mistress. He could not be both Peace and Peacekeeper. I didn't know that."

Candy blew out a breath.

"Nate said when the gathered affinities discovered Luke was a fraud, that he was Peace, not Peacekeeper, they'd tear him to pieces. It was time to drop the charade for Luke's own wellbeing. If I confirmed that Luke stood the circle with you, Nate would see him out of this mess. Charlie and I could go home, and Luke would be free."

The room fell silent, waiting for her to continue.

"He didn't want to be Peacekeeper. He didn't want anything to do with it. He wouldn't even know what the Peacekeeper was if Charlie and I hadn't told him about it. To make it worse, we apparently gave him bad information."

She wiped at her tears before continuing. "I would not have Luke trapped in a future he doesn't want, nor would I see him dead. I thought I'd been offered a way out for all of us. I didn't think 'free' meant that Luke would be dead. It's not how I interpreted it.

"Call me selfish if you want. Call me a traitor. I don't care. I've lost everything now. Out of contact for over a week, I'm sure I've been fired. I'm probably being evicted at this moment. My brother won't even meet my eyes. I'm sure my parents have disowned me. I don't even know where they are. Nate said Mom and Dad would be in the stands somewhere, but who knows? And Luke almost died."

Her voice broke on the last words, more tears leaking down her cheeks as she sniffled. "It doesn't matter. I was wrong. If I have to pay for that with my life, so be it. If it costs me my dignity, that's fine too. Call me whatever you want."

"Call you friend," Luke mumbled, eyes still closed. "Sorry, Candy."

The room waited for more words that didn't come.

Charlie stared at his feet, silent.

Sianna stared at the hand joined with Luke's. She didn't respond.

Edgar shook his head. "I didn't know. I'm sorry, Candace."

William's eyebrows shot up. "You're apologizing to her?"

Sianna cleared her throat. Her voice still came out as a whisper. "My brother was psychotic and dangerous from his first transformation. He enjoyed torturing and killing prey. He's killed every mate he's ever claimed, usually during the mating. Without saying the words, my father promised her a horrible death that wouldn't help in the end."

"How did he know about Luke standing circles?" I asked, eyes narrowed.

There was no response.

"Jen may be able to answer that when she wakes," Micah

suggested. She was fast asleep in one of the spare bedrooms upstairs.

Neither Micah nor Ethan had forgiven me, but they'd come when needed. That had to count for something. I sighed to myself, blinking hard. I hated the part of me that did what was necessary, regardless of the cost. I hated it, but I did it anyway.

"Whether he stands as Peace or not, he is Peacekeeper," Edgar said finally. "I would usually agree with Nate. Those that are Peace cannot serve as Peacekeepers. They do not have the capacity for both. Once the name of Peace ties them to the Walker and Mistress, they cannot help us.

"We've seen it before. When I was Overlord, we attempted it. I would accept help for my people in any form. The gentle soul that stood as Peace at the time offered assistance, but he could not hold our energies. The worst among us reacted as Nate described, tearing the poor empowered person limb from limb. The desperate hope for a Peacekeeper being dashed broke many of us.

"Long past history aside, Lucas is Peacekeeper, even if he is Peace to you. My brother cannot remain Overlord. He is wrong about this, and I don't believe he's capable anymore. I have not seen him transform since before Sianna was born. He intended the Peacekeeper to die to hide his own lack of control."

Rage circled the room again, this time from William. Adrian quirked an eyebrow at his older brother. "William, you're Fear. I'm Rage. You're stepping on my toes, man."

"That's unfortunate," William said without humor, passing on the opportunity to joke with Adrian.

That can't be good, I realized.

Edgar sighed, meeting Sianna's eyes. "We are in trouble,

dearest child. We must remove him. There will be war over this if we don't move quickly."

"It's too late," Will said lightly, his rampant rage belying his tone.

Edgar sat back, staring at William.

"I'll rot in hell for all eternity, but those I love will be safe. No. If he wants to strike at one of us, he'll face the wrath of *all* of us. If he wants a Trellis head for his mantle, let him try for mine. Nathaniel is about to learn a hard lesson. We each reap what we sow."

The doorbell rang on some existential cue, sounding like the ding at the end of a round of boxing.

"It's for me," Luke said, eyes half-opened.

Luke's adventure continues in *Reaping, available now for pre-order and scheduled for release on July 23, 2021.*

THANKS FOR READING!

As always, if you enjoyed this story, your Amazon rating and/or review would be appreciated. As a new author, reviews are imperative to attracting readers.

For updates on my releases as well as **bonus content,** please subscribe to my newsletter at https://maggielilybooks.com/sign-up/.

You can find me on Facebook, Instagram, and Bookbub.

Want to chat? My Facebook reader group is cozy and fun with next to no smarmy sales pushes. Otherwise, you're welcome to email at maggie@maggiemlily.com.

ALSO BY MAGGIE M LILY

Peacekeeper's Harmony Series

Ransom

Reaping (July 23, 2021)

Rise

A Lovely Twist of Fae Series - Fall 2021

Ainsley

Aurora

Arbor